PRAISE FOR MELODY ANNE

"A second chance story packed with suspense, heat, and family."
—Harlequin Junkie on *Owen*

"The Undercover Billionaire series is a great contemporary romance series about this family of billionaire brothers who live normal everyday lives even though they are rich."
—Fresh Fiction on the Undercover Billionaire series

FINN

Other Titles by Melody Anne

Billionaire Aviators

Turbulent Intentions
Turbulent Desires
Turbulent Waters
Turbulent Intrigue

Billionaire Bachelors

The Billionaire Wins the Game
The Billionaire's Dance
The Billionaire Falls
The Billionaire's Marriage Proposal
Blackmailing the Billionaire
Runaway Heiress
The Billionaire's Final Stand
Unexpected Treasure
Hidden Treasure
Holiday Treasure
Priceless Treasure
The Ultimate Treasure

Undercover Billionaires

Kian
Arden
Owen

FINN

AN
ANDERSON
BILLIONAIRES
NOVEL

MELODY ANNE

Montlake
Romance

Published by Montlake Romance, Seattle
www.apub.com

Amazon, the Amazon logo, and Montlake Romance are trademarks of Amazon.com, Inc., or its affiliates.

ISBN-13: 9781542015936
ISBN-10: 1542015936

Cover design by Letitia Hasser

Cover photography by Wander Aguiar Photography

Printed in the United States of America

This book is dedicated to Doug Whichman. You changed this entire story with your help and military knowledge. Some friendships start in the best ways.

Acknowledgments

The first book in a new series is always the most difficult to write. I'm very lucky to have Joseph Anderson, who seems to make his way into every series I write, helping me out in the beginning. And with this series, it's a continuation of my very first series I ever wrote—my ever-important Anderson family.

But this time I wanted to stretch my limits, and I also wanted to write about something that matters. I was thinking of doing a center for domestic violence to center the series around; then I talked with my editor, and we decided a veterans center would be much better. And I'm so grateful for that because once that was worked out, this story took off. But I was still struggling with what direction to go with it. And then I met the fantastic Doug Whichman, who this book is dedicated to. He's been in the service for eighteen years and shared so much of his journey with me! I lost my writer's block, and the story changed and flowed after that.

One of the greatest aspects of my job is the research I get to do. Doug invited me to the National Guard base in Salem, Oregon, and I was like a child in a candy store as I got to tour this fantastic place. It's a search and rescue unit, and all the people who talked to me were so helpful and amazing. I want to give a special thanks to Dittman, O'Brien, and Nelson for taking the time to talk to me and help me make this story as accurate as possible. I always worry when I write military stuff because I don't want to fail these men and women who dedicate their lives to all of us. On this tour I got to sit in a Black Hawk helicopter, take pictures, and hear amazing stories. I have four books left in this series, and I can't wait for my next visit. I'm trying to make my way up into the air in one of these amazing machines. I don't know if that will happen. :)

As always, I don't write a book alone. I have a team of people who make it possible for me to do what I do. My besties, Stephanie and Ridgley, sat with me as we outlined this series—and possibly finished a few bottles of wine. Then my editors, Lauren and Lindsey, worked through the story with me to perfect the characters and the journeys they will take. And the Army National Guard base in Salem changed the entire direction the series will take with their knowledge and help.

I'm so blessed to do what I do. I never forget that. I hope you love this new series, as it's become so special to me. I'm excited to see where it goes next as I grow and change in life. This year has been an adventure for me, and I'm not even close to seeing it end. So my characters of course will grow as well.

Joseph is so happy to be back on the pages again, meddling in the lives of his newest family members. Come and take a ride with us as we get to hear some real stories from real military members and have some fun along the way.

PROLOGUE

Joseph Anderson wasn't a man who lived with regrets. He'd enjoyed a blessed life with family and friends, and even if there had been bumps in the road along the way, he figured that was all just a part of who he was today.

He was in the prime of his life, in his humble opinion. He didn't care that his hair and beard had gone white many years earlier. He didn't care that his smooth skin had become wrinkled, and he didn't care that it took him a few extra seconds to rise from his favorite easy chair in his den after having a drink of fine scotch and possibly sneaking a few puffs from a favorite cigar.

Age was just a number, and it wasn't something that would define him or slow him down. There was still a lot of life to live, and he wasn't going to waste a single moment of time. Right now he was sitting back in his favorite chair, a smile on his lips.

Family.

At the end of the day, it all came down to family. Whether a man was rich or poor in the financial sense, he'd die a wealthy man if he had a good family. Maybe there had been a time or two in Joseph's life he'd . . . um . . . helped his family along, and maybe, just maybe, they might've called that meddling, but to date he hadn't steered a single one of his children or nieces and nephews wrong. And he'd even been kind enough to help some of his friends out in expanding their beautiful families. That was commitment, in his humble opinion.

Instead of making accusations at him, they should be throwing big parties in his honor, thanking him for seeing what they needed before they were even aware they needed it. But a man didn't do what he did to be praised. He did it because he loved big-time. Everything Joseph did was done on a grand scale. And that was something that would never change.

"Charlie, can you get the car ready?" Joseph asked over his speaker.

"Yes, sir. Where would you like to go?"

"The hospital," Joseph told him.

It took a few seconds longer to stand than it used to, but soon he was moving toward the door. After a couple of steps, the kinks in Joseph's back were gone, and he picked up his pace as he made his way to the front of the house.

That morning Joseph had received a phone call that had stunned him. It took a lot to surprise a man who'd lived many lifetimes in his short years on this earth. But this call had at first shocked him and then brought him immense pleasure as he'd sat there for a while, basking in the news he'd been given.

Joseph had nearly hung up the phone when no one had answered his *hello*, but something in him told him to wait. Then *she'd* spoken. He hadn't recognized her voice. Why would he have? It had been over thirty years since he'd last seen her.

Sandra Anderson.

She'd been married to his awful uncle, Neilson Anderson, who had faked his own death, then run away like the coward he'd been his entire life. Joseph hadn't expected to ever hear from his uncle's wife again. She'd come many years before, a baby in her arms, and then she'd disappeared into the night. Joseph had used his unlimited resources trying to find her, but it had done no good. She'd vanished without a trace.

Now, over thirty years later, she was back . . . and sadly, she was dying. And one of her last requests was to speak to Joseph.

Sandra had been twenty-five years younger than Joseph's uncle. But that man had always been a terrible person. After faking his own death, he'd waited for his wife and infant son to collect the insurance money; then he'd grabbed her up and whisked her away to South America, where he'd had four more children with her.

Once her husband had died, Sandra had scrimped and saved and brought her children back to Seattle, but she'd been ashamed of the money she'd stolen from Joseph many years before. It broke Joseph's heart that he'd missed out on knowing his family because of a little bit of cash. Money came and went, but family was forever.

But it was never too late. He'd make things right with his newest family members. After all, they were Andersons. And that meant something in Joseph's book. They had no idea where they came from, but they were about to find out.

Once family, always family.

Joseph smiled as he climbed into the back of his car. It looked like he had a new project to keep him occupied. That was why he'd never grow old. He had too many family members needing him—and he was more than willing to give them a hand—whether they realized they needed his help or not.

It didn't take long for Joseph to arrive at the hospital. And George was right behind him. One of their triplets, Richard, was out of town on business, but he'd want to be a part of this new addition to their family, too. He'd already been informed.

By the time Joseph and George left Sandra's room, Joseph had to turn away to hide the tears shining in his eyes. She was sorry she'd taken the kids from him, sorry to have deprived them of a loving family.

Joseph wasn't a man to hold a grudge. She'd been scared and lied to for years by the man who should've cherished her—the man who'd married her—Joseph's rotten uncle. It wasn't her fault, and Joseph truly meant it as he told her he'd take care of her children and that he found her brave to come to him now.

He and George didn't speak as they exited the hospital. Then the two of them stood there for a while as they took in this new information they'd been given. Finally Joseph turned and smiled at George.

"It looks like we have five family members in need of our help, brother," George said with a sly smile.

Joseph beamed. "Why, I believe you are correct, George," Joseph said with a chuckle.

"We'd better get started. We've lost a lot of time already," George said.

"I couldn't have said it better myself," Joseph replied.

The two of them fist-bumped like they were teenagers as they moved toward the awaiting vehicle. They had too much to plan to take separate cars. They had five boys to take care of, none of whom were married. Joseph felt like a kid in a candy store.

"Let the matchmaking begin," he said as George poured each of them a scotch.

They clinked glasses and put their heads together. Life was good—it was always so, so good.

CHAPTER ONE

Three Months Later

The slight limp Finn Anderson was still experiencing as he walked into the posh room at an expensive lawyer's office had him scowling, something he'd found himself doing too much of lately. It had been three months since the bomb that had ruined his career had gone off, and he was still dealing with the repercussions of the incident.

For a man of action, having any limitations whatsoever was something very hard for him to swallow. He followed the hall to the room he'd been summoned to, and when he opened the door, he was glad to see one of his brothers waiting.

"Do you know what this is about?" Finn asked Noah Anderson, the second oldest in his line of siblings.

"Not a clue, but I was told it was important," Noah replied.

"Maybe we're getting a big inheritance from a supersecret ninja society," Brandon, the comedian of the family, said as he stepped in the door right behind Finn. Finn was irritated he hadn't known he was back there. Even his senses seemed to be messed up from the explosion.

"Keep on hoping, little brother," Finn said.

"Well, this *is* a pretty classy office," Brandon pointed out.

"Yeah, way too nice for the likes of you to be stepping foot inside," their youngest brother, Crew, said as he entered the room.

"Look, Shrinky Dink, I think we're all here because you messed with the wrong patient," Hudson said as he entered.

"I'm the only sane one in this family," Crew pointed out as he sat down.

"Are you supposed to say that?" Brandon asked. "Don't you have a code of ethics or something?"

"Shut up," Crew told his brother with a smile.

"Now, I know you aren't supposed to say *that*. You make your money off of people talking too much. Should I lie back and tell you all my problems?" Brandon persisted.

"I don't have enough time in the world to hear *your* problems," Crew said.

That got a chuckle from the entire group.

"Man, it's been a while since we were all in the same room. We can be thankful for at least that much in being called here," Noah said.

"Well, hopefully someone is going to tell us what in the hell it's all about," Finn said. He was impatient and not in the mood to be in the fancy offices.

"If you hold on to your big-boy panties, then maybe we'll find out," Crew told him.

"At least I wear proper underwear," Finn pointed out.

"Have you been going through my drawers again?" Crew asked. "Jealous that I can fill mine out?"

Brandon laughed at that.

"Trust me—there's no problem in me filling *anything* out," Finn growled.

"I don't know. You seem a bit broken still," Crew persisted.

"You're an ass," Finn told him. "I'm just fine."

"Knock it off before someone walks in and thinks we're utterly uncivilized," Crew said. He was always the calmest of all of them.

"Yeah, yeah, shrink away at us," Noah grumbled.

"This family needs me more than I'm able to help," Crew said.

"Wait a minute—" There was a noise at the door that stopped whatever Finn had been about to say.

"Thank you all for coming here today."

The room went dead silent as all five brothers turned to see the infamous Joseph Anderson filling the doorway of the conference room. What in the hell was a man who was basically royalty doing with them?

This man owned half the businesses in Seattle, provided tens of thousands of jobs, donated tens of millions of dollars each year, and ran many charity organizations. On top of that he was known as a family man. There were rumors he was a meddler, but no one ever had a bad thing to say about Joseph Anderson—and many reporters had tried to dig up some juicy gossip. There was just none to be had.

As the oldest brother, Finn had always taken the lead in any new situation in their lives. Slowly, he rose to his feet, which encouraged his brothers to follow suit.

"Mr. Anderson, is there something we can help you with?" Finn asked.

"Good. You know who I am," Joseph said as he waved a hand in front of his face. "Sit down. There's no need for us to be formal."

Finn had to hide a smile at Joseph's words. Of course they knew who he was. Was there anyone who didn't?

Joseph moved to the head of the table, where a seat was still available. No one sat until Joseph was seated; then, with confused looks, they followed suit.

"It would be very difficult not to know who you are," Brandon said with a smirk. "Considering you own half of Seattle."

That earned a chuckle from Joseph, which shocked Finn. He hadn't expected a man as powerful as Joseph to have a sense of humor.

"I wouldn't say I own exactly *half* of Seattle," Joseph said, zero humility in his tone. "But I definitely own a lot of it. I like business, and I like helping others find their calling in life." He paused for a moment as he looked each of the brothers in the eyes. Finn wasn't easily intimidated, but he found this moment a bit over the top.

"Well, I don't believe in beating around the bush, so I'll get right to the point," Joseph said. Finn found himself tensing as he waited for whatever words were next to come out of this man's mouth.

"Your father was my uncle. I won't talk about him because I don't see a point in dredging up the past. He took you away, and we weren't able to find you. Your mother called me on her deathbed, apologizing and explaining it all to me. That means . . ."

There was another long pause as Joseph looked at each of them again. Finn was in total and utter shock. He couldn't have said anything even if a 9 mm was pointed at his head.

"You're my family. Technically we'd be cousins, but you're the age of my kids and nephews, so feel free to think of me as your uncle." He smiled as if he was bestowing a blessing on them. Some people would think that was exactly what he was doing.

He continued talking. "And as such, I have an inheritance for you. I know your mother didn't have a lot, but her wishes were for you to have family and have a true start in life. I don't believe in just handing something over. It's not how I was brought up, and it's not how I raised my kids. Money, just like everything else in life, has to be earned. Money comes and goes, as well. But at the end of the day, family is what matters—family is our legacy."

There was another pause. No one said anything.

"You're my family, and I want to know you. So I've come up with a project that we can work on together. That means we can get to know each other, and I get five new additions to my already beautiful family. I know you might need some time to think about this, and I'm okay with that as well. You're Andersons, which means you're stubborn as hell, but it also means I know you'll make the right decision."

Still no one said a word. A storm could've ripped through the room, and none of them would've moved. Yes, they had the last name

Anderson, but that was a common name. Lots of people had that name and weren't related to *the* one and only Joseph Anderson.

"I'm not going to pry right now. We'll meet at my place in three days, once you've had time to process all of this. Once the shock wears off, I'm confident you'll be excited to not be alone. Here's the project we'll be doing together, and here's my home address. I look forward to speaking more with you."

With that a man stepped forward and passed out a folder to each of the boys. Then both Joseph and the man left the room. No one spoke for a very, *very* long time.

Finn was in utter shock. He'd thought they were alone in the world. Losing their mother had been one of the hardest things he'd ever experienced, and that was saying a lot, considering he'd been shot at nearly daily at some points in his career.

But to find out he had a huge family out there threw him for a loop. He wasn't sure what to think of it all. Family hadn't been something he'd thought much about. He'd had a terrible father, a wonderful mother, and pretty decent siblings. But discovering there was a massive number of family members who shared his blood was overwhelming—and not necessarily a welcome gift. And he couldn't care less about the inheritance Joseph had briefly mentioned. He'd been smart with his money in life. He wasn't a billionaire, but he could hold his own.

He knew how his brothers' minds worked and knew they were having similar thoughts as him. Even though their father had been a monster, their mother had been Mother Teresa. She'd raised them with values, integrity, and morality. They didn't always follow her advice, but they could consider themselves assets to society.

"What does this mean?" Crew finally asked after a long, long silence.

"I have no idea," Finn said. "But we won't find out unless we read what's in here."

"Do you trust him?" Noah asked.

9

"No," Finn said. Then he shook his head. "I don't think he's a man to lie, not with his business ethics, but he can't just be told we're family and automatically want to take us under his wing. Who in the hell does that?"

"We know his business practices, but we know nothing about the man himself," Crew pointed out.

"How much do we want to know?" Finn asked.

"If he's family, we should want to know a lot," Hudson said.

"He doesn't need us in his life, since the man is basically God, so maybe he does want to know us if he's putting in this much effort to come up with a project," Noah said.

"He's just a person," Brandon pointed out. "Definitely a powerful person, but still just a man—definitely not God."

"Keep on saying that a few more times," Hudson said. "Maybe we'll actually believe it eventually."

The room went silent again as the brothers reached for the files and opened them. They had no idea what was about to happen in their lives. If they had known the storm that was descending upon them, they might've run from that room without ever laying a finger on the folders Joseph had given them as casually as a mother giving a piece of chocolate to her child.

Chapter Two

Finn didn't know what to think as the large Hummer limo pulled up the long driveway lined with giant oak trees. They turned a corner, and the famous Anderson mansion rose high in the sky in front of them.

Finn wasn't that guy to be awed by much, but it was impossible not to be impressed or in shock at the massive building before them. Yes, he knew how wealthy Joseph was, but seeing his property brought that into clear perspective. It also brought home the fact that he shared the same blood with the man who'd built such an impressive empire.

But what in the hell did that matter? Finn was the oldest of the five siblings; therefore, he had the most memories of his deadbeat, alcoholic, selfish father. The man had been a monster. He'd abused his wife and children and hadn't known the meaning of the word *love*.

The Andersons had a hell of a lot of wealth, but what did that matter if they didn't give a damn about the people who should mean the most to them in this world? It wasn't the Anderson blood that flowed through his veins that made him who he was. No, that was from his sweet mother's side.

Finn wasn't sure he wanted to know this family. He'd heard good things about Joseph, but everyone was capable of slipping on a mask, then hiding their true selves in the darkness behind closed doors.

"Damn, could you imagine growing up in this place?" Brandon asked.

Finn shrugged. "Just because the house is huge and filled with what I imagine is every luxury known to man doesn't mean it was a happy home."

"You gotta admit it'd be a lot better than the two-bedroom home we all had to crowd into," Noah said.

"I disagree," Crew said with a smile. "Do you have any bad memories of that place?"

Hudson smiled. "Luckily I was too young to remember the old man, and once Mom moved us back to Seattle, he had nothing to do with our house; so no, I don't have bad memories there."

"See, size really doesn't matter," Brandon said with a laugh.

"Ha ha, not a problem with size in our family," Finn said, feeling a bit better about having to step into this monstrosity of a house in a couple of minutes.

"You guys seriously need to grow the hell up," Crew said with a roll of his eyes.

"Why is that? We're just chatting here," Hudson said with an innocent smile.

"Mm-hmm," Crew said as the car stopped.

"Why does your mind have to immediately go into the gutter? Do you need some counseling?" Hudson asked.

"You're such an ass," Crew told him.

"Now, now, is that any way to speak to a patient?" Hudson said, not able to keep a straight face.

"I'd quit my profession for life if you were my patient," Crew said.

"I'm crushed. Seriously. Down to my soul," Hudson told him as he patted his heart.

The door to the car opened, shutting them all up.

"Here we go," Finn said. The smile he'd been wearing fell away as he stepped from the limo, then waited for his brothers to follow. They all got out, almost battle ready as they stood there and looked up and up at the huge mansion. It had to be an optical illusion, but it appeared as if the thing went up ten stories and stretched out farther than the eye could see.

"Seriously, who in the hell needs this much space to live?" Finn asked.

"Apparently Mr. Anderson," Brandon said with a chuckle.

"He's been described as larger than life," Crew pointed out. "Maybe large men need more room."

"We aren't exactly small," Finn said with a grimace. "And we've been just fine in normal-size homes."

"But I can still imagine all the adventures our cousins had growing up here," Brandon said.

"You're referring to them as our cousins already?" Finn asked, feeling a bit of disgust.

"Hey. When in Rome . . ." He paused for a moment. "I don't know, wear togas?" he finished with a shrug.

That had them smiling again.

"Right this way," the driver said as he held out a hand toward the huge cement staircase. They could walk side by side up them and still have room for dates on their arms.

"Here we go," Finn said as he led the group up the stairs. As they reached the top, the door opened. Was someone just standing there waiting for them to step into the right position? It was such an odd place.

"Good evening. Mr. Anderson is waiting in the den," an elderly gentleman in a nice suit said as he held the door wide open.

Once they were inside, the door shut, and the man led them down massively oversize hallways in a maze that would've confused most people. Luckily, Finn was always aware of his surroundings. If there was an emergency, he'd know exactly how to exit this place.

He tried not to look around too much, not wanting to be impressed with the furniture and artwork that definitely cost more than he'd made in his entire lifetime. But as much as he wanted to fault this huge place, he had to admit it was done tastefully. Yes, there were a lot of expensive pieces, but there were more family portraits than priceless collectables.

Finn had heard Joseph was a family man, but again, a person could show the world exactly what they wanted the world to see. But it was hard to keep a hard edge when he was walking down hallways lined with family pictures of adventures Finn would've loved to have taken when he was a child.

He wasn't complaining about the way he'd grown up. His mother had loved them, and that was more important than any amount of money. They'd gone camping and fishing, and she'd taught them how to take care of themselves. No, they hadn't taken any trips to Disneyland, but he didn't care all that much. Because she'd tried her best to bring the adventure to them in their own backyard. That spoke a lot of her character and who she was.

"It's good to see all of you again!" Joseph's booming voice pulled Finn from his thoughts as they stepped inside the massive den filled with a fireplace Finn could have walked straight into and several couches and chairs in a circle.

"Sit, sit," Joseph continued as he stood in front of a chair that looked like it should be a throne for a king. Of course, Joseph had been described as royalty, so it was actually pretty fitting.

"Thank you," Crew said, taking the lead since Finn appeared to have lost his voice. That was something new for him.

"Did you read over my proposal?" Joseph asked after they were all settled. Finn's brothers looked to him, and he sighed.

"I want to know why you're doing this?" Finn asked instead of answering Joseph.

"I don't understand the question," Joseph said.

Finn knew Joseph wasn't a stupid man. He'd had far too much success in his lifetime. So he clearly wanted to know what Finn's thoughts were before he answered a question like that.

"You don't know us. You don't owe us anything. Why are you creating this massive project that just so happens to fit all of our careers?" Finn said. He couldn't spell it out any better than that.

Joseph smiled as he leaned back with a lit cigar in one hand and an amber-filled crystal glass in the other. He took a sip and sighed before setting it down. Then he looked Finn in the eyes.

"I believe in family. I also believe in hard work. I didn't just pull this project out of the seat of my pants. It's something very special to my Katherine. When I discovered I had five nephews, I knew there was no one better for the job," Joseph told him.

"I'm sure there are people out there with a lot more experience than us," Finn pushed.

Joseph chuckled. "You can check into my many businesses, son, and you'll see I have a special place in my heart for the underdog. If no one ever gets a chance, then how do they get to prove themselves?" he asked.

"We prove ourselves with our actions," Finn told him.

"And I've done my research, boy," Joseph said with a wink. "You *are* Andersons, whether you like that or not. Not only have you served in the military, which is noble and honorable, but you've worked hard your entire lives. That deserves respect."

"This is a big task," Noah said. "What if we don't do it justice?"

"I have no doubt how hard you'll work on this," Joseph told him. "But you all have to be in agreement. You *all* have to be in on it, or no one is. Family should stick together, and I want this to be a family project from beginning to end."

Finn looked at each of his brothers. Yes, they were all independent, but he could see they wanted to do this. He also knew that if he walked away, they'd go with him. But was he truly going to let his anger over his father—and his own pride—make him take something this huge from his siblings? No, he'd never do that.

"Okay, Joseph, I think we're up for the task," Finn said. "Tell us more about it."

"That's the attitude I like to hear," Joseph said with a smile.

They spent the next several hours going over Joseph's vision of what he wanted. Finn was surprised by how much he agreed with him. Maybe Finn didn't want a new father figure in his life. But he definitely had a new direction he was taking, now that he couldn't finish the career he'd loved.

Whatever was going to come next might just blow him off his feet again. But this time he was going to be ready for it, and he was definitely going to have his guard up.

Chapter Three

Brooke Garrison wasn't your typical anything. Never in her life had she been described as *average*. She'd been called many things in her time, but never *boring*, never *ordinary*, and never *girlie*.

She took pride in who she was, in what she had accomplished, and what she was capable of still achieving.

She'd grown up tough—had to grow up that way, with an older brother she'd idolized. A pang of sorrow ripped through her at even the thought of her big brother. Three months. It had been three months since she'd lost him, and she still had days she couldn't breathe she missed him so much.

But at least she had the knowledge that he'd been proud of her. Just as she'd idolized him, he'd always encouraged her to live her dreams and had never stopped telling her she could be anything she wanted. He'd made her promise to never compromise and never back down and never settle for anything less than she deserved.

And because of him she hadn't. The two of them might've had a completely worthless father, who'd walked out on them without so much as a glance backward, and a mother who was too busy looking for her next fix to be a good mother, but it hadn't mattered. Because the two of them had each other, and at the end of the day, that had been all that mattered.

She was now lost. She wasn't sure how to survive in a world without her best friend, her coach, her family, her heart and soul. She wasn't sure she wanted to be happy in a world he didn't exist in anymore.

For a month after the soldiers had shown up on her doorstep to tell her Jack was gone, she hadn't done much of anything. She'd barely survived that horrific visit she'd prayed she'd never get. She'd collapsed in their arms. Then she'd been in denial. She was *still* in denial. She kept his phone active and called it at least once a day just to hear his cocky greeting. She cried every single time.

A tear rolled down Brooke's face as she moved down the street in her sleepy little town of Cranston, Washington, which was just outside of Seattle. She'd never leave her hometown. Only three thousand people lived there on a good day, but Seattle was less than an hour away if she needed anything from the city, which she rarely did. It was a slice of heaven in an otherwise busy metropolis kind of world.

But the town boasted three bars (of course), a medical clinic, a small theater, a martial arts studio, several small restaurants, a great grocery store, and a heavenly coffee stand. What more did a person need? Nothing, in her opinion.

But if the rumors were true, her town was soon going to become a media circus. She had severely mixed feelings on that. It appeared the Andersons had bought the huge parcel of land to the north of town and were beginning a massive project—for veterans.

This was a two-hundred-acre parcel of land that the rumors were flying around about. The town mill was saying it was going to be several buildings with all sorts of services for current and past veterans. The sky was the limit when Joseph Anderson put his backing behind something.

She didn't want the circus, but she was all for doing anything involving veterans. There was no way she couldn't be involved. Maybe it would help her feel closer to her brother; maybe it would help the pain of his loss dim just a little bit. She didn't see how that was possible, but miracles did sometimes happen.

Brooke was a nurse practitioner with a lot of experience under her belt, considering she was only twenty-nine. But she'd grown up quick as a medic for the military, and that was like working three times as many years at a regular facility.

She'd heard a rumor that a new set of Andersons was heading up this brand-new project, and she was determined to find out exactly what they were doing. If they were building a veterans facility, then she definitely wanted to know everything about it.

Brooke stopped as she reached the martial arts studio. She could hear a deep male voice from inside and then a round of laughter from what sounded like a *lot* of females. She smiled, the feeling of her lips turned up almost foreign on her face now.

If there was a new Anderson in town, it made sense that any eligible females would swarm to him. Rolling her eyes, she opened the door and found herself with a smirk on her face at the first words she heard.

"Now, ladies, try not to hurt me too badly," that rich, sexy voice said.

Another round of giggles followed the man's words. Brooke wasn't sure what to expect when she turned the corner. But what she got wasn't it.

Brooke had been surrounded by strong, sexy men her entire life. Her brother had been two years older than her, and he'd been great looking, athletic, humorous, and all-around amazing. His friends had matched him. But Brooke hadn't been interested in guys in that sense. She'd wanted to play sports with them, roll in the mud in a nonsexy way, and watch sporting events while spitting seeds. She hadn't had her first boyfriend until she was nineteen, and then she'd beat him at basketball, and he'd dumped her. She'd learned early on that guys were nothing but trouble.

But the man she saw standing in front of a roomful of women immediately stopped her in her tracks. She didn't want to swoon like all the other ladies, but she found her knees slightly weak. *What the hell?* That wasn't a reaction she liked or wanted.

He had to be standing at least six feet three, with shoulders that appeared as if they wouldn't fit through a doorway and arms that instantly made her want to run her fingers over them. His T-shirt showed the hint of a tattoo she was almost desperate to see the rest of. His short dark hair was slightly tousled, and his high cheekbones and clean-shaven face were made for midnight fantasies. If ever there was a man who could be described as perfect, it was the guy standing in front of her.

Just as she was able to suck in her first breath since seeing him, his head turned, and then crystal-blue eyes were gazing straight at her—right into her very soul. Never in her life had she experienced something like she was feeling right then, right at this moment.

Time completely stood still as she gazed at the man, at this stranger. She tried telling herself it was nothing, that she was simply messed up from grief and loss. Otherwise she'd feel exactly zero emotions toward this guy who meant nothing to her. But she couldn't shake how intense the feeling was.

"You're a bit late, but we'll make room," he said, his voice like butter melting on top of a mile-high stack of buttermilk pancakes. It cascaded over her, making her fall into a trance.

"Hey, Doc Garrison. You here to learn some self-defense?" Brandy, one of her patients, asked.

The woman's voice finally managed to snap Brooke out of her insane stupor. She ripped her gaze away from the man and focused on her patient instead.

"Nicolette told me about the self-defense training, and I wanted to make sure it was being taught right. You know my patients are important to me," Brooke said.

"Yeah, you're the best, Doc," Cindy piped in. Several heads nodded.

"Wanted to make sure it was being done right?" the man asked with a smirk and a raised eyebrow.

She turned back to him and felt immensely better when she didn't grow faint at looking into his eyes. That cocky little smirk was exactly what she'd needed to see. Oh, how she loved to wipe a look like that off a man's face.

She hunched her shoulders as if she was just a sad, weak female and sauntered up to him, looking as innocent as a python in a bunny costume.

"I'm the town practitioner, Brooke Garrison," she said, holding out her hand.

He paused for just long enough to make her uncomfortable. She had zero doubt it was a control thing. She had to grit her teeth to keep the innocent expression on her face.

"Finn Anderson," he said. His fingers curled around hers, squeezing just slightly. A buzz ran through her that she refused to acknowledge.

"Great to meet you, Finn. What are your qualifications for teaching this class?" she asked. It was making her slightly sick to use the tittering female voice. But she liked to surprise people, and because she was naturally petite, she was often underestimated.

"I was military for seventeen years, so I think I'm pretty qualified," he told her. There was something in his voice as he said the word *was*. She knew there was a story there. She wondered if she'd find out what it meant.

"Hmm, that doesn't necessarily mean you're *qualified*," she told him.

"Why don't I demonstrate with you, then?" There was zero doubt it was a challenge he expected her to refuse. She kept her facial expression innocent.

"If it helps my patients, I'm more than willing to help," she told him. She turned and walked over to her students, set down her purse, and took off her jacket. Her size truly did make people underestimate her. She loved it.

"Okay, class, I'm going to show you what not to do, and then exactly what to do, if a man comes up behind you and grabs ahold," Finn said.

Brooke stood in front of him and smiled at the girls, who were beginning to giggle again as Finn crept up behind her. She could feel his hot breath as he stealthily began to surround her.

She waited.

This was the fun part.

Finn's arm wrapped around her middle, and before the other one could connect, Brooke jumped into action. She twisted so quickly she knew he wasn't sure what was happening. Her foot wrapped behind him, and within two seconds, she had him on the ground . . . pinned beneath her body with her legs trapping those beautiful arms to the mat.

The look of utter shock on his face was a priceless moment she was sure she'd live over and over again while dreaming and daydreaming. Her innocent expression evaporated as victory showed in her eyes. Who was teaching whom now?

"Is that what I'm supposed to do?" she asked as she batted her lashes and desperately tried not to giggle.

Then it was her turn to panic, because she saw the gleam in his eyes about a second too late. Before she had a chance to so much as inhale, she found herself being flipped over, with Finn's massive weight trapping her beneath him. Their breathing was heavy and loud as she found herself gazing into his intense blue eyes. Damn, she could get lost in them—she *was* getting lost in them.

"I haven't been surprised in a long time, Doc," he told her, his voice husky. For just a moment she forgot they had an audience. Her gaze dropped to his sexy, full lips, and she felt a tingle in her belly that was lighting her on fire. A low growl escaped his throat, and that made her realize exactly where they were.

"It's good for you," she said, her voice breathless and telling. "Too much confidence can make you weak and vulnerable." Now she wasn't sure if she was talking about him or herself. She didn't want to analyze that too closely.

"I think we're going to be friends," he said as he licked his lips. She had to bite her tongue and do everything in her power not to respond to this man.

"I don't think so," she said. "Now get off me."

He pressed more intimately against her for just a second, making her gasp, before he was suddenly on his feet, his hand held out. Brooke was too scared to touch him again, not while her hormones were going totally crazy. She stumbled her way to her feet.

She didn't meet his eyes this time as she said, "I think you're qualified." She then moved to her stuff and put on her coat, irritated her hand was trembling. There was no way she was staying in that studio with him.

"Bye, Doc," one of the girls called out, and she waved, afraid of turning around.

"I'll be seeing you soon, Doc," Finn promised as she reached the studio door.

She went outside and inhaled a deep breath of air, grateful the scent wasn't full of Finn Anderson.

"Not a chance will I be seeing *you* again," Brooke mumbled to herself. "I don't know what in the hell happened in there, but I can tell you're a dangerous man."

"What did you say, Doc?" Theo, an eighty-year-old patient, asked as he stopped next to her.

"Oh, sorry, Theo, I was just muttering to myself," she said, feeling heat in her cheeks.

Theo laughed. "I love it, Doc. I'm not the only one," he said. "Where are you heading?"

"I'm going home to eat and sleep," Brooke said.

"Then I'll accompany you. A pretty young lady shouldn't be walking alone, and my doc told me I need more exercise."

"I'd love the company, Theo," she said, putting her arm through his.

Finn Anderson was just a blip in her otherwise organized life. She'd forget about him by the time she woke up. She wasn't worried—not in the least.

CHAPTER FOUR

"I'm going to marry Brooke Garrison."

The room went utterly silent as four sets of eyes stared back at Finn as if he'd lost his mind. Well, technically he had lost a bit of his mind when he'd gotten his concussion and been forced into early retirement from the military.

But right now his thinking was more than clear. The moment he'd laid eyes on the sexiest woman he'd ever encountered, he'd needed to know her—it hadn't even been a choice. The second she'd taken him to the ground, he'd wanted her with a passion he'd never felt in his life. When she'd batted those eyes at him, victory in her gaze, he'd known he was going to marry her.

"Um . . . we didn't know you were seeing someone," Crew finally said after the silence dragged on and on. Finn was so in his own head about this woman he wasn't noticing much of his brothers' reactions.

"I'm not yet, but I'm still in love," Finn told them with a smile that wouldn't stop.

Brandon, who was always the first to make a joke in any situation, laughed. "Well, *now* you're making total sense," he said. "Go on and tell us more."

"She came to the studio last night and took me down in about two seconds flat. I mean she *literally* had me pinned to the ground without me allowing it. She's the woman of my dreams," Finn said.

"Wait! Hold the fort! A woman took you down?" Hudson said, his lips turning up in a beaming smile. Now his brothers were getting more into the conversation.

"She sure as hell did," Finn replied, not in the least worried about the mocking he was surely going to receive. He was hella impressed she'd done it. "I never would've thought she could do it. She can't be more than a few inches over five feet, and I could seriously wrap my hands around her waist. The girl is as petite as they come."

He couldn't quit grinning.

"Damn, maybe we're going to have our first family wedding," Noah said with a whistle.

"She's the practitioner here in town. I need a fake injury," Finn said, completely serious.

"What? You need what?" Crew asked, his brows wrinkling.

"An injury," Finn said, feeling completely reasonable. "Maybe you should punch me in the eye. Make it really black." He looked from brother to brother.

"Oh, hell yeah, I'm up for that," Brandon said, standing as he knocked his fists together.

"Simmer down, Rambo," Crew said. "No one needs to be punishing anyone. What we need is to realize our brother is in need of some serious help."

"He asked for it," Brandon said with a pout, looking incredibly disappointed.

"What in the hell is wrong with this family?" Crew asked, throwing his hands in the air. "Am I the only sane one?"

"On most days," Hudson said with a laugh. "That's why we needed one psychologist in the family—so the rest of us wouldn't go totally bonkers."

"It's too late for us," Noah piped in. "We're so far off the deep end, not even *you* can fix us, Crew."

"Yeah, that's what I've always feared," Crew said. "But still, no one in this family is punching anyone else in this family. Why don't you try to be a normal human being and simply ask the girl out?" The suggestion seemed completely foreign to the rest of the brothers, making Crew sigh.

"I don't think she likes me yet. Nope. I *definitely* need another plan," Finn said. "Come on, Brandon. Give it a go."

Before Crew could stop him, Brandon stepped up, and his arm flashed out with a right hook that nearly knocked Finn back. He shook his head to clear the stars. He'd been hit many times in his life, but his little brother had some power in those arms.

"Good job," he said as the fog cleared. "Am I bleeding?"

"Not yet," Brandon said with a laugh. "Want another one?"

"No, it's *my* turn," Hudson said with glee. "You had your shot. I get to help out, too. Our brother's in need, and I'm willing to give a fist to the cause."

"Stop this nonsense," Crew said. But it was too late.

Hudson got the next hit in, and this one caught the corner of Finn's mouth, and he immediately tasted blood. He moved to the garbage can and spit, then grinned at his brothers.

"Good enough?" he questioned.

"Yeah," Noah replied with a pout. "Guess I don't get to hit you next."

"Sorry, brother. Maybe next time," he replied, feeling pretty damn good. "But just remember, I get payback on those two," he pointed out.

"Hey, you asked for it," Brandon said.

"And we were just helping you," Hudson piped in.

"And I'll be willing to return the favor," Finn assured them.

"I'm out of here," Crew told them before storming from the room.

"Wait, you're the one I need to help come up with a story," Finn shouted. Crew kept on walking. Finn turned back to his other three brothers, at a loss. This wasn't going to work if he didn't have a hell of a story.

"Okay, here's what you say . . . ," Hudson began.

Finn smiled. He was *so* going to get the girl.

CHAPTER FIVE

There were days Brooke loved her job and days she wondered what in the world anyone had been thinking to give her a medical license. This day happened to be a day she was a bit worried about the medical profession in general.

It seemed she couldn't think. And no, it had nothing to do with a sexy military guy who'd kept her awake for two nights in a row. That was just foolish. It was a Monday, and she obviously was just recovering from her wild weekend of Netflix and an overdose of popcorn and Coke Zero.

"How many patients do I have left?" she asked her favorite assistant, Rose.

"Just one, and he's pacing," Rose told her.

"Okay, send him in. I need this day to end," Brooke said.

"I don't mind him hanging out in the lobby with me," Rose told her with a wide grin.

Rose was seventy-three but didn't look a day over fifty, and the woman could run laps around high school kids. Brooke hoped she had half the life Rose did when she was her age.

"Then we'd never get to go home," Brooke told her.

"You can leave him with me. I'll diagnose him, but I'm sure it'll take a full-body exam," Rose told her with a wink before turning and walking out of the exam room.

Brooke was smiling when Finn Anderson walked in her door. The smile fell away as she felt heat rush to places she didn't want it rushing.

"Hello, beautiful. How has your day been?" Finn asked as he moved with confidence to her exam table and hoisted himself up, towering above her.

"What are you here for?" she asked, though the swollen eye and cut lip were pretty good indications. It seemed odd, though, as he didn't seem the type of guy to rush to the doctor for a few fighting injuries. Her eyes narrowed as she kept her distance.

"I might have a concussion," he told her. "Better safe than sorry, I always say."

"What happened?" she asked, though she could probably figure it out.

He grinned, seeming completely unaffected by his injuries.

"There was this sweet old lady walking out to her car at the grocery store, when out of nowhere ten guys swarmed her and demanded her purse. I couldn't let that happen. I rushed to her side immediately. A couple of them got in a few hits, but I ultimately won," he said, his chest puffing out a little.

"Ten guys, huh?" she said, trying desperately not to laugh.

"Maybe more. I was too busy fending them off to *really* count." The total innocence in his eyes made his story that much funnier. She would not laugh. No way. No how. She turned away and composed herself before facing him again.

"Want to tell me the real story?" she asked.

"What? I'm hurt you don't believe me," he gasped.

"You might have a career in acting if the martial arts stuff isn't working for you," she said, crossing her arms against her chest.

"I wouldn't act with such a beautiful woman," he told her. "I'm hurt, Doc. I really need your assistance."

"You look fine to me. Put some ice on it, take some Advil, and try not to get in any more brawls for the next few days," she told him as she moved over to her desk and sat.

"Didn't you take an oath to do no harm?" he asked.

She spun around on her stool and glared at him. His beautiful blue gaze was boring straight into her eyes, just like it had at the studio.

"I'm not the one who punched you, but I can see how it could've happened. You seem the type of guy to get punched a lot," she told him.

"I'm a fun-loving guy. Ask anyone. I was just trying to protect the elderly," he said. "Now you better check me out, 'cause if I do have something wrong—and if I go home and die—you'll have to live with that the rest of your life."

She sat there for a few more moments before letting out a frustrated breath and rising. She didn't want to touch him, afraid of what would happen if she did. But he was right. She was the only practitioner in town, and it was her duty to see every patient who wanted her help, whether she wanted to or not.

"Did you pass out?" she asked, still standing three feet away.

"No, didn't pass out, but I saw stars," he told her.

"If you have a concussion, it can last for hours, days, or weeks. Some extreme cases last months. You'd have to stay with family." Maybe if she scared him enough, he'd give up this ruse.

"Can't stay with family right now. Maybe you should host me overnight," he said with a wink.

"That's never going to happen," she told him.

"Never say never," he easily replied.

"Have you had a headache or felt pressure in your head?" She was hesitating on actually touching him. It was foolish. She was a professional. Touching him was no big deal. She touched people all the time. She needed to pull it together.

"Yeah, slight headache and a bit of a fuzzy feeling."

"Are you telling me the truth?" she pushed.

"I wouldn't lie to you, Doc," he said, batting his big beautiful blue eyes.

She had no choice but to move closer. She grabbed her light and leaned in as she shined it in one eye and then the other. Their mouths were only a few inches apart, something she was very much aware of.

His breath smelled like mint and honey, of all things. Without her wanting it to, her tongue slipped out and wetted her suddenly dry lips. She was practically trembling as she stood this close to the man who'd haunted her dreams for two nights in a row. It was insane.

"Do you have any gaps in your memory since the fight?" she asked, hating the slight edge of huskiness in her voice.

"No memory loss, but a bit of dizziness."

"What about ringing in your ears?" she asked.

"When I was hit in the eye, I heard some ringing," he told her. His own voice had dropped a couple of levels, and each word he spoke sent a rush of hot air across her face that had her wanting to lay him down on the exam table to take advantage of him.

"When did this fight happen?" she asked.

"It wasn't a fight. It was a rescue," he told her. "And it happened this morning."

"Yeah, the bruising looks fresh. If anything, you have nothing more than a mild concussion. Why don't you go hang out with some friends—maybe have someone stay the night with you and check on you a few times? I don't see anything alarming."

"Come on, Doc. I just told you I don't have anyone. Show some mercy on me," he said.

She took a step back from him, taking a deep breath that was still full of his scent, and tried to get her rapidly beating heart back under control.

"This is highly unprofessional. I don't appreciate you trying to give me a guilt trip into going out with you," she told him in her sternest doctor voice. She'd had patients like him before, but none she'd ever felt the need to take the offer they were giving.

"But you don't want something to happen to me, do you?" he pushed.

"I'm not worried," she told him. "Go home and ice your face. Here's my number if more serious symptoms occur."

He let out a sigh as he accepted the card she handed him. "Can I page you anytime for *any* reason?" he asked with a wiggle of his brows.

"No, you can't. That's for emergencies only. If I get disturbed too much after hours, I get cranky, and no one wants a cranky woman with access to needles and scalpels."

His grin fell away for the briefest of moments. "You're a hard one, Doc. But I don't give up too easily," he said.

"I'm incredibly stubborn, Mr. Anderson," she told him.

"And I'm incredibly determined, Brooke," he quickly replied.

Her gut clenched again. There was nothing quite like a strong alpha male to make her feel more like a woman. She was stubborn and independent, and she valued her life. She didn't let anyone tell her what to do, and she'd earned respect in her line of work. It was hard for her to date because most men couldn't handle her.

She had a feeling Finn Anderson could not only handle her but also satisfy her in ways she couldn't imagine. Shaking her head, she looked away from him. This wasn't the time or place in her life for her to want anything from a man—especially a man like him.

"I need to close up," she told him.

She heard his feet hit the floor as he jumped off the exam table. She kept her back to him.

"Plan B it is," he said from behind her, his hot breath rushing across her skin, making goose bumps spread down her arms.

Before she had a chance to reply, he was out of the office. She didn't move for what felt like forever. She really had no idea what he was talking about with a plan B. And though she didn't want to, she was curious. Would he give up? Did she want him to? She wasn't sure.

"I know exactly how you're feeling. That man has charisma," Rose said, making Brooke turn and look at the doorway where Rose was standing, fanning herself with a magazine.

"And he knows it," Brooke told her with a crooked smile.

"That just makes him all that much more sexy," Rose said. "I'm going home now. I'm going to listen to a hot audiobook while taking a bath and picturing Finn's hands all over my soapy body."

"Rose!" Brooke gasped. "Please, for the love of everything holy in life, don't put images like that in my head."

Rose just laughed as she turned and walked away.

Brooke wasn't thinking about Finn's hands on Rose as she locked up the clinic and began her mile walk home. No, she was picturing her and Finn together in a large tub filled with scented oils, their skin slipping and sliding . . .

"Stop it!" she muttered as she moved a bit faster, trying to outrun her thoughts. She wanted nothing at all to do with Finn Anderson. She didn't want anything to do with any man.

She was too broken in her life right now, and it would be nothing but a disaster if she were to even try. She'd had her brother as a good role model in life, but her father had been worthless. Losing her brother had nearly destroyed her. She wasn't in a place she could take a chance on falling for someone, of going through another loss like how she'd felt from the moment she'd learned of her brother's death. Not that she thought Finn was the type of man who could be hurt, but it wasn't fair for her to date when she wasn't in a place she could give of herself.

Still, as she walked in her front door, she knew it was going to be a very long night—hell, a very long week, month, possibly even year. Maybe she should find some stranger and get laid. That would at least take one ache out of the equation.

But as soon as she had the thought, she knew she'd never do it. She wasn't that kind of girl. She wished like hell she was, but she wasn't. Finn was just a small obsession right now. She'd forget about him soon enough.

Maybe it was just because he was so persistent, and that was something that turned her on. He didn't seem at all intimidated by her, which was a complete novelty. Maybe . . . no! There was no *maybe*. She wasn't dating, had no desire to date, maybe never would again.

This was a time in her life when she needed to focus on herself. But no matter how much of a pep talk she was going through in her own head, it was blowing right out her ears, because as soon as she closed her eyes, she could see those bright-blue eyes looking down at her again . . . and she wanted him.

CHAPTER SIX

A rainbow rose from the ground in a perfect arch as fog drifted over the gently rolling hills, looking like an army of soldiers all coming to settle at the very spot the heart and soul of the veterans center was going to be built. The morning sun was just cresting over the top of the mountains, casting a halo of light upon it all.

Finn was a strong man; he had been through the depths of hell and clawed his way out of that dark place. He'd held men in his arms as they'd taken their last breaths, and he'd consoled friends over the unbearable loss. He'd been shot, stabbed, and tortured, and he'd led battles he hadn't wanted to lead.

He'd lived a life that would've traumatized many men and women, but his love of family and his desire to be a good man in spite of his father had kept him from leaping over the edge into oblivion. He did feel lost at times, but he never allowed himself to wander too long before finding an anchor to hold on to.

But as he stood in this place, he felt a tremor shake his body, felt a sting of tears in his eyes, and, though he'd never admit it out loud, felt an ache in his soul. He could almost hear the cries of those lost soldiers who'd died for his freedom and the freedom of so many others.

Finn had once been asked why he did what he did. He'd been a Navy SEAL and had been through a training regimen most people in this world couldn't survive and certainly wouldn't choose to go through.

And yet he'd been one of the few to volunteer, to take his career and his life one step further. One of the men at a base had asked him why he'd go through that—what made it worth the torture?

He hadn't been offended and certainly hadn't felt even the slightest hesitation in his response to the man.

"There's a brotherhood among soldiers—something you will learn the longer you're in this world. We will die for one another—that goes without saying, but it's so much more than that. We will hold on to each other's secrets, be there for every event that matters, and know it's reciprocated. Sometimes in this life being great isn't good enough. Sometimes we have to rise from the ashes we've turned into and become a man we can be proud of, a man we can look in the mirror and know we gave our all."

"But why a SEAL?" the soldier had persisted.

"Because I knew I was capable of more. I knew mediocre wasn't a word in my vocabulary, and I knew I had to push myself or else die a mental death. We don't go through a training program like that to show the world who we are. We do it to show ourselves who we're meant to be."

The kid had stood there without any further questions, and Finn had walked away. Some men had what it took to lead an army, and some were meant to follow. There was nothing wrong with that. Not everyone in this world had to be a leader. But saying that, everyone had it inside them if they wanted to dig deep enough.

Too many men and women settled for mediocre. Finn wouldn't settle for less than extraordinary.

"What do you think?"

Finn tensed at the loud voice behind him. Sure, he'd heard Joseph's vehicle pull into the otherwise quiet place, but he hadn't bothered to turn around. It had only been a few weeks since he'd learned Joseph Anderson was related to him.

But just because a man shared the same blood as you didn't make him family. What made a person family were the blood, sweat, and tears of years upon years of a relationship. Blood mattered, but brotherhood meant more.

Finn could truly say he had that brotherhood with his siblings. He could also say the same for fellow soldiers. Joseph might be in his family tree, but that didn't mean he trusted the man or respected him. Respect was something that must be earned. And it wasn't something easily earned, in Finn's eyes.

"I wasn't thrilled to jump on board this project when you put it before us," Finn told him. He was aware of how stiff his shoulders were and how he moved six inches to the left when Joseph stood beside him. There was nothing Finn did that he wasn't aware of.

"Why is that, son?" Joseph asked. The man's normally booming voice was a bit more subdued in this sacred place. Finn gave Joseph a morsel of respect for that.

"I'm not your son, Joseph. I don't want to be disrespectful or rude; I just want to set boundaries with you," Finn said.

Silence greeted his words. He was used to the art of a good silence. As thirty seconds turned into a minute and then two, Finn had to fight a curve to his lips. He didn't want to like Joseph, as the man was related to his late asshole father, but Finn couldn't help but wonder if a piece of his own stubbornness had come from this man.

"I respect boundaries," Joseph finally said.

Finn was so surprised by the words he wasn't sure what to say. For one, Finn hadn't been sure of Joseph's response, and that hadn't been at all what Finn would expect to hear.

"Good. Then we shouldn't have a problem," Finn said. If Joseph could compromise, then maybe he could as well.

Compromise wasn't something that had been much in his vocabulary, either. Finn was a leader through and through, and as such, he didn't often have to meet somebody in the middle. They either did it his way . . . or they died. That was the sort of situation he'd been in for a lot of his life.

"I agree," Joseph said with just enough power and edge to his voice to show Finn the man might be willing to compromise but never would he grovel. Finn could respect that as well.

"What made you decide to build this center if it wasn't for us?" Finn asked. He was watching as the rainbow began to fade, and the fog slowly sneaked away. He was wishing he had a camera on time lapse to capture the moment.

"I'm doing it for my wife," Joseph said. "As I told you, this project means a lot to her."

Whenever the man spoke of his wife, his voice softened, and his body relaxed. There was one thing Finn had no doubt about when it came to Joseph and Katherine. The man loved her more than himself and loved her more than anyone else on this earth.

She was his rock, his foundation, his world. That was something Finn had never understood before. Why in the world would a person give up everything for another human being? Why would they put themselves through the possible trauma of loving someone they couldn't live without?

But Finn's view on this was beginning to change. One chance encounter with a woman he couldn't stop thinking about was making that change. It was softening him. That wasn't necessarily a good thing. But no matter if he wanted to stop it now or not, it wasn't in his hands.

He was a powerful man, confident and ready to take on the world. But this woman could drop him without much effort at all. That was true power. That was power he knew nothing about.

"Was Katherine a veteran?" he asked Joseph.

"No. But her father was. And she lost him because of terrible care. The man shouldn't have died the way he did, and Katherine has been an advocate for veterans ever since. It was time to do something on a grander scale," Joseph said.

Finn didn't want to respect this man, but it was increasingly more difficult not to when he gave so much to others. That was something that couldn't be faked.

"So what do you envision?" Finn asked Joseph.

"No, son . . ." Joseph stopped and shrugged. "I'll apologize for that; it's a habit for me. I won't apologize for loving you, but I'll give you time to accept you have family before I push too hard."

There really wasn't much Finn could say to that, so he shrugged and waited for Joseph to continue.

"As I was saying, that's not for me to decide," Joseph went on. "This project is for you and your brothers to work out. I can't wait to see the magic that happens."

Finn did smile then.

"In this place, magic won't be a problem," he told Joseph.

"I'm surprised to hear those words from you. In my humble opinion, you don't seem to be a man who believes in fairy tales and unicorns," Joseph said. "And that's what magic is all about."

Finn did laugh a bit at those words.

"Yeah, I never have believed in the impossible," Finn admitted. "But I'm realizing I might not have all the answers after all." He was quiet for a while longer, but Joseph seemed to be very good at reading others. He didn't interrupt—just waited for Finn to continue.

"When it comes to soldiers, I've seen miracles. I've watched the hand of God come down and heal an unfixable wound. I've seen a bullet miss a head by a hair, and I've watched a man rise from an ambush without a scratch. I've also seen some horrific things that should've never happened. But those miracles changed my mind about magic. Those miracles made me begin to believe."

Joseph nodded but didn't say anything for long moments as they watched the rainbow fully fade and the last vestiges of the fog hide behind the mountain. Only then did he turn to Finn.

"This place will be a refuge. It will offer the best services, but it will also hold that magic you speak of. The reason for that is love," Joseph assured him. "It's being built out of love."

The walls around Finn's heart where family was concerned cracked a little with those words. He decided he'd better leave before a grenade took the walls completely out. There was no goodbye as the two of them parted. Finn had a lot to think about.

CHAPTER SEVEN

"Do you know how unbelievably stupid it was for you to get hit in the face, with the injuries you suffered only three months ago?" Denny Michaels, his friend and military doctor, said with a scowl.

"It was just a couple of punches, and I needed a reason to see the doc. I'm going to marry that woman," Finn said with a shrug.

"Dammit, Finn!" Denny thundered as his fist slammed down on the desk. "You were nearly killed by that bomb. It ended your career and could've easily taken your life. You need to take this seriously."

Finn grew solemn as he sighed. "Believe me; I've been taking it seriously. I've been a military man for seventeen years. I don't know how to be anything *but* a soldier. I was so pissed off for months my family couldn't stand me. Then this last week I've found myself smiling again."

"So you're smiling again, and the first thing you do is get in a fist-fight?" Denny questioned.

"That was to have an excuse to see the girl," Finn said.

"You couldn't come up with a better plan?" Denny pushed.

"One of my brothers said the exact same thing. But it seemed perfectly reasonable to me," Finn told him.

"It was idiotic," Denny said. Before Finn could defend himself again, he held up a hand. "Tell me what has you smiling again."

Finn's smile grew. "I don't trust Joseph. I'm not saying he's a monster, but why in the hell would he be pushing so hard to be around us? It makes no sense. But I do have to say, it's nice we have family. We've been on our own for so long I haven't imagined life any differently. Joseph might be a man pushing to get into our lives, and I'm certainly leery, but the rest of the Anderson clan doesn't seem too bad. That certainly isn't terrible," Finn told him.

"So you like having cousins?" Denny asked.

"I don't know them real well yet, but my brothers and I agreed to meet them at Joseph's place. There was a big family barbecue. What was nice is no one was pushy. My brothers and I have been on our own for a long time. You know that, and at first we weren't going to go, but in the end we don't run from anything, so we accepted the invite."

"How did it go?" Denny asked.

"We stayed about eight hours. At first it was a bit like boot camp with everyone sizing everyone else up, but I have to admit, my cousins have married well, because the wives told us all, including their husbands, to quit posturing and maybe try to get to know each other."

"That would certainly break the ice," Denny said with a chuckle.

"Well, they made us feel slightly foolish, where we could laugh at ourselves. And man, there are a ton of miniature Andersons running all over the place, and it's impossible to remain aloof when a blue-eyed, curly-haired little girl crawls into your lap and demands you tell her a story," Finn said with a smile.

"Hope you didn't tell her any war stories," Denny said.

"I have more class than that," Finn said. "I didn't know any fairy tales, so I just talked until she fell asleep in my lap."

"You're looking a little dreamy there," Denny told him with another chuckle.

"Don't think I'm going soft," Finn growled. "But I do have to admit, I wouldn't mind one of my own sitting where my niece was."

"Well, if you're calling her your niece . . . ," Denny said with a big grin.

"I guess technically she's my cousin or something, but the kids just automatically started saying Uncle Finn. I was a goner," he admitted.

"So why then don't you give Joseph the same chance you're giving the rest of the family?" Denny asked.

Finn stiffened the slightest bit. Then he forced himself to relax and take in a few calming breaths.

"You know I had a crappy excuse for a father. Joseph was his nephew. I just don't know that I can trust him."

"Trust has always been hard for you," Denny told him. "And I can see where you'd have reservations about the guy, but I've only heard good things about him."

"Which is a red flag for me. Everyone has something to hide. Everyone!" Finn insisted.

"Not a person who opens his doors for the world to step inside."

Finn thought about that for a moment. Then he shook his head. "It doesn't matter. I'm not going to let that man ruin how I'm feeling now."

"And how is that?" Denny asked.

Finn's smile grew. "I never believed in love at first sight. And then I met Brooke. And man, when she took me down to the ground with that cocky attitude and sweet-ass smile, I fell instantly in love, and all the anger I'd been feeling drained away. I've got to know this girl."

Denny smiled. "Why don't you just ask her out?"

"She has a wall the size of China around her. I have to be smart about it," Finn said.

"How do you know that?"

"Well, she keeps walking away from me, for one, but this is also a small town, and people like to gossip. She lost her brother a few months ago, and they were tight. She has a deadbeat father who walked out on her when she was little and a mother so high she doesn't know what day of the week it is. I have to be smart here."

"Is she worth it if it's this much work?" Denny asked.

"Hell yes, she's worth it. But I promise not to take any more knocks in the head. You didn't have to drive all the way here to check on me."

"When Crew called, I knew someone had to talk to you. Yes, I've been your doctor a long time, but I'm also your friend, and I know you rush in when you should be running out."

"I have a hero complex," Finn said with a shrug. "I'm the oldest of five kids, with my own stories of a deadbeat dad. I like rushing in."

"And you don't often take time to think about the consequences. You were injured badly, Finn. This isn't just a bullet wound or a broken bone. Your head was messed with," Denny said.

"I know. Trust me; I know. I was in a fog for six weeks. I can't remember much from the explosion that took some of my men's lives, and I'll carry the guilt of it for the rest of my life. I should've listened to my instincts. I knew something was wrong; I still did nothing."

Finn didn't want to think about that day, didn't want to think of the men who'd died under his command. The world was seriously messed up when one man could kill himself to kill so many others.

"It wasn't your fault. You know that. And yes, men died. But many are still alive, and the fighting will continue until hatred isn't so easily accepted."

"In a perfect world, we'd all appreciate each other and our differences and realize that's what makes us unique. But I fear it will be a long time before that happens."

"Yeah, I hate to agree with you, but you're right," Denny told him. Then he got into doctor mode again. "Now take off your shirt. I want to look at your chest."

"I'd rather Brooke examine me," Finn said with a laugh.

"Well, you're stuck with me, so don't be a pain in my ass."

Finn rolled his eyes as he removed his shirt. Yes, he had many scars on his body. He'd already had a few bullet holes in him and more than a few stitches, but the bomb that had ended his career had sent shrapnel all over his chest and side. But it could've been so much worse. He didn't care about the marks on his skin.

He wasn't worried Brooke would find fault in his battle scars. She didn't seem the type of girl to judge another for imperfections. Besides, Finn was a confident man. He kept himself in great shape, and he knew he was good looking and charismatic. The many numbers slipped into his pocket at bars had been happening his entire life.

One-night stands had always been enough for him. Maybe it was the fact that he was now thirty-five, or maybe it was just that his career was over. Maybe it was all the changes in his life. He didn't know what the reasoning was; he just knew that he hadn't so much as glanced at another female since the night he'd set eyes on Brooke Garrison.

One thing about Finn that hadn't changed in all his years was once he made a decision about something, he followed through on it. And right now, he'd decided to hunt Brooke—and he wasn't letting her out of his sight.

She could run all she wanted, but she'd never dealt with anyone like him before. She wouldn't have to again. Because even if she didn't know she was his, she was. And one thing was for damn sure—Finn didn't let go of something he truly wanted.

CHAPTER EIGHT

Brooke didn't know what to say or think when she stepped out of her clinic and found Finn leaning against the low brick wall beside the sidewalk. The man was absolutely exasperating, but she couldn't deny the tinge of excitement at seeing him.

She might not want to be a typical anything, but when it came to Finn Anderson, she felt like a girlish schoolgirl waiting for her crush to give her a bit of attention. It was absolutely ridiculous.

"Hello, beautiful," Finn said as he pushed himself off the wall and moved toward her.

"Finn," she said, showing no expression. There was no way she was encouraging him, but she was beginning to forget why that was.

"I couldn't let you walk home alone on this perfect night, so I thought I'd accompany you," he told her as he moved beside her and held out his arm.

She wasn't going to take it, she told herself, absolutely not, but somehow she found her hand sliding through that tempting crook of his elbow. And then they were walking before she knew it. What was wrong with her, dang it?

"Do you think I'm not capable of taking care of myself?" she asked with a smile.

"Oh, I have no doubt *you* could defend *me*," he said with a chuckle. "I was just looking for a reason to see you."

She laughed at his words. "I do respect honesty," she admitted.

"I love your value system," he told her.

His easy use of the word *love* wasn't missed by her. Brooke didn't often use that word in casual conversation. She never said things like "I love those shoes" or "I love a good sunset." She used the word *like* a lot, but not the word *love*. Maybe it was because love was reserved for something sacred, such as the love between her and her brother.

"Why would you put so much effort into courting me when I'm not interested?" Brooke asked. To some people, the question might come across as rude, but she knew Finn would think about it and answer honestly.

He paused as they made it about a block down the street. She did respect how he wouldn't just spurt out what he'd think she'd like to hear, but that he actually thought about his words. She couldn't help but have respect for him.

"I like you, and if I didn't think you had some genuine feelings for me, too, I'd give up, but that's not the case," he told her simply.

She chuckled. She wasn't going to try to tell him he was wrong. They'd both know she was lying, and it wouldn't do her any good.

"You haven't lived a civilian life very long," she pointed out.

She felt him tense the slightest bit before he forced his body to relax. That was another thing she respected and liked about this man. He seemed to have it together when she knew he'd been through things that would make most people lose it.

"No, I was forced into early retirement," he told her. There was the slightest tinge of bitterness in his voice at those words. She'd spent years in the military. She could relate to what he was feeling.

"Tell me what happened to push you out," she said. From one soldier to another she knew this could be tricky, but he was the one pursuing her. If he wanted to know her, then she certainly would need to know him.

"It's not a light story," he said.

"None of them ever are," she assured him.

They walked a few more steps, and she gave him time to decide if he was going to share with her or not. It wasn't something she could push from him. It was personal and difficult.

"One of the first lessons I learned in the military was to trust my gut," he told her. "I'm sure it was the only reason I was alive most of the time, since I've always been a man addicted to adrenaline, women, and danger."

"Women, huh?" she said with a chuckle.

"Yep, women," he answered as he squeezed her arm. "But that's all changed. It seems I'm addicted to only one now."

A warm glow she didn't want to feel indeed filled her.

"Quit being Casanova and go on," she told him.

"Well, you know there are five of us in my family. I don't think you know I had an abusive father who died when I was ten. I'd had no choice but to be tough. Before I was a teenager, I'd known I'd one day join the military. I think the way I grew up is the reason I thrived in a setting where early death is a very likely possibility."

"I think the tougher we are, the more easy we can face a situation, but I think that even the softest of souls can become a great soldier once they find who they really are," she said. "I used to be a lot stronger. Too many losses make us weak." She hated to admit something like that, but the words just spilled out.

"I agree with that. I've watched boys become men more than once. And it's okay to admit we need help sometimes. We don't always have to be strong."

She had to fight tears at his words. But she wasn't going to delve any deeper into that at the moment, so she addressed the first part of his statement. "And girls become women," she pointed out.

"There's no doubt about it," he said. "I just worked with far more men than women. It doesn't lessen the impact female soldiers have in the military world."

"No, it doesn't, and times have changed, but it's still difficult for a woman to rise in a man's world," she said.

"Not for the best—not for ones like you," he said.

She smiled. "I never knew there was a challenge. My brother always told me I was the best, so I walked in there *knowing* I was and never doubting that for a second." She loved being able to talk about her brother with a smile instead of tears. "But enough about me. I want to hear your story."

"I could hear about you all day long," he said.

"Yeah, yeah, yeah, now talk," she said with another chuckle. She was truly surprised how much she smiled and laughed around this man.

"I was sitting in the lead Humvee of five vehicles, with four more MRAPs behind me," he continued. "One of my men asked what we were gonna do. There was a sense of unease among all of us."

"I've been in situations like that," she said, wishing she could take some of his pain away. This wasn't a good memory for him.

"I told the guys I didn't like it, but ultimately it was my call, and they were going to do whatever I told them to do. I scanned the small village that contained about fifty citizens in a remote area of Afghanistan."

"I served there," she said. "I can picture the scene." He nodded.

"It was early on a Sunday morning, and we were doing humanitarian relief, bringing medical supplies, clothing, and food. Normally, as you know, when we showed up, the citizens would walk out and greet us with some hesitancy, for sure, but also with an underlying excitement at what they were about to receive."

"So no one was coming up, which would be a major red flag," she concluded.

"Yeah, for sure," he said. "I told my men to keep at full battle rattle. Then I opened my door and stepped out. My men followed me. We were all leery, all on red alert."

She waited, not wanting to interrupt. She felt almost as if she were there with him; the scene was so familiar for her.

"It took a good couple of minutes before the village elder stepped from one of the houses about forty yards in front of us. He nodded, then moved forward. I couldn't suppress the unease I was feeling and told my men to stand at full attention."

She was well aware of how easy it was to follow a commander you respected.

"I told the elder we had supplies when he was about ten feet away from us. Then I asked him where his people were. I didn't like how this was going down. Right after I asked the question, doors began opening, and the people stepped out with those expressions we'd come to recognize."

"I did it a few times. Those first steps they take are always hesitant, but then they move a bit quicker in anticipation of the new goodies. It was hard to stay on full alert sometimes when a small child was wrapping his arms around your legs, thanking you for a toy he'd never thought he'd own."

"Yeah, giving toys to the kids was probably my favorite thing to do," Finn told her.

Her heart softened even more for the man, dang it.

"I was talking to the elder when one of my men alerted me to look to my left," Finn said. "A man stepped around the corner of a building, a thick coat covering him in hundred-degree weather. We knew instantly this was bad."

"Very bad," Brooke agreed, feeling Finn's body tense.

"One of my men told him to halt. The man stopped about twenty-five feet in front of the nearest soldier to him, who demanded the man open his jacket." A shudder passed through Finn.

"The next few seconds were the slowest and longest of my life. Everything happened too quickly for anything to be done to stop it. I knew what was coming, but there was nothing I could do about it. All I could think about is how foolish it had been for me not to trust my instincts in the first place."

"If we're always running scared, then we'll never get a single thing done," she told Finn.

"There was a massive flash of light as the man literally exploded, the suicide vest he was wearing instantly disintegrating him. The soldier standing about six feet in front of me disintegrated, his body ripping apart before either of us even had time to blink. It just happened so damn fast."

"Oh, Finn," Brooke said, feeling his pain.

"The Humvee windows shattered as rocks flew through the air with added pieces of blood, flesh, and bone." He stopped talking as he cleared his throat. He was trying to get through the story, but he couldn't do it without emotion.

"My body was thrown back about ten feet as I crashed into the Humvee behind me. My ears were ringing, and I was desperately trying to get to my feet, but my legs weren't reacting to the command. I couldn't move."

"I'm sure you were injured more than the adrenaline running through your body was allowing you to know."

"There was so much chaos all around. The villagers who'd been farther back ran into their homes, slamming their doors shut. So many men, both soldiers and civilians, lay still on the ground around me. Body parts were scattered all over the place. I wasn't computing all I was seeing, but the nightmares I've had since have reminded me in vivid color what happened."

"The man did maximum damage," Brooke concluded.

"Yes, he'd had a powerful bomb, and he hadn't cared who he hit. It didn't matter if it wiped out his own people, as long as he was taking down US soldiers at the same time."

"They never care because they aren't human," Brooke said.

"One of my men was talking to me, but I can't remember this part. I've read it in the report, but I was fading fast. He called in a 9-line. I tried acknowledging him, apparently, the response so ingrained in my brain, but all I was seeing was darkness. All I was hearing was a deep ringing in my ears."

"Do you remember any of it?" she asked quietly.

"I remember the soldier telling me to hold on, that everything was going to be okay. My men were trained well, and they knew what to do. He stayed with me, his hands pressed against my chest. There was so much blood. My blood, other people's blood, so much blood. I've seen a lot in my years, but I'd yet to see anything like what I saw as that bomb went off."

"I'm sorry."

He didn't acknowledge her empty words. That's all they were. She was sorry, but she had nothing to do with it. It was odd how people apologized for things they didn't do. You could say you were sorry they were feeling what they were feeling or had gone through what they'd gone through, but even then, they were just empty words. It was something she really wanted to quit saying.

"The last conscious thought I had of that day was realizing I was smelling charred flesh. I prayed at that moment it was something I'd never smell again, something I'd never see again."

She waited for him to conclude as they reached her house. She wasn't going to apologize again. She also wasn't going to leave him standing on her doorstep right after he'd shared something so personal with her.

"When I came to next, I was in a hospital getting patched up. It was days until I found out we'd lost six of our men in that explosion, and eight villagers. It was a lose-lose situation all the way around. I didn't know for another couple of weeks that I'd never go out in the field again."

"How did that make you feel?" she asked.

"Angry," he admitted. "I was forced to come home."

She wanted to comfort him, wanted to take some of his burden away, but she was already falling for this man she didn't want to fall for, and she didn't want to keep encouraging that. She had her own demons she was fighting. How could two broken people have a healthy relationship? She didn't see that as possible.

"Finn, this is a lot," she told him. "I think you need someone to tell your story to, someone to help you, but I really don't think that person is me. You didn't want to come home, and home is where I feel the safest. Right there is a big difference between us."

He turned them so he was pulling her against his hard body. His expression changed as his lips turned up the slightest bit. His eyes still looked lost, but there was a light in them that intrigued her no matter what she'd just said.

"I didn't want to come home—not because I don't love my family, but because I identified more with the soldier I was than the man I am," he said. Then his lips turned up more. "But then I met you. You might not think you're the person to help me, but maybe, just maybe, we're supposed to help each other."

Her heart thudded hard at his words. "Finn," she warned.

He leaned down and gave her a kiss. It wasn't slow nor fast. It was firm and gentle at the same time, and when he pulled back he took her breath with him.

"I'm glad to be home," he said. The last of the shadows in his eyes had evaporated.

He didn't allow her to respond. He just turned and walked away, leaving her swaying on her feet. And Brooke was in serious trouble, because she found herself wanting to call him back to her.

CHAPTER NINE

Confidence was a funny thing. It was easy to feel when everything was going your way. And for Finn Anderson, from the time he'd hit puberty, *everything* had certainly gone his way.

That was, until he'd met Brooke Garrison.

Something Finn had decided early in life was *not* to chase women. He didn't need to. They chased him. If he asked a girl out, and she said no—that might have happened maybe once in his life—then he moved on. And he never thought about her again.

But nope. That certainly wasn't the case with Brooke. He'd been to her office twice, sent her flowers, and even managed to walk her home, where he'd felt a great connection with her and knew she'd felt it, too. And yet she was still keeping her distance.

If he truly thought it was because she wasn't interested, he'd have given up. Rules were created for a reason, after all. But he knew she wanted him, knew she was more than interested. He could see how she reacted to him.

Her breath hitched, her skin broke out in goose bumps, and her cheeks flushed. She didn't want to like him, but she did. So that meant he had to get more creative. He had to find out more about her and win her over by giving her something she couldn't say no to.

"So you still striking out?" Brandon asked with a laugh as he took a long pull of his Corona.

"I wouldn't exactly call it striking out," Finn grumbled.

"It's Friday night, and we're sitting in the bar together instead of with beautiful women on our laps. I'd call that striking out," Brandon told him.

"I like this bar. They have a good band on Fridays," Finn corrected.

"So you're telling me you'd rather be here with me than one particularly sexy doctor?" Brandon pushed.

"No, I'd rather be naked with Brooke in my house, but I have patience," Finn said, making Brandon choke on his swallow, bringing Finn slight pleasure.

"Well, she's right over there. Why don't you give it another try?" Brandon told him when he was done choking.

Finn's head whipped around as he watched Brooke walk into the room with two women. His heart instantly raced at the sight of her in a pair of skintight jeans and a fitted top. She wasn't overdressed, but she didn't have to be. There was such natural beauty about her she could seriously cause a freeway jam just by walking along the side of the road.

"She's with friends. I'm not going to bother her," Finn said as he held up a hand. The pretty waitress who'd been flirting with him for the past hour was instantly at their table.

"Another round, sugar?" she asked as she batted her ridiculously long eyelashes.

"Yeah, and I'll take a double whiskey on ice as well," Finn said.

"Make that two," Brandon piped up.

"Be right back," the waitress said.

"Damn, she's cute," Brandon said as he looked at the woman's ass as it swayed.

"Can you even describe her face? Your eyes have been on her ass all night."

"When you wear shorts that short, of course eyes are gonna be on your ass," Brandon said.

What Finn found interesting was he'd of course noticed the woman's curves, but he hadn't felt a single lustful thought. There was only one woman he wanted to be thinking about, only one woman he seemed to find the least bit attractive. He was so totally screwed.

The drinks arrived, and he pounded the whiskey, loving the burn down his throat. He needed to calm his nerves before he did something stupid like stand up, walk over to Brooke, and throw her over his shoulder.

Maybe she'd respond to a little caveman gesture.

Most likely not.

He'd probably find himself pinned to the ground again. But that wasn't such an unpleasant thought, either.

"Just go talk to her. You're going to be absolutely no fun now that she's here and you're obsessing," Brandon told him.

Though he was feeling a slight buzz, his senses weren't nearly dulled enough to handle watching as two men walked up to Brooke and her companions, standing far too close. When Brooke laughed at something one of the men said, Finn felt his blood boil.

"Calm down. You don't own her," Brandon said with a laugh.

"You never *own* a girl. Maybe thoughts like that is why you're still single," Finn snapped.

Brandon laughed. "I'm single because I'm too selfish to be in a relationship," he said with a shrug. "And I like my freedom. There's no one out there worth giving it up for."

"I'm gonna laugh my ass off when a woman takes you down," Finn said.

He wasn't laughing at the moment, though. The man got a little too close to Brooke, and he felt his muscles tense with the need to jump up and push him away.

"I'm laughing right now. Damn, you look pissed."

Just then the man's hand shot out and wrapped around Brooke, pulling her against him as he grabbed her ass. Finn was on his feet in less than a second. He was going to kill the guy.

Brandon stood right beside him, his smile fading at the raw fury in his brother's face.

"We're getting in a brawl, aren't we?" Brandon asked.

Finn took a step forward, but there really was no need. He stopped in his tracks as Brooke spun around so fast the guy groping her had no chance of retaliation. In about two seconds she flung him to the ground, her high heel poking into his chest.

"Don't ever grab me like that," she said, her smile still in place.

The man lost all color in his face as he looked over to his buddies, who were roaring with laughter.

"Let me go, bitch," the guy said as he struggled beneath her.

"Gladly," she told him.

She turned away, grabbed her drink from her friend, and completely ignored the guy. She might be tough, but she obviously had no sense of preservation. The bar was crowded, and Finn began pushing people away as he tried to reach her in time.

The man stood up, fury written all over his drunk features.

"Don't do it," Finn said, but his words were drowned out by the band and the crowd.

The man lifted his arm, getting ready to slug her. What kind of a pig was he? Finn reached them just in time to stop the man's fist from connecting with the back of Brooke's head.

She whipped back around and saw what had just about happened. She didn't look scared; she looked absolutely livid.

"You were going to hit me from behind?" she gasped, looking at the mortified man in shock and anger. "What kind of man hits someone from behind?"

"You bitch!" he screamed, struggling against Finn. He really wanted to knock this asshole out.

"Don't do it. He's so not worth it," Brandon said. "Let me walk him outside."

Finn felt adrenaline ripping through him. The need to punch this man was so extreme it was taking all the willpower in him to stop himself.

"Come on, brother. Let it go," Brandon said, a hand on his arm.

Finn looked at Brooke, who appeared just as pissed as him. That helped calm his nerves . . . some. He nodded, afraid if he spoke he'd explode.

Brandon grabbed the man's arm, twisted it behind his back, and smiled when the guy yelped. Then he began moving, giving the guy zero choice but to move forward. His friends looked away, obviously embarrassed and not willing to get into a fight.

Finn turned back to Brooke.

"You look nice," he said.

Her mouth gaped open as she stared at him as if he was insane. He felt as if this woman was making him head in that general direction.

"Um . . . well . . . um . . . thanks for the help. I totally wasn't expecting him to hit me," she said. "I could've taken care of it, but I appreciate not having a bruise on the side of my face. He'd have gotten his ass kicked, but . . . well, thanks."

"Hmm, do you have a hard time thanking someone? That came out a little hesitantly," he said, his mood instantly improving just speaking with her. Damn, this woman must be using black magic or something because she had him hook, line, and sinker.

"I don't normally need to thank anyone. I take care of myself," she told him, her shoulders going back and that confident gleam appearing in her gorgeous eyes. That look made him want to push her up against the nearest wall with her legs wrapped around him.

He shifted, his pants becoming ridiculously uncomfortable.

"Hi, I'm Sarah," the dark-haired girl sitting at Brooke's table said with a friendly smile.

"And I'm Chloe," the blonde girl spoke up somewhat shyly. "What Brooke meant to say was, 'Thank you so much.' She truly appreciates you helping."

Brooke glared at her friend. "I did say thank you," she said.

"Yeah, in your 'I don't really mean thank you' tone of voice," Sarah said with a chuckle. "She's all bite, you know. She's as smooshy as a marshmallow underneath it all."

"Shut up," Brooke muttered.

He was sure he wasn't supposed to have heard that, but he was so damn tuned in to her he could hear her breathe.

"Don't give up, 'cause I've never seen her react to a man the way she's reacting to you," Chloe told him.

"I think we're going to be great friends," he said as he looked at Brooke's friends. They both grinned at him. Brooke glared.

"I do appreciate the help, but we're having a girls' night, if you don't mind," Brooke said when she looked at Finn again. She barely met his gaze before her eyes dropped to his lips, making his pants even more uncomfortable.

"Are you kicking me out?" he asked with a smile. He was in no way offended. He wasn't sure if this woman could do anything that would offend him. He was too smitten. It was an incredibly odd feeling, but one he was growing to like . . . a lot.

"Not a chance," Sarah said. "I'm buying him a drink for rescuing us."

"It's a girls' night," Brooke said with her brows raised.

Sarah just laughed while Chloe spoke up. "I'm buying him one, too."

"I couldn't turn down such a generous offer, or it'd be rude," Finn said, feeling pretty good. All the adrenaline had simmered down, and now that he was with Brooke, even if she was trying to get rid of him, his Friday night had completely turned around.

"Well, if you guys want to be alone . . . ," Brooke said with a shrug.

Sarah and Chloe laughed in unison, and Finn couldn't help but grin. It showed a lot about a person by who they chose to hang around, and Brooke had great taste in friends. He was liking her more and more by the minute.

"So we hear you've been stalking Brooke. According to her she's turned you down several times, but you haven't run away yet with your tail between your legs. That's impressed me already," Sarah said as she put an arm through his, and they moved toward a table.

"I don't give up too easily," he said.

Sarah and Chloe were both incredibly beautiful women, but there wasn't even a spark of attraction. Nope. The only woman he wanted was an irritated brunette who was giving him some pretty fantastic dreams.

"We'll see," Chloe said as she sat down next to him. "I've watched Brooke make grown men weep."

"Then she's hanging around the wrong men," Finn assured her.

"I think you might be right about that," Sarah said.

"I'm right here," Brooke said, her hands flying up in the air as she sat down across from him.

"Don't worry, beautiful; I always know where you are," Finn told her with a wink.

Her cheeks turned a delightful shade of pink, and he had a sudden image of her hair spread out on his pillow, her cheeks flushed, her lips gaped open in a gasp of pleasure. His pants were now painfully tight. He tried to shift, but it did no good.

"Quit calling me that," she muttered as she looked away.

"I'm just stating the obvious," he told her.

"Oh, I like you, Finn," Sarah said.

"Yep. Me too. Don't give up," Chloe said.

"Not in my nature," Finn told the girls.

Brandon made it back and ordered another beer, and Finn took his time grilling Brooke's friends. If he was going to win a date with the girl, there was no better way to do it than getting her information from other females. By the end of the night he had a solid plan of action.

Brooke didn't talk a heck of a lot, but she did manage to relax some as she chatted with Brandon. His little brother had a way of easing people's nerves. He was a good guy, genuine and funny and a pleasure to be around.

If Finn had jealous tendencies, he might've felt a little threatened at the way the two of them chatted so easily. But since Finn wasn't worried in the least about his brother doing anything more than trying to make him jealous, he remained calm.

Never in their lives had the brothers ever let a woman come between them. If one of them staked their claim, it was hands off to the rest of them. That rule had never been broken.

For the first time since meeting Brooke Garrison, Finn had a good night's rest. He had plans for the next day. And whether Brooke knew it or not, she was a part of those plans.

He was so going to win the girl.

CHAPTER TEN

Seven in the morning on a Saturday wasn't Brooke's favorite time of day. Especially when she'd been out until one the night before and had downed maybe five too many tequila shots. When her phone rang, it felt like thunder booming through her house.

She covered her head and prayed for the noise to stop. But the fates weren't aligning with her because it began ringing again just as she started to drift back to sleep. Fury filled her as she ripped the pillow from her head and threw it across the room.

Sitting up, she glared at the phone. How dare it ring so early on her day off? She didn't pick it up. But now she was awake, and her head was pounding. She rose from her nice, comfy, warm bed and slowly made her way to the bathroom. The image gazing back at her wasn't a pretty sight. Her hair was sticking out in all directions, and last night's makeup, though light, looked like raccoons had taken up residence under her eyes.

She made her way to the kitchen, and it took three tries to get her coffee brewing. Then she stood there and stared at it longingly as it slowly dripped into the pot. That wasn't helping, so she grabbed a glass of water and downed a couple of Advil, praying for the pounding in her head to diminish.

A knock sounded on her door.

Maybe it was a wrong address. No one in their right mind would show up at her house this early on a Saturday. On the best of days Brooke wasn't a morning person, but her friends would all be snuggled up in their own beds right now. They wouldn't be out. Yes, Brooke had probably drunk more than both of them combined the night before, but they'd had their own fill.

The knock sounded again.

An actual growl escaped her throat as she stomped her way to the front door, not bothering to check who it was. Whoever was rude enough to be at her house that early deserved a fright at the sight of her.

She yanked open the door . . . then froze.

Finn was standing there, looking far too fresh and happy, a grin on his beautiful lips, and wearing an outfit that left little to the imagination. He was in running shorts and a skintight black shirt that molded to his body the way she wanted to be wrapped against him.

"Good morning," he said all sunnily, as if he wasn't completely out of line for being at her place. "Is that coffee I smell?"

Much to her horror, the man stepped inside her door and moved right past her. For about five seconds she was motionless and unable to utter a sound. Finally, it clicked that the guy she'd been trying to avoid, who seemed to be everywhere, had not only monopolized her night but was now at her place six hours later.

She slammed her door shut and stormed into the kitchen, ready to have it out with him. She stopped again as she saw him pull two coffee mugs down from her cupboard and pour the steaming liquid into the cups. He moved with ease in her kitchen as if he'd been there a million times before.

She was still unable to speak as he opened her fridge, looked around for a second, then pulled out the half-and-half. He moved over to the counter and poured a dab into his cup, stirred it, and took a sip.

"Perfect. Just what I needed," he said with a smile. She was standing with her mouth dropped open, not knowing what to do. "And I have fresh doughnuts to go with them." He held out a box she hadn't noticed. When she didn't take it, he set it on the counter and opened it. The smell of sugar and yeast made her stomach growl. He pulled one out and took a bite. "Delicious. Eat up. You'll need the energy."

Finally, Brooke broke through her shock. She stood there with her hands on her hips as she tried to form the right words. She wanted to yell, but she had her brother's voice in her head telling her people listened to you a lot more when you used a calm voice.

"What in the hell do you think you're doing?" she asked through clenched teeth. Her words rose a little at the end of the sentence, but she felt she was controlling herself quite well under the circumstances.

"Picking you up for a race," he said, as if it was something they'd had planned.

"What are you talking about?" The smell of the doughnuts and coffee was finally too overwhelming, and as much as she wanted to physically kick him from her house, she had to have the energy to do it first.

She moved over to the coffee, poured creamer in it, and took her first sip, a sigh escaping her grateful mouth. There was nothing quite like that first sip of hot coffee in the morning, especially when your head was fuzzy and a hangover was overtaking your senses.

"You took me to the ground in front of an entire class. I've decided to challenge you to a race to regain my manhood," he said.

It was way too early for her to try to figure this out. She was utterly lost. Without even realizing it, she grabbed a doughnut and took a bite, groaning at the taste as it practically melted on her tongue.

"What race?" she asked. "And I have no doubt your manhood is firmly intact." She turned away and moved over to her island, sitting.

The look Finn gave her as his eyes gazed over her, from the tips of her messy hair to the soles of her feet, finally made her realize she was in a tiny pair of silk shorts and a tank top that left little to the imagination. She didn't like sleeping with a bunch of clothing.

With a gasp, she dropped her doughnut, jumped up, and moved quickly to her room, where she grabbed a robe. Her face was flaming as she cinched it around her waist. She'd been too irritated by his interruption to notice what she was wearing. When she came back out, he was sitting at her breakfast bar, still gazing at her with the same heated look.

"Still look amazing," he said with a wink.

"This is so inappropriate; I don't even know where to begin," she told him. She grabbed her coffee and the last bit of her doughnut and moved away from him. "I'm not doing a race with you. I think you should leave."

She drained her coffee and poured herself another cup. She wasn't human until she had at least two. As much as she didn't want to give him the satisfaction, she grabbed another doughnut, too. Drinking always made her hungry the next day. Maybe it was her body's way of trying to recover.

"Are you chicken?" he asked, a clear taunt in his eyes.

That firmed her shoulders as she glared at him.

"I'm not afraid of anything," she informed him. She'd been in some pretty harrowing experiences when she was a flight medic. There wasn't a lot in her small town that could make her shake. Maybe spiders. They were creepy and could sneak up on a person. Absolutely terrifying.

"Good. Then we'll race," he said, as if it were a done deal.

"What makes you think you can show up on my doorstep, walk into my house, get into things in my kitchen, and then challenge me?" she snapped.

"I'm doing it," he said.

She was trying desperately not to yell.

"Why are you so determined to see me? I've made it clear I don't want to date you," she told him. She hated being mean, but it appeared a direct approach was all that was going to work on him.

"I get that, but I like you. So let's be friends," he suggested. She wasn't buying the innocent look in his eyes one little bit. There was no way she could be friends with him, not when she wanted to rip his clothes off and run her mouth down those solid abs she was sure he was sporting.

"We can't be friends," she told him.

"Why not? I'm a great guy," he told her.

"Because you don't want to be just friends," she said.

"I can be friends. It's a place to start. And I want to take you for an adventure today. That's what friends do."

Brooke loved races. She loved anything that challenged her, anything that raised her adrenaline. He was proposing something that made it really hard for her to say no. And from the look in his eyes, he was very much aware of that.

"What kind of race is it?" she asked. Her headache was fading, and even though she didn't want to be intrigued by the prospect of getting out and challenging herself, she was. Plus, she really, *really* wanted to wipe that smug look off his face.

Yeah, he might be bigger than her and stronger. But that wasn't an advantage in a race. She could move fast. Because of her petite size she was often underestimated. The more she thought about it, the more appealing the idea became.

"It's an obstacle mud run, and we're already signed up," he told her.

"You were pretty confident I'd do this," she said. She so wanted to tell him to stick it, but she loved mud runs, and she had no doubt she could kick his ass at it. The more mud that got on him, the heavier he'd become. Plus she'd learned a few tricks. If she rubbed her scented oil on her arms and legs, a lot of the mud slid right off. She wasn't teaching him *that* trick.

"I've asked some questions," he said as he stood. Damn, the man had incredibly sexy legs. They also had a lot of hair, another thing for the mud to stick to. She was so going to beat him.

"What questions? And with who?" she asked.

"I can't reveal my sources," he told her.

"You're a royal pain in the ass, you know that?" she said.

He just laughed as he poured himself a second cup of coffee and grabbed another doughnut.

"I have four siblings. I've been told that a time or two," he said, not even a little bit offended.

"Does anything get under your skin?" she asked.

"Yeah, a man trying to hit a woman," he told her, his smile fading. "If that guy had made contact with you, he would've left that bar with broken bones." The way he spoke the words was with cool confidence, and she had no doubt he was speaking the truth.

"I don't need someone to protect me. I'm capable of taking care of myself."

He moved closer, and she lost her breath when he stopped with their bodies almost touching. The heat coming off him made her want to strip away her clothes and see how good it would feel to be pressed against him.

"We all need to be taken care of once in a while," he said in that deep husky voice that absolutely melted her.

She had no retort. And she knew if she didn't move now, she was going to cave in to her desires. So, too quickly for her still-hungover body, she turned, practically threw her coffee cup on the counter, and ran from the room.

Brooke didn't like running away from anything, but in this case, she decided to give herself a break. The man could charm his way into a lion's den and have them all purring like kittens. And she wasn't as strong as a lion. Not at this point in her life, and not when Finn reminded her of all the wonderful qualities of her brother.

They were so much alike it was scary. But she definitely wasn't having brotherly thoughts about Finn—that was for damn sure.

Retreat was the smartest option. She felt much better at leaving him in her kitchen for over an hour as she took an extralong hot shower and went through her workout clothes, deciding on the best outfit to wear.

Brooke was definitely competitive, and she needed to gain the upper hand when it came to Finn Anderson. He'd had it from the moment their eyes had first connected. But she was more than determined to steal it from him.

And maybe if she could do that, she'd try out her lion-taming skills next.

CHAPTER ELEVEN

It was a surprisingly warm day for a suburb of Seattle. The sun was actually out, which was a good thing, since Finn was about to drag Brooke through muddy water and over obstacles.

From what he'd learned about this woman in the last couple of weeks, he knew a regular date just wouldn't do. She liked adventure, loved to be challenged, and was a strong woman. If he wanted to win her over, he had to think outside the box. That was a real treat for him.

"This is only three miles?" Brooke asked, making Finn laugh. Before his injury he'd run an average of ten miles a day. Now, he knew this course would actually challenge him, but his doctor had told him to exercise and to just be careful of his head. He could do that.

"Three miles of nonstop activity," Finn told her. "You up for it?"

The look she sent him had him wanting to throw her over his shoulder again to take her to the nearest secluded area. Damn, she was sassy as hell and more than a match for him. He wasn't going to ever let this woman go.

"Just try to keep up," she told him as the announcer called them to the front of the line. She was practically jumping where she stood, very eager to get started.

The gun went off, and Finn was so busy fantasizing about Brooke that she definitely got a head start. He didn't mind that, either, because he had one hell of a view of her backside—and it was a great ass.

This particular course had been designed by a former military group, and it wasn't for the faint of heart. They ran about a quarter of a mile before the first mud pit stood before them. Brooke didn't even hesitate as she jumped onto the rope above the pit, her feet practically flying over the wobbling line.

While Brooke made the obstacle look easy, Finn took a moment to watch people falling into the mud left and right. By the time he could actually take his eyes off of her, she was on the other side. He had to get moving, or she really would smoke him on this course.

With a smile, he launched himself onto the rope and caught up with her at the rope ladders. She looked like a spider monkey as she easily made her way over the ladder, then made a graceful jump down, not getting a single speck of mud on her.

He kept pace with her the entire time, preferring the view from behind. Every once in a while she glanced back; her eyes lit up with happiness and victory as she figured she was beating him. He didn't mind her winning.

When they came to a muddy pit filled with cars that they had to hop over, Finn again stood back and watched. She was poetry in motion. She looked as if she was barely hitting the hoods of the cars before leaping to the next one. People were slipping and sliding all over the place, and her laughter was ringing out as she skated across the obstacle.

He was falling deeper and deeper in love with this woman.

He didn't want her getting too far away, so he ran over the cars, nearly slipping at the end. He had to take a major leap, and still his foot hit the mud, the gooey mess splashing up the back of his thighs. Much to his bad luck, she turned at that particular moment, her lips turned up as she laughed at him.

And he immediately looked around for the nearest place to haul her to. If he didn't kiss her soon, he might implode. This woman was driving him crazy in all the best ways.

They had to next belly crawl beneath army netting, and there was no avoiding getting dirty this time, especially with paintballs and fire hoses aimed straight at them. He stayed right on her feet as she easily navigated her way through it. She had hardly anything on her, while he was covered in blue, green, and red. Looked like the shooters thought she was too damn hot to hit.

They were right.

She was oblivious to her appeal, though. As they came out the other side, two of the firemen literally were stopped in their tracks as they stared at her, trying to get her attention. She ran right on by. Their heads turned as they followed her. If he was a jealous man, he might've wanted to stake his claim. But Finn wasn't. She was his even if she didn't know it.

Brooke crossed the finish line two seconds in front of him, then turned and did a happy dance around him as she giggled in pure joy.

"I won. I won. I won. I won. I won," she said in a singsong voice as her fingers poked at his chest, shoulders, and arms. "You couldn't catch me." The pure joy in her voice was enough to send him off the deep end.

"That deserves a prize," he told her.

She made another circle around him, still in her taunting mode. This time when she was standing before him, he grabbed her. She immediately stopped what she'd been about to say, and her eyes grew wide as her lips parted, and her already flushed cheeks turned a deeper shade of pink.

He didn't give her time to think, just wrapped his muddy arms around her and pulled her to him. The gasp escaping that delicious mouth of hers sent his hormones into overdrive.

"This should've happened more than just once," he said, giving her the only warning he was capable of.

She didn't fight him as his head lowered and their lips connected. The first taste of her cherry lips had his head spinning. She didn't fight him, not one bit. Her body melted against him as she opened her mouth and kissed him back.

Finn forgot they were at the finish line of a race, forgot there were hundreds of people around them. Hell, he forgot his own name as this strong, stubborn, beautiful woman gave herself to him.

Finn's hand moved lower as he prepared to grab her luscious ass and pull her legs around him. But they were rudely interrupted as cheers and catcalls echoed around them.

"Yeah, you go, man," someone shouted.

"Mmm, that's a prize I want," a woman said in a giggling voice. "I'm sooooo next."

Brooke gasped as her lips ripped away from his. She looked at him in horror before glancing at the crowd circling them, laughing, everyone in good moods to have finished the race and witness a hot kiss.

"I can't believe I did that," Brooke said as she lifted her hand and ran a delicate finger over her swollen bottom lip.

"You make me forget where I am," he told her. "That's something that's never happened to me. You were magnificent today."

She shyly looked away from him, which shocked him all over again. She was so damn confident, seemed to have her life together in so many ways. But she didn't see herself the way he saw her. He placed a finger under her chin, forcing her to meet his gaze.

"You are beautiful, strong, talented, and amazing, and I'm utterly obsessed with you. Don't hide. Don't fight it. Just accept who you are and what an honor it is for me to be with you."

Her mouth gaped open as she gazed at him. A sheen of tears appeared in her widened eyes, and she tried to turn, but he wouldn't allow it. He was completely mesmerized.

"I don't know what's happened in your life that you don't see your-self, but I'm damn determined to show you exactly why I like you." He wanted to tell her he was in love with her, but he knew she wouldn't believe him. He knew it was far too soon. Hell, they'd just shared their second kiss. He'd never told a woman he loved her before. He'd never even come close to thinking he was in love.

"Nothing happened to me. I'm fine," she said, but there was a slight shake to her voice. She wanted the world to think she was a hell of a lot braver than she actually was.

"You are more than capable of taking care of yourself," he told her. "But I want to lift the burden you carry. I want to show you it's okay to let another stand by your side—not in front of you, not behind you, but right at your side. I'm that person. You'll learn to trust me."

She didn't say a word, and he could see she was fighting tears. He decided he'd said enough for now. He let her go, wrapped her fingers in his, and walked toward the cleanup area.

Their time together was just beginning. They had a lot more adventures ahead of them, and he was looking forward to every single moment.

CHAPTER TWELVE

Brooke paced her house, unsure of what she was feeling. She'd been filled with something unlike anything she'd felt before after that mind-boggling kiss Finn had laid on her at the end of the race.

She tried convincing herself it was no big deal. She'd been full of adrenaline, on a high from doing so well. It was perfectly natural to think there was more to the kiss than there really was.

She reached up and touched her still-tingling lips. But then the man had driven her home and dropped her off without so much as a peck goodbye, and for the last few hours she'd been an utter mess.

The spray from the shower had felt like tiny needles poking her over and over again because her entire body was overly sensitized. She was a nurse practitioner, dammit. She knew hormones, knew about the release of chemicals when a person was turned on. It was how the human species survived, after all.

But at the moment she didn't feel like a nurse, doctor, or any other professional. She felt like a needy woman, but she wasn't sure what she wanted to do about it. She didn't like it one little bit.

It was a little past ten when her doorbell rang, giving her a definite sense of déjà vu. She absolutely despised how her hand shook as she reached for the doorknob. There was no doubt in her mind who was on the other side of that door. She just wasn't sure what to expect or what she wanted to happen.

"Hello, beautiful," Finn said as he stood before her.

"Finn," she replied, her voice a bit too husky.

"I had a lot of fun today," he told her, not attempting to push his way inside this time. Brooke didn't even care if her nosy neighbor was staring out her window right now. She felt frozen in place as she stood in front of this man who'd been driving her crazy.

"I did, too," she admitted. "Thanks for the race." It was a little bit lame, but she couldn't seem to help herself. She didn't know what to say around this man, which was something new for her.

"I had full intentions of leaving you alone for the rest of the weekend, but then I was lying in bed, and I knew there was no way I was going to sleep until I did this," he told her.

He didn't move.

"Do what?" she asked. Her stomach fluttered at the intense look of his gaze.

He smiled. Then without another word, he closed the gap between them. She didn't even pretend to fight it when her body pressed against his. For a few intense seconds he looked straight in her eyes, and it was as if she could read every thought going through his brain.

He wanted her. There was an intensity about him that belied anything she'd ever felt or seen before. It was truly hard to resist a man who so obviously desired her. And it had been a very, *very* long time since she'd felt even the remotest resemblance to passion.

His head descended, and though she'd been expecting an explosive kiss, his lips were gentle as they slowly caressed hers. She couldn't stop the murmur of delight escaping her mouth as he softly bit down on her lower lip.

He took his time giving her gentle kisses, his tongue whispering out and tasting her mouth before retreating. She squirmed against him, needing more, wanting more, wanting it all. But she also loved the slow seduction. She was an utter mess. And for once in her life she didn't care.

Finn deepened the kiss as his hands moved up and down her back, touching every inch of her, making her tremble in his arms. They went lower, sliding over the curve of her butt before moving upward again. She pressed closer to him, needing so much more.

His tongue slid inside her mouth, and she fully opened to him. She'd thought the kiss earlier had rocked her world. It was nothing compared to what he was doing to her now. And this time she couldn't use adrenaline as an excuse.

No, this man turned her on. And it wasn't just sex appeal. He was the total package. He was everything. He made her yearn, he made her laugh, and he frustrated her. And she was scared. But not scared enough to push him away. No. She pressed closer instead.

He took her mouth in a punishing kiss as he grabbed her butt and pulled her against him. She felt his arousal, felt what the kiss was doing to him. Her breasts filled and ached as her nipples poked against her bra. She hurt all over—an unbearable ache that had her whimpering in his arms.

She felt pressure building in her core, and she knew there was no one but him who could relieve it. She was ready to pull him into her bedroom, beg him to hold her tight, to slip inside her and never stop what he was doing.

But then he did stop. She whimpered as her eyes slowly opened. His bright-blue depths were shining down at her, the hunger and need obvious. He reached up and cupped her cheek, letting his thumb rub over her swollen lip.

"You are so damn beautiful," he whispered. "So extraordinary."

Much to her horror she felt tears sting her eyes. She didn't feel that way. She was confident in life, not so confident in relationships. But this wasn't a relationship. She wasn't exactly sure what this was.

"I want to lift you in my arms, carry you to your bed, and please you all night," he told her. Yes. She wanted so desperately to tell him yes, but she couldn't get that one simple word past the lump in her throat.

"But I'm not going to. I promised myself I was going to come and give you a kiss, because I can't get you out of my thoughts, because I want you twenty-four-seven. But I want you for more than a night. So I'm going to let you go, and then you're going to think about me as I'm going to think about you. And then the next time we come together, it will be that much better," he told her.

She wanted to argue with him. She wanted to beg and plead. She was so hungry. He'd done that to her. He'd made her feel this desire, this want. He couldn't leave her hanging like this.

But she wasn't able to utter a single word. He leaned in and gave her one more chaste kiss, and then he pulled back. She stared in a bit of horror as he backed out her door. She gripped the side of it to keep from falling.

"Soon," he said with a smile.

Then he turned and walked away. She was left standing there, watching him go. It wasn't a bad view to watch him walk away, but he'd left her with such an unbearable ache she wasn't sure what to do with herself.

Brooke wasn't sure how long she stood there, gazing at the empty street. But finally she managed to shut her door. She stumbled to her bedroom in an absolute daze and fell onto her bed.

She'd been willing to give him her body, but she wasn't in a place she could give her heart. That had been enough before—it wasn't now. Not with this man, not after the loss of her brother, not after the heartbreak of trying to figure out how to live in a world she didn't seem to recognize anymore.

Finn was breaking down the walls she'd erected to protect herself. He was doing it by being good to her, by making her feel what she didn't want to feel. And she was even more scared now than she'd been when she'd been in Black Hawks with bullets whizzing past.

That was a matter of life and death. This was a matter of her losing something she hadn't even realized she might want. Finn was more dangerous to her peace of mind than anything else she'd ever experienced. She just didn't know what that meant or what was going to happen next.

She had a feeling she wasn't going to sleep that night. But even though she was hungry, needy, and highly frustrated, she also found herself smiling in spite of the fear. The man was doing things to her no one had ever done. And he'd accomplished one goal indeed—she needed to see what came next, and she definitely needed to see this man again.

CHAPTER THIRTEEN

Finn sat at a large round table with his brothers, a smile resting on his lips. He wasn't complaining with how much he was smiling lately—not one little bit. It felt natural, though he hadn't been a man to smile easily for most of his life.

It wasn't that he had been unhappy; it was just that he'd lived so long in a world where he had to be on constant alert that he'd forgotten the art of true happiness, forgotten how good it felt to do something so simple as smile.

He took a moment to reflect on the perfection of a round table. Finn had also been the man in charge most of his life. He'd taken over as head of the household at the tender age of ten, and then he'd led a group of stubborn, determined, and very, very tough men on the battlefield. A leader always needed to emerge, and Finn didn't mind filling that role. It was who he'd been born to be.

But he didn't have to be the leader anymore. His brothers were all good men, all natural leaders on their own. They didn't need a leader. They needed a brother, and he was more than happy to fall into that role again. So he loved that they were sitting together at a round table. There was no one greater or lesser in this setting.

He'd once read that King Arthur had a round table for himself and his knights to show that no one was above another. It was perfectly fitting. He hadn't been thrilled being forced into civilian life, but as time lapsed, the more comfortable he was with it.

"The more time that has gone on since Joseph dropped one hell of a bomb on us, the more I'm appreciating what he's given us," Noah said as he looked at each of his brothers.

"I agree. I know life takes us in all directions, but I've missed this time together, and now that we're working on this project, we aren't living such separate lives," Hudson piped in.

"Are you saying you have to have a reason to hang out together?" Brandon asked with his trademark smirk.

"With you hobos? Without a doubt," Finn said with a punch in the arm that would've knocked a lesser man right from his chair.

"I might have to agree with that statement since you're all certifiable," Crew said with a chuckle.

"Ah, a shrinky joke," Brandon said. "Better be careful, brother, or we might think you have an actual sense of humor."

"Shut up, Brandon," Crew said with another chuckle. "I'm hella funny, but I have to be careful around you lunatics."

"How are we ever going to get any work done when we can't seem to focus?" Hudson asked.

"We can work and play at the same time. Isn't that why we all picked something we love to do?" Noah asked.

"I'll never forget when Finn told us to choose our careers wisely, as we'd spend more time working than living," Crew said. "Until I became a psychologist, I didn't realize how true those words were."

"So what you're truly trying to say is I'm the smartest of all of us?" Finn said with another smirk.

"That's not even somewhat accurate. I'm the one with a PhD," Crew told him as his chest puffed out.

"It doesn't count when you got that degree lying on a couch," Brandon told him.

"My clients lie on the couch, not me," Crew said.

"Oh really?" Brandon said. "Any hot female clients?" He waggled his brows.

"You're a pig," Crew told him.

"I'm not denying that," Brandon assured him. "But I still want the question answered."

Crew tried not to smile, but he couldn't help himself. "I don't look at clients that way. They come to me for help, and I wouldn't belittle them in the slightest by acting so disrespectful."

The great thing about his brother was the truth in those words. The man had more integrity than any other man Finn had ever known, and that was saying a lot, because there were a lot of men in his life he knew he could count on. Finn really was a lucky man to be surrounded by so many incredible people.

"All kidding aside, you're a pretty badass dude," Hudson told his brother.

"I think considering where we came from, we've all turned out pretty great," Noah said.

They paused for a moment as they thought about the guy who'd been married to their mother. The man may have donated the sperm that had created them, but he'd never be considered a dad. A true father was a man to be respected and was supposed to challenge and support you. He was also supposed to teach you. Their mother certainly had given them morals and a code of ethics, and she'd apologized she hadn't chosen a better man to be their father. It broke all their hearts knowing that she'd spent one minute worrying about how they had begun in life.

Each of them had grown up knowing they could do anything they truly wanted to do. For Finn a military career had been all he'd been interested in. He'd joined young and had loved every minute of it. He was only thirty-five, and now he had to find a new path. This center was doing that for him. He had a passion to help veterans. He wished more people felt that way.

Noah had been born to be an architect. He'd served in the military as well to pay for his schooling. But his brother had been creating buildings since he'd received his first LEGO set at the age of three. There was no doubt he'd design things for the world to see, use, and appreciate.

Hudson had been playing with Lincoln Logs at the age of one. He'd built his first structure at the age of nine—it had been a Mother's Day present for their mom—a beautifully designed chicken coop she'd loved and used until the day she'd passed. There had been no doubt he'd one day own his own construction company.

Brandon had always been the joker in the family, a laugh readily escaping his smiling lips, and had a passion for danger and puzzles. He'd struggled the most in trying to find his passion in life, but the first time he'd wired something, he'd known he'd be an electrician.

And Crew—well, Crew was the calmest of them all. He'd been the mediator when they'd fought, been the voice of reason, and had always been the first to step in and listen if they ever had problems. It took someone smart and talented to get through as much schooling as he'd gone through to become the doctor he was. It also took a hell of a lot of empathy and compassion to hear the horrors people spilled on him and to be able to keep smiling day after day.

Finn loved his brothers and was more than proud of them. And this project had something in it for each of them. How had Joseph known that? How had he done it? Finn wasn't quite sure.

"Joseph has been trying to be good and give us space, but I think his intentions are good," Noah finally said when a long silence quieted all of them for a while.

"I don't know about him," Finn admitted. "I don't have a lot of faith in anyone trying to step so easily into our lives."

"What about him don't you like?" Crew asked.

"Is this my brother asking or the shrink?" Finn asked.

"I'm both. You can't separate me," Crew said with a shrug.

"I don't have a lot of experience with fathers. Even some of the men I've known and trusted my life to have turned out to be shitty ones, so Joseph trying to fill that role makes me uncomfortable," Finn admitted.

"I think it makes us all a bit nervous," Brandon said. "But this project is pretty incredible, so that's a gift I can truly appreciate. If Noah would ever finish the plans, then maybe I can get to work."

"Well then, let's stop trying to talk about all our girlie issues and get to work," Noah said.

"What have you got so far?" Finn asked.

It was odd for him to feel the least useful in a situation, but he sort of felt that way now. Noah was designing the facility, Hudson was building it, and Brandon was wiring it. Crew would work there with the patients when it was finished. What was Finn's role in all of it? He wasn't quite sure.

"What do we need the most, Finn?" Noah asked. "I'll show you what I have, but since you served the longest, I need your input to make sure this is perfect."

"What do you have?" Finn asked, feeling instantly better. Of course he was needed in this project. He'd worked with many soldiers with PTSD, and he wanted only the best for them.

"So far we have the main lodge, where families can come spend time, patients can visit and feel comfortable, and staff can become more family than help," Noah said as he laid down the map of what he'd designed.

"Over here are the private cabins," he said as he pointed out a wooded area with a couple dozen small housing units that had porches and privacy fences to give the patients time to recover without eyes on them. "And the main housing unit is here."

The next hour they went over the buildings, and Finn piped in where necessary, saying what he felt was needed at the facility. This wasn't a cheap project, and when they were finished with it, Finn truly hoped more centers followed suit and gave back to the men and women who had given their all for a pretty thankless career.

"I think we're ready to present to Joseph," Noah said after another couple of hours passed.

"Yes, I think we are," Crew agreed.

"We're going to be breaking ground before we know it," Hudson said, sitting back with a look of awe on his face.

"This is the biggest project you've ever done. Are you ready for it?" Noah asked.

"I'm more than ready," Hudson said.

"I've got to meet with Sarah tomorrow so we can finish these designs. She's going to be furious I didn't have her here today," Noah said with a wince.

"Uh-oh, in trouble with the girlfriend?" Brandon mocked.

"I'm constantly in trouble," he said with a laugh. "Damn, that woman turns me on."

This made all the brothers laugh.

"Looks like it's not only Finn who's falling right now," Brandon said. "Good thing I'm too smart to fall for a girl."

This time all eyes locked on Brandon. "Oh, little boy, you're so gonna go down someday," Finn assured him.

"Nope. I'm a lover, not a fighter. I see too many couples start out all giggly and in love, and soon there's nothing left but nagging and resentment. I won't fall into that."

"It's only bad like that when you allow it to be or when you're with someone you're not supposed to be with," Crew pointed out.

"If I'm in a relationship where we have to start seeing a Shrinky Dink like you, then something is seriously wrong," Brandon said with a shudder.

"Most problems in relationships come because of a person's internal demons, not because of what their partner is doing," Crew said.

"I have no problems. I'm a perfect specimen," Brandon said as he flexed his impressive bicep.

"Ha! That's a laugh," Finn said.

"Laugh all you want, brother. But I'm the one wining and dining multiple ladies while you're running after one with your tail between your legs."

"I'll gladly chase after Brooke each and every day, and I'm not even a little bit ashamed of that," Finn said.

The cocky look fell from Brandon's face as he analyzed his brother. "Hmm, this is interesting," he finally said. "I never thought I'd see the day you fell, but you really have fallen."

"I really have fallen," Finn said, proud of the fact.

There really wasn't anything more that could be said. Finn wasn't ashamed of his feelings, so his brothers could mock him all day long, and it didn't bother him. He was falling totally and irreversibly in love—and he was damn happy about it.

CHAPTER FOURTEEN

"I absolutely, positively, one hundred percent don't like the man!"

Chloe and Sarah burst into laughter, making Brooke glare at her best friends. There was nothing like having women in your life who didn't put up with your b.s. and who weren't afraid to call you out when you were being an utter moron.

"I mean it. He's been nothing but a pain in my ass from the moment I met him." The laughter continued. "Okay, I'll admit there's chemistry between us. But that's just hormones, and those are a dime a dozen. Besides wanting to rip the man's clothes off, there's absolutely nothing appealing about him."

"Mm-hmm," Chloe said as her giggles began dying down. "I'm not buying anything you're selling right now."

"That's because you're as bad as I am. I'd much rather talk about *your* love life or, I should say, the *absence* of a love life," Brooke said.

That wiped the smile from Chloe's face. "Just because I haven't dated in a very long time doesn't mean there's anything wrong with me. I'm just . . . picky."

"And what about you?" Brooke asked as she turned to Sarah.

With her smile firmly in place, Sarah stuck out her tongue. "I had the best sex of my life last month. Oh, I shall miss Fabio," she said with a sigh.

"Dream sex *absolutely* doesn't count," Brooke told her friend, who laughed again.

"Hey, I'd say it counts when I have better sex in a dream than in real life," Sarah pointed out.

This made Brooke's frown fall away as she laughed with her friends. They were a perfect match—had been from the moment they'd met in middle school. They were the Three Musketeers. Nothing happened in any of their lives without them immediately rushing to each other to spill all. That also meant they couldn't get away with deceiving one another.

"Okay, I might like the man, but I really, really, *really* don't want to. I've been such a mess since losing my brother. I've barely managed to hold it together. If I dare let my guard down, I truly fear Finn's going to step right in, conquer whatever it is he's trying to conquer, and I'm going to be left smashed against a wall. I don't need that right now. I don't know if I could survive it."

At the vulnerability in her tone, her friends' smiles faded away as they pushed a box of cookies toward her. She rolled her eyes, but she pulled one out and took a bite.

"What if he's exactly what you need? What if it's time to live again?" Sarah asked.

"Men love the chase," Brooke said, finishing her cookie in record time. She might have a bit of a sweet tooth. It was a good thing she was as active as she was. "But when they catch the person, they lose interest. And if I'm not careful, I'm going to fall apart. And if he is serious, I'm not, and maybe I'm the jerk who hurts him."

"Or maybe he wants to catch and *not* release," Chloe pointed out. "And it doesn't matter what you do, 'cause we love you, so you can never be a jerk to us."

Brooke smiled. There truly was something special about a sisterhood that most people couldn't understand. It superseded almost anything else in life. They really would do anything for one another, even if it meant losing something.

"Even if he did want to keep me, I'm not in a place in life that I want to be in a relationship. Too much has happened this past year. Sure, I wouldn't mind some smoking-hot sex, but I don't want anything to do with love."

"I don't think we get a whole lot of choice in that," Chloe said. "Sometimes it just hits us like a sledgehammer, and there's nothing we can do about it."

"Really?" Brooke asked. "And when's the last time you were in love?"

She knew she was being pouty and petty at the same time, but the last thing she wanted to do was think about love, romance, and happily ever afters.

"Ah, it was Jeremy in the sixth grade. That's why I've never fallen in love since. He broke my fragile heart," Chloe said with a dramatic sigh.

"I remember that, and no hearts were broken. I do remember after the tragic breakup how you went into the library and found him playing a game with another girl," Brooke said with a giggle, loving that her friends could pull her out of a bad mood.

"Oh my gosh, I totally forgot about that!" Sarah exclaimed. "I don't remember what game it was, but you marched up to the two of them, making the girl practically shake in her cute little boots, and then you flipped the game board up into the air, making the pieces scatter all over the place."

Chloe's face turned a nice shade of pink. "I'm so happy that of all the things you have forgotten from childhood, that memory stays clear in your mind."

"That was a fantastic moment. Jeremy probably peed his pants right then and there," Brooke said.

"Yep. See why I've never fallen in love again? It was so traumatic I can't even think about it," Chloe said.

"Yeah, you forgot about him the second you fell for the star basketball player. What was his name again?" Brooke asked.

"Don't you dare even say his name. We promised *he* wouldn't be spoken of again," Chloe reminded them, which made Brooke and Sarah burst into more giggles.

"Okay, okay, we'll behave, but only if you leave me alone when it comes to Finn," Brooke said.

"Fine. We'll have a truce . . . for now," Chloe said, grabbing a cookie and viciously biting into it. "But this is far from over."

"Didn't his name start with a *T*?" Brooke asked.

"I said fine," Chloe said with a glare.

"So we're all agreed that love and lust are two different things, and we agree that hormones won't dictate our lives," Brooke told her friends.

"We don't fully agree with that, but we can have a truce, at least for now," Sarah said. "Otherwise Chloe might kill us."

"Hey, those middle school dreams have an impact long into our future. That's the first taste we have of emotion and young love. Sure, we evolve, and it changes and we grow, but we have to start somewhere. I don't think we ever forget our first few loves," Chloe said.

"No. I think if there comes a time we forget them, then we're broken beyond repair," Sarah said.

"Maybe it's better to be broken. If we're already too damaged to be fixed, then we can't be hurt any further," Brooke said, feeling she was really beginning to put things together.

"I don't want to be that broken. I might be afraid to fall in love, but I'm not fully discounting it. I'm just being very picky. No one likes to eat a pint of ice cream while crying and watching *Dear John* for the hundredth time," Chloe said.

"Who says that's a bad night?" Brooke asked. "I don't mind watching Channing Tatum over and over again."

"I'd rather watch *Magic Mike*. Then I get to see Matthew McConaughey, too," Sarah said with a sigh.

"We're all hopeless if we're more in love with ice cream and movies than real life," Chloe said.

"Sometimes broken is a good place to be," Brooke told them.

"As long as it doesn't last that long," Sarah said.

"I'm working on myself. I have you two in my life. I don't need to date," Brooke said.

"That might be all of our problem. We enjoy each other so much we don't give anyone else a chance," Chloe said.

"What's wrong with that?" Brooke asked.

"I can't think of a single thing," Sarah said.

They all went silent as they grabbed another cookie. It was a Friday night, and they were perfectly content being with each other. Maybe that was healthy, or maybe it wasn't. But at the moment, Brooke didn't really care.

Except, just when she least expected it, thoughts of Finn popped into her mind. And it wasn't just sex. He challenged her, made her laugh, and made her think about what she wanted in life. He was a very, *very* dangerous man. And she was looking forward to whatever was coming next with him.

Chapter Fifteen

Finn gazed at the large and very empty house before him. He strolled through the hallways, his steps echoing off the bare walls. It was an odd feeling to put one foot in front of the other as he looked at room after room.

He was the oldest of five children, and he'd never owned a home before. It wasn't something he'd ever cared about. He'd been deployed so much of his adult life that it would've been a waste to have a mortgage. So he'd stayed on base. One advantage of being a career military guy was that he had few expenses, and he was frugal.

So he'd been able to save a lot of money. And that had been before he'd discovered he was a part of *those* Andersons and been given an inheritance. But for the first time in his life, he wanted roots, wanted a home to call his own.

There were days he felt he couldn't breathe when he thought about the fact that he'd never be deployed again, never lead a group of men on assignment. It had been his entire world for seventeen years. He still felt slightly lost.

But then he thought about Brooke, and that panic immediately dissipated. She was like a bright ray of sunshine in an otherwise dark world. She was exactly what he'd been searching for without ever realizing it.

It was such a strange feeling for a man who'd never wanted more than a night or two with a woman. He'd never spoken words of love. Yes, he'd lusted after women, and he appreciated their curves, their smiles, the glint in their eyes. But never before had there been one he'd dreamed about, been consumed with, wanted to put a ring on.

Brooke had blown into his life on a strong summer storm, and she wasn't going anywhere. Ergo, he'd bought a house. He was a changed man, a man ready to settle down and become part of a community.

Never before had Finn felt as if there was a missing piece to his life. But again, that had been before Brooke. Sure, he knew it was too soon to feel this need toward her. The rational side of his brain was telling him to slow down. But he pushed that side down. For once in his life he didn't want to be rational.

His brothers would continue giving him hell the further he fell. But he also knew they'd support him. That's what family did. And yes, it had hurt more than he'd ever imagined possible to lose his mother. But he and his brothers had also been blessed by gaining uncles and cousins. They had more people in their lives now than they knew what to do with.

Though money hadn't ever come easy to him or his brothers, they'd always worked hard, and they'd managed to have successful lives. Maybe they hadn't achieved every dream they'd ever imagined, but they'd come pretty damn close.

Finn walked to the front door of his home and looked out at the cheery neighborhood he'd never wanted to live in before now. There were flowers and trees and manicured lawns. There were neighbors and dogs and people walking by.

A mother pushing a stroller stopped on the sidewalk and waved, a bright smile on her lips. It was too far from his front door to shout out a greeting, but he raised his hand. It was almost odd to wave instead of salute. He wondered how long it would take him to adjust to normal civilian life. Maybe he never would.

Just as he was about to go back inside, a big black truck pulled down his driveway. Finn smiled. His first real guest. Of course, all that was in his home right now was a bed and some power cords for his phone and laptop. Hell, there wasn't even beer in the fridge yet. But still, he could count this as his first guest.

Joseph Anderson stepped from the passenger door of Finn's brother Noah's truck. Finn stood up just a bit taller. He was certainly on guard around this man, and he wasn't looking for a father figure, but the man did command a certain amount of respect, and that was something very difficult for Finn to deny.

"Well, look at you, boy, a homeowner," Joseph said in his booming voice. The mother who'd been passing by was almost a block away and turned her head with a smile. Yeah, Joseph had that effect on people.

"Hello, Joseph. What are you doing here?" Finn asked. "And with the bum of the family, at that?"

"Ha. I'm a professional. If anyone's the bum of the family, it would be you," Noah said with a laugh.

Looking at the two of them, that was probably true. Noah was wearing a dark suit and crisp white shirt, while Finn was in a pair of worn jeans and an old college hoodie. But he'd been in a uniform for too many years. There was no way he was switching from one dress code to another. And Finn had no doubt a suit was just another uniform.

"He told me you bought a house, something *you* should've told me," Joseph chastised. "So I insisted on coming to see it. We were just going over the revised plans for the center."

"I want to be in those meetings," Finn said as he looked from Joseph to Noah. "It's important to get this right." He wasn't happy about Joseph needing to know everything about his life, but he wasn't going to chastise the man again. He'd already told him about boundaries. Joseph wasn't a person who needed to be told something twice. But he was a man who'd push those boundaries to the very limit every single time.

"That's why we came," Noah said. "I know what this means to you." He didn't add anything about Finn's personal injuries. There truly were too few places for injured vets to heal or get help. The fact that Joseph and Katherine were investing so much into the project gave Finn instant respect for the relatives he hadn't known he had.

"Sorry. I'm a little on edge today," Finn said, feeling bad for jumping to conclusions. "You're absolutely right. This center means a lot to me. I just want to make sure the stuff we've been talking about is getting implemented."

"We have plenty of time to go over things," Joseph said. "But we'll leave these notes for now, so you can see the changes and add to it. Make some extra slashes just to annoy your brother," he added with a wink.

"You *are* quite the meddler, aren't you, Joseph?" Noah said with a laugh.

"I'm hurt you'd think such a thing. I'm a gentleman," Joseph said with utter innocence in his eyes. Noah laughed. Finn didn't want to soften toward Joseph, but it was difficult not to when the man was so damn charismatic. "Now, quit dawdling and show me your home."

Finn thought about refusing the request, but he didn't see why he should. This wasn't something too personal. Hell, he'd shown his neighbor, who was happy the place was no longer empty and wanted to hear about the plans Finn had for it. So he figured he could give Joseph that much courtesy.

Finn walked the halls again, this time with Joseph and Noah at his side. The halls were wide, the rooms oversize, and the views incredible. He'd chosen well.

"There are some lots across the field for sale," Joseph said. "I know the seller, if any of your siblings are looking."

"I'm looking," Noah said. "It's time to move out of the condo. I want a dog."

That stopped Finn in his tracks. "You? *You* want an animal?" he said.

"I don't know," Noah said with a shrug. "I thought it'd be nice."

"But you're a clean freak," Finn told him.

"People can change," Noah said. "Shut up about it."

"I can't wait till the first time the dog rolls in the mud and tracks it through your entire house." Just the thought sent Finn into a burst of laughter.

"Not *my* dog," Noah said. "He'll be too well behaved for that."

"Yeah, good luck with that," Finn told him.

"I'll just have a trail from my place to yours. If he misbehaves, I'll send him your way," Noah said.

"I'm building a fence," Finn told him.

"Well, now that you have a large home, it'll be time to fill it," Joseph said, interrupting the banter.

"I need to hire a decorator. I don't care how it looks as long as the furniture is comfortable," Finn told him.

"That's not what I meant about filling it. There's nothing like the pitter-patter of tiny feet," Joseph said.

Finn burst out laughing before he could stop himself. This was a hard boundary Joseph certainly shouldn't be crossing, but it was hard to stay on guard with the man when things like that were coming out of his mouth. His new cousins had already warned him Joseph wouldn't be happy until his newest nephews were married and getting their wives pregnant. Finn had assured them he knew how to handle men like Joseph. Apparently he wasn't so good at that.

"I've already found the woman I'm going to marry." Finn was shocked when those words came out of his mouth. How was he supposed to make Joseph take him seriously when he was sharing something so personal with him?

Joseph stopped what he'd been about to say, and Noah gaped at him.

"You were serious about that," Noah said.

"Dead serious. Brooke doesn't realize it yet, but our fate is already written."

"Who in the hell are you?" Noah asked.

"You hush now," Joseph said. "He's a man who knows what he wants and isn't afraid to go after it." Finn didn't like Joseph defending him. That made him uncomfortable. The man was getting too personal, but Finn wasn't doing a hell of a lot to stop it from happening.

"You're never with a woman more than a night—two at most," Noah insisted.

"The moment I met Brooke, I knew she was the one. I can't explain it. I wasn't looking, wasn't ready, but none of that matters. I want her, and though she's fighting it, she wants me just as badly."

"It's fate, my boy. When you know you know. I knew the second I met my Katherine, and I can't imagine my life without her. When it's *the one*, you don't let her go, and you show her every single day what she means to you." It almost sounded as if Joseph choked up there at the end. But he turned away for a couple of seconds, and when he looked back at them, he was completely fine.

Finn wanted distance from this man, but it seemed impossible to keep it when he was feeling all aflutter thinking of the woman he loved. But he still wasn't going to share his personal life with Joseph. He turned and looked at Noah, letting Joseph know his words weren't for him. He reminded himself he didn't need a father figure in his life. He didn't need an overbearing honorary uncle, either.

"I look at this woman, and I know it's right. I can't explain it. When I got my injuries and was released from the military, I thought my life was over. I was wrong. Slowly it's coming together, and I know she's a huge part of that. It'll take a while to convince her, but I'm not worried," Finn told him.

"Then I truly am happy for you, brother," Noah said as he patted him on the back. "Maybe you should just put some basics in here. Because I heard a woman likes to decorate her own home."

Finn hadn't even thought about that. "Good idea. Or maybe I'll get some truly horrible things, bring her here, and she'll have so much disgust she'll insist on helping me. She can decorate it now, and then it'll be ready when she finally accepts we're a couple."

"Isn't that a bit dishonest?" Noah asked.

"Nope, it's sly," Finn said.

"Sometimes we have to do things a little differently to reach the same results we would going another route," Joseph piped in.

Noah threw his hands in the air. "I can't keep up with either of you. And since you don't have any beer, I say we get out of here."

"Good idea. I can at least go get a coffeepot. No way can I wake up in the morning without caffeine."

"I love shopping," Joseph said.

"Then you guys have at that. I have work to do," Noah said.

"Nope. You showed up here, little brother, so you can help me with my house."

Noah grumbled but then shrugged. "Fine," he said.

"I'll take you to my store," Joseph said.

"That's not necessary," Finn quickly told him.

"Oh, quit being a pain in the ass. I heard you loud and clear about boundaries. This is shopping, not a father-son camping trip."

Finn was taken aback at the words. He'd never experienced something like that, never gone and done something fun with his father. The pang in his chest told him that it actually bothered him that he'd never gotten an experience like that.

"I don't see a problem with it," Noah said as he broke into the somewhat awkward silence.

"I suppose," Finn said, not finding a reasonable way out of it.

Once he agreed, things moved fast. Six hours later Finn felt as if he'd been through basic training all over again. Joseph Anderson certainly didn't act or look his age. The man had taken him and Noah to one of the huge Anderson complexes and stocked a lot of Finn's kitchen and pantry—all of the items already on their way to be delivered and set up.

The amount of wealth in the Anderson family boggled Finn's mind. He was a part of that wealth now, and he wasn't sure how he felt about it. Corporate jets, unlimited money, unlimited power, and people willing to go out of their way to make them happy.

It wasn't necessarily unpleasant, but it was a huge change, and there were definite advantages to it. But there was also something to be said for humility, for always working hard for everything you needed and wanted. Finn appreciated his upbringing. He was also appreciating this new life.

Maybe he'd somehow manage to merge the two halves together and find a decent balance. He was sure he could do just that with Brooke by his side.

CHAPTER SIXTEEN

Seattle and sunshine weren't something that went hand in hand. So when there were sunny days, everyone and their dog came out to play. It didn't matter if the temperature was only in the midsixties; it still felt heavenly to have sunshine on your face.

And though sun might be a luxury in the Pacific Northwest, the luscious greenery and mountains of flowers made up for the wet state they were typically in. But on this particular day, none of that mattered, 'cause the sun was indeed out, and all was well with the world.

Because of the beautiful weather, the last of Brooke's patients had canceled on her, which she wasn't upset about. She wanted to play outside as much as they did. She found her favorite coffee stand and then made her way to the Town Center Park. It was crowded this afternoon, and she was lucky to find a nice sunny bench with a seat open.

She sat down, sipped on her white mocha, and sighed in pure joy as she watched a father chase his son through the monkey bars and up to the top of the play structure before they slid down the huge windy slide.

A little punch in her gut made her wonder if she was changing her mind about having children. It wasn't that she didn't love kids. How could anyone not be affected by the joyous laughter of a happy child? She wasn't uncaring. It was just that she was horrified at the thought of ever getting married, and she truly couldn't imagine raising a child on her own.

She'd been raised by a mother who made it clear she and her brother weren't her first priorities, and Brooke was afraid she might not love her child enough, since she'd never truly been shown how to love your own kid. She did care about her patients, and it broke her heart when a child was on her table, but that was about empathy, not love.

She could barely use the word *love*, let alone feel it toward another human being. She had loved her brother more than just about anyone else on this planet, and losing him had ripped a piece of her soul away. What if she did have a child, and then that child grew up to hate her or, even worse, died on her? Would she be able to handle that? She didn't think she would.

It wasn't that Brooke was meek or felt she was incapable. She was just very aware of her strengths and weaknesses, and giving love certainly wasn't a strength of hers. Brooke was able to appreciate her weaknesses because she was so aware of her strengths. Without accepting what you couldn't do, you'd never know the joy of succeeding at what you did best.

Losing her brother had taken something deep from her. She knew he'd kick her ass for how pathetic she was feeling and acting. But she didn't know how to change it right now. That should be enough to move her into action. She was discovering depression was a real thing. It scared her how Finn could lift that sadness. She felt guilty about living when Jack was no longer alive.

No one was made perfect. How boring would the world be if that were the case? It was the simple imperfections in life that made the world so wonderful. If everyone was the same, there'd be no joy, no reason to rise, no reason to truly experience life. If she'd never experienced sadness, then she wouldn't know what true joy was. She was as grateful for her weaknesses as she was for her strengths.

She heard a deep male laugh that had her head snapping to the right, her thoughts vanishing as she recognized it. Though it wasn't something she wanted to acknowledge or think about, she was connected with

Finn Anderson. The more she learned of him, the more that connection grew. It was hard not to like the man—especially when he made it so damn obvious how much he liked her.

She was glad to find he wasn't looking at her, giving her a chance to study him longer without his knowing gaze searing straight into her soul. He had a way of reading her that scared the hell out of her. He saw too much, knew far too much, and she felt as if he knew her better than she knew herself.

She'd bet her life he'd been an ideal leader. She had no doubt if she'd served under him, she would've gladly followed him anywhere he'd wanted to lead her. Her lips turned up at that thought. She would've been quite pleased to be under him, too, dammit.

He was currently playing a rough and rowdy game of basketball with his brother and a couple of the local teens, who looked utterly exhausted. She recognized two of the kids immediately as the star players at their local high school. The kids had scholarships to two of the best colleges in the country, but at the moment they looked worn out while Finn and his brother Noah looked as if they could easily play for hours.

Finn with his shirt off was a sight to behold. That was for damn sure. Signs of war marked his skin, but they took nothing away from him. If anything they only added to the man's appeal. He was a fine specimen, and nothing could take away from that.

His chest was meaty, his stomach hard and lined, and his back was truly beautiful. He turned and dunked the ball, and the many muscles in his back flexed as his shoulders were all angles and ridges, making her drool. He took her breath away with his masculine beauty. She found her fingers twitching with the need to lay her fingers across his hot skin.

As if he could feel her gaze boring into him, he turned, and just that quickly his warm blue eyes captured hers, leaving her frozen to the spot at the power of the look. He didn't look away from her as he said something she couldn't hear, and then he was moving.

His brother looked bummed he was leaving, but the two boys they'd been playing bent forward, relief on their sweaty faces. If Brooke wasn't so mesmerized by Finn at the moment, she might've laughed at the kids.

Finn jogged over and immediately sat next to her, his sweaty thigh brushing against her now-trembling leg as he leaned back, his arm snaking out behind her and resting on the bench, his fingers brushing her hair.

It was far too familiar a gesture, but it felt way too good for her to try to pull away. She hadn't realized how much she'd missed the connection of a man being this close to her, how much she'd missed intimate touching. It was something everyone needed, even if they didn't realize they did.

"I'm pleasantly surprised to see you out here in the park at two in the afternoon," he said, his voice a low baritone that rested easily in the pit of her trembling stomach.

"My patients canceled on me. I think they're playing hooky from work and soaking up the sun like we are," she said. She lifted her cup and took a sip to keep herself occupied and to keep her from tossing the drink aside and using her fingers on him instead of the cup she was holding.

"Ah, sounds as if you have very wise patients," he told her with a chuckle.

"I do indeed. And I didn't complain one bit because that meant I got to play hooky as well," she said with a genuine smile. It was hard not to when the man was looking at her with such a mischievous and adoring look.

"Well, I was going to make my way to see you after my brother and I taught these boys some lessons on the court," he said.

She laughed at the cockiness of his words. "Are you really bragging about beating some kids on the court?" she asked with a raised brow.

"Hey, they aren't your typical kids," he defended before laughing. "And they had the nerve to call my brother and I old, so we had no choice but to show them who the bosses were."

"Oh, how dare they call you such an offensive name," she said, giving him a properly horrified expression.

"I'm so very glad you understand," he said before shifting the slightest bit, his leg pressed even more tightly to hers. Then his fingers stopped playing with her hair and began to make little circles on her neck and shoulder that were causing her insides to stir in the most fascinating of ways.

She really should stop him, and she was planning on doing just that, but maybe just a second or three longer. That surely couldn't hurt anything—and it felt so damn good.

"Why were you coming to see me?" she asked, remembering what he'd said what felt like forever ago. He continued to rub her neck, and she didn't stop him.

"I'm taking you out on Friday, so I wanted to give you ample warning to not make other plans." It was hard to think when she was all gooey from his touch, and though they took a few minutes longer to process than they should have, his words eventually penetrated her muddled brain.

"What makes you think I don't already have plans on Friday?" she asked. She might've been offended he'd think he could ask her out so last minute, but considering she hadn't been on a date in what felt like eons, it was hard to take offense.

"Because I'd change them anyway," he said, as if his words were perfectly acceptable.

"Just for that I believe I'm going to say no," she said. She hated how stubborn she could be sometimes, to the point she would hurt herself just to win.

"I don't think I'm going to let you say no," he said with a sly smile. Her mouth gaped open. She wasn't used to people talking to her this way. She wasn't used to men she couldn't chase away.

Finn was a complex man she didn't quite know what to do with. She could be around him a dozen years, and she had a feeling she still wouldn't be any closer to solving the mystery that was him.

"Finn . . . ," she began, but she wasn't quite sure what she was going to say.

"Okay, hurry it up, Finn. You're giving these kids much too long of a break," Noah called out with a laugh.

"Don't worry about it, man; take your time," one of the kids called out.

That made Finn chuckle before his hand shifted from her neck, and then he stood. Her leg felt instantly cold where his had been pressed to her. She didn't want him to leave. That shocked her more than anything else that had happened so far.

"I'll see you Friday at five," he said. He gave her one hell of a wicked smile before his gaze settled on her lips for three heart-stopping seconds. Then he turned and was gone.

Brooke told herself not to watch him play basketball, but for the next fifteen minutes she found herself sneaking glances his way, and each time she confirmed the view was just as delicious as the last.

She had no doubt she was going to meet him for that date. He'd get his way—but then again, she'd be getting hers as well, so she could actually call that a win-win. Whatever it was, she was in deep, deep trouble.

CHAPTER SEVENTEEN

When a date starts out in a private jet, you have a feeling it's definitely not going to be ordinary. Brooke had no idea what she'd agreed to, but so far Finn hadn't disappointed her. If she was being totally honest, she'd admit that scared her. But she was pushing her fears aside because she couldn't wait to see what he had planned next.

"Can I get you something to drink?" a young blonde flight attendant asked with a smile.

"Um, I guess I'll take a Coke Zero," she replied. She could really use something much stronger, but Finn had told her no alcohol until the date was over.

"Make that two," Finn said as he walked into the cabin and sat next to her.

"Yes, sir," the woman replied.

"Where in the world did you get your hands on a private jet?" Brooke asked. "Normally, military guys can't afford something like this." She'd never lived a life of luxury. Yes, she made good money at her job, but not even close enough to afford something like this.

"I can't reveal all my secrets," he said with a laugh. She just raised a brow and waited. "Fine. I have a very generous uncle who gave me access to one of his jets," Finn admitted.

"What's that like to find out you have this entire family you didn't know about?" Brooke asked. She couldn't even imagine how his life had changed with that revelation, especially since she didn't even know the meaning of family.

Her father had run off before she could ever know him. Her mother had been a drug addict, and now she'd lost the one member of her family she'd loved and relied on. Finn had been given a gift she couldn't imagine being given. It sent a pang through her heart. But right now she wanted to know more about him, not feel sorry for herself.

He was quiet a moment. She liked how he took time to answer an important question, liked that he wasn't going to just spit out the first words he thought of. He took his time to think about things. She was liking him far too much already, but she couldn't seem to prevent herself from talking to him, so she might as well go with it.

"At first I was at a loss. My father was a terrible person, but Joseph has never said a single bad word about him. He's never blamed my mother for keeping us away. It's a slow process. Neither I nor my siblings are that trusting with people, but it's hard to keep distance with this family. Sure, they're rich as hell, but they're also so damn human, so family oriented. It makes it impossible not to get to know them. And it's becoming increasingly hard to not like them."

"You can't live in this area and not know the Anderson family. They're practically celebrities. It'd be easy to not like them because of their wealth and influence, but they do so much for the community, and they do it without fanfare. I have a lot of respect for them," she said.

"Yeah, that's what I've learned. Of course I knew of them. I just never imagined we were related," he said.

"Even though you share the same last name?" she questioned.

"Do you know how many Andersons there are in the world? It's about as common as Smith or Jones. No, it never crossed my mind they were family. But even if it had, I would've probably assumed they didn't want anything to do with us. Like I said, my father was a bad man, and if I'd have thought we were related, I guess I would've assumed we were the black sheep of the family, which I guess we kind of are. But Joseph hasn't treated us like that. Maybe it would be easier if he did."

"So what comes next? You're obviously in his jet, but what comes next?" she asked.

He laughed. "Hell if I know." The stewardess dropped off their Cokes and left again. "For now, I guess we just get to know them. I have cousins who are pretty cool. And Joseph and Katherine have this big project he wants us all working on. So that's a start. I don't want anything from them, but . . ." He trailed off, and she wanted to push him, to find out what he'd been about to say, but she also knew it was none of her business.

"I was skeptical of the veterans center at first, but now I'm getting a little excited for it," she told him.

"It's kind of funny because it's the perfect project for all of us to be in the same place at the same time. I'm a retired vet, though that's still processing in my mind. I want to see a place soldiers can go that they can get help. For the first couple of months after my accident, I was utterly lost. I know a lot of men never come out of that, so if I can be a part of helping other men and women, then I'm all in."

"What will your brothers do with it?" she asked.

"Noah's an architect, so he's designing the facility. Hudson owns a construction company and will be building it. Brandon's an electrician, so he'll wire it all, and Crew's a psychologist, so he'll work there when it's finished. It really is something that we each get to put our part in."

"I think it's amazing how much it means to you. You're not who I was expecting you to be," she admitted.

"Did you expect a god complex?" he asked with another laugh.

"You are a SEAL," she said, as if that was all the explanation she needed to give.

He winced. "I *was* a SEAL," he corrected.

"I've heard once a SEAL, always a SEAL," she told him.

"Yeah, it's really tough for me to let it go. It was my entire life for a long time. I've seen some things that'll never leave me. But I know we helped a lot of people. I just wish I was still helping." He gave her a halfhearted smile.

"But you *are* still helping. You're running the classes for battered women, are helping plan this facility that will help thousands, and I saw you at the grocery store last week, loading bags into Ms. Patterson's car. You seem incapable of walking away from any situation where a person needs help."

He smiled again. "I'm the oldest of five kids. I guess I sort of took over in the dad role, and it's never stopped. I like being needed, being counted on. I'm in no way perfect, but I figure if I do the best I can on a daily basis, then I can close my eyes at night with a clear conscience."

"You're not an easy man to walk away from, are you?" she said, feeling all sorts of nervous again.

"I hope not," he told her with a wink.

"What are we doing tonight? You still haven't told me. I've never been a girl who likes surprises."

"Well, you might have to get used to it, because I love to bring the unexpected."

"Oh, you're frustrating," she said.

They'd only been flying an hour when the jet began its descent. "Where are we?" she asked.

"Montana," he said.

"Want to be more specific?" she asked, knowing he wasn't going to be.

"You'll see," he said.

She gave up pushing him and felt a stirring of excitement in her gut as the jet touched down. She had zero clue what they were going to do, especially in Montana, but she didn't even care. She was having a good time with him, and she had a feeling it wasn't going to end anytime soon.

When the jet door opened, she wondered what in the hell they were getting into. Finn was grinning like a fool, and before her on the private runway were a bunch of soldiers, a sleek black helicopter, and a couple of Humvees.

"What are we doing?" she gasped.

He held out his hand. "You're about to find out."

CHAPTER EIGHTEEN

"You'll need to come with us, ma'am," a straight-faced soldier said as Brooke reached the bottom of the stairs.

Brooke looked over her shoulder at Finn, who was clearly trying not to smile. She knew this was all part of his plan, but she couldn't figure out what in the world was happening. She did feel her adrenaline begin to pump as fight or flight kicked in. She needed to just calm herself and go with the flow.

She never had been into surprises, but she was realizing she trusted Finn, and because of that trust she was starting to feel excitement brewing in her.

"Under whose orders?" she asked as she stood with her shoulders back, keeping just as straight a face as the man in front of her. If he was a soldier, he'd recognize her posture, know she hadn't been a grunt in the military. If he was an actor, this pose had intimidated bigger men than him.

She saw he was trying not to smile, and she had to fight to keep her own composure. The longer she stood there facing the guy, the more fun this adventure was becoming.

"I have orders to take you to the tents to change and then escort you to the helicopter," the soldier said.

"Whose orders?" she repeated.

"That's classified," the man said, never breaking his role. She could keep fighting this, or she could go with the flow.

"I'll accompany you," she said, feeling almost giddy.

"Thank you, ma'am," the kid said, showing obvious relief.

"I hate being called ma'am," she pointed out.

"Sorry about that, ma'am," he said with just a bit of sass.

She was taken to the tent without another word, and when she stepped inside she found jet-black clothing, including a helmet and face mask. She couldn't help but smile as she moved over to the items. There was even a bag with a note on it that said to place her civilian clothes inside, and they'd be safely taken back to the jet.

There really wasn't anything Finn hadn't thought of with this adventure. She just wasn't exactly sure what was happening yet. But she didn't hesitate any longer as she began stripping away her clothes and placing them in the provided bag.

She put on the sturdy black pants, top, vest, and jacket before grabbing the face mask and helmet. She wasn't putting those on quite yet. But they were high quality and lightweight. Only the best for an Anderson, she supposed.

She stepped from the tent. "Please place your helmet and face mask on. This is a dangerous situation," the same soldier said.

This time Brooke didn't argue as she did what he said. She was more than impressed with the quality of the items. There was a button on the side of the goggles that gave her instant night vision. Whatever they were doing required her to see in the dark. Her heart picked up its pace.

She heard a noise to her left and turned to see Finn stepping out of an identical tent to hers. Her breath caught in her throat at the sight of him all in perfectly fitted black clothes, his mask and helmet firmly in place. He was a dream come true, so damn sexy she could eat him up. How in the hell had she resisted him as long as she had? She really didn't have an answer to that. "Mmm, you look good enough to devour," Finn said as he stopped right in front of her.

"I was thinking the same thing," she told him before she could even think of holding in her words. She had no idea if that made him smile or not, as their faces were hidden from each other.

"You take my breath away, woman," he told her.

"That's because you can't see me," she reminded him.

"Oh, believe me, baby; I have a perfect vision of you in my mind," he murmured.

"Sir. We have your weapons," a man said, interrupting them.

They both turned and watched as a table was wheeled toward them with boxes on top. Finn and Brooke stepped up to the tables, and the boxes were opened. Inside were several very real-looking guns. Upon closer inspection, she could see they were airsoft guns, but they were about the best quality money could buy.

"What are we doing?" she asked, feeling positively giddy.

"This is an important mission," Finn said as he strapped ammo to his belt and picked up two handguns and an AK-47.

"Okay, okay, I'll stop asking," she said with a giggle while she secured her own ammo and chose her weapons. They might be using airsoft guns, but they felt good in her hands, the weight perfect to what a real gun would be and the size right on.

"This way," another soldier said as the helicopter blades began spinning.

"We're going in that?" Brooke gasped. This night just kept getting better and better.

"Looks like it," Finn told her as if he didn't already know.

They stepped inside the helicopter, and soon it was lifting into the air. They didn't go too far before a voice spoke in Brooke's earpiece.

"Hold on, the doors are opening."

She was belted in, but she still found herself gripping her seat. She'd flown in a lot of choppers, and she wasn't afraid of them, but she never did like when the doors opened. Sometimes the machines ripped. She didn't see the reason behind opening the doors. The chopper lowered until it was about twenty feet off the ground. Then it just hovered right there.

She watched in a bit of horror as two soldiers pushed out ropes, then turned to her and Finn and saluted before grabbing the ropes and leaping from the chopper.

"You're next," a soldier said to Finn, who saluted, then stood. He turned back and looked at Brooke once before grabbing the rope and easily disappearing as he climbed down.

"Ready, ma'am?" the original soldier asked as he held out a hand.

He might not be able to see her face, but her eyes were the size of flying saucers at the moment. "You want me to climb down a rope from a moving helicopter?" she gasped.

"It's not moving at the moment, ma'am. It's hovering," he told her.

She felt the blood drain from her face. She could refuse, demand they land the chopper. But her sense of adventure wouldn't allow her to do that.

"Ready," she said, almost shocked when she stood and moved toward him. He didn't let her go as she wrapped her hands around the rope.

"It's real easy, just like you've done a thousand times in the gym," the man told her. His words actually helped. She had gone up and down the ropes in the gym hundreds of times. This truly was no different. She smiled again, though no one could see it.

"Geronimo," she said as she jumped from the chopper and began making her way down, easily and quickly. The difference from the gym was a slight swaying, but it was a thrill beyond anything she could imagine. This date was starting off more than great. Nothing would ever compare to this night. She was forever ruined to a normal date now.

Finn was at the bottom of the rope as she leapt off. She giggled in pure delight as she threw her arms around him, not even caring if she was breaking her role in this game. If the date ended right then and there, she'd go home a very happy woman.

"I did it. I can't believe I did it. I never thought I'd do something like that," she said with another laugh.

"You were incredible," he told her. "Now I'm regretting this damn mask because I really want to kiss you right now."

"I know the feeling," she said with a long-suffering sigh.

He was reaching toward his mask when they were interrupted again.

"Come this way, please. The matter is urgent," a new soldier said. "We need your help."

Finn growled, making Brooke quite happy that he was frustrated. But he obediently turned toward the man. Before them was a huge complex of some sort. It looked like a medical facility.

Suddenly noise broke out, the sound of gunfire making Brooke automatically drop to the ground as she pulled out her weapon and eyed the building in front of her. Too many years as a soldier were ingrained in her to not respond to the sound of danger. She got in battle position as she'd been trained to do.

Laughter came through her earpiece before it was stifled.

"You have good training," Finn told her as he stood above her, holding out a hand.

She couldn't help but giggle as she accepted his offer of help and got to her feet.

"I guess old habits die hard," she told him, feeling a little silly. But as she turned and looked at the soldiers around her trying to hide their own smiles, she felt better. "If I forget to tell you later, this is the best date I've ever had."

Finn pulled her against him for a moment before the soldiers began moving forward and waved at them to follow.

If Brooke didn't know for sure this was nothing more than a game, she might think she was in a real situation. They entered the building, six of them in total, to the sound of gunfire, smoke, and people crying out.

Their mission was to find the shooters and rescue the innocent civilians huddled in different places. Finn was so detailed in his planning every scenario imaginable was presented to her.

There were multiple bad guys fighting back against them, and about a hundred innocents. At the end of the night, they saved them all. Brooke was covered in sweat, and her cheeks hurt from smiling so much. Her adrenaline was pumping, and she knew beyond a shadow of a doubt she was falling in love with the man who had made it all possible.

What she didn't know was exactly what she was going to do about that.

By the time they came out of the building and took off their masks, Brooke didn't have any desire to fight against what she was feeling. She turned to Finn, who appeared just as happy as she was at the moment. Her guilt was fading at feeling happy, because she had no doubt it would be what her brother wanted for her.

"Take me home, Finn," she said.

Her tone must've indicated exactly what she wanted, because his smile fell away, and his body went still as he gazed down at her.

"With pleasure," he said as he took her hand.

CHAPTER NINETEEN

Never in her life had Brooke been gazed at so intently she felt it through her entire body. But as she looked at Finn, she felt utterly consumed— something she'd never even come close to feeling before.

She had to have him, had to take this next step with him. She didn't want to desire him, didn't want to like him. But the choice was no longer hers to make. He'd gotten to her, whether she wanted that or not.

He moved closer, no hesitation in his step. His hand cupped her cheeks as those burning eyes looked at her, showed her every intention he had for her on this night. And there was nothing in her that wanted to fight it.

"Kiss me," he demanded.

A shiver raced through her at the low velvet of his voice. He didn't lean forward, didn't try to connect their mouths. He waited for her to reach up, for her to close the small distance between them.

In life Brooke was confident. She knew exactly who she was and what she wanted—most of the time. But when it came to this man, she felt like an utter mess. She wanted to do as he commanded, but she was nervous, unsure. She wanted the choice taken from her, but she couldn't admit that, couldn't give him that power.

"Kiss me, Brooke," he said again with a hint of danger and authority in his tone.

She moaned as her body swayed toward him. Frustration was building. This thing between them had grown out of control. If Finn made love to her, she was sure she'd get some of her senses back.

He smiled—a predator smile, a victory smile. He knew he had her in the palm of his hand. He knew he could take anything he wanted from her. But he wasn't making it that easy. No, he wanted her to give it all to him—he wanted her to give up her control.

With a frustrated sigh, she moved forward, closing the final distance between them, and it was so worth it as her lips touched his. One little taste was all it took for her to feel utterly out of control. His fingers caressed her face as he ran his tongue over her bottom lip, making her savor the moment.

Finn had her trembling within seconds as he moved his hands down the sides of her body and reached around her hips, firmly cupping her ass while he deepened the kiss. He moved, pushing her back against the wall as he slid his fingers to her butt and squeezed.

She grew greedier as she slid her hands behind his head, holding him in place, not ever wanting his lips to leave hers. He became more urgent as he pressed against her, showing her exactly how turned on he was. There was no way of stopping the moan that was ripped from her body.

She was hungrier for this man than she could ever remember feeling. And it seemed nothing was going to satiate the desire. She wanted more and more and more. She couldn't get enough of him. The throbbing rushing through her body was almost more than she could bear.

When he pulled his lips from hers, she whimpered in frustration. But then he dropped in front of her and laid his head against her stomach. Her legs were shaking so badly she wasn't sure she could keep standing.

He lifted her shirt and kissed her shaking stomach as he undid her pants.

"Finn, wh . . . what are you doing?" she asked, though she wasn't even sure her words were coherent.

He didn't look up, didn't stop what he was doing as he ran his tongue across her stomach while he pulled down her pants. Then his mouth moved lower, and she gripped the top of his head as his tongue swiped across her core.

Her legs almost buckled at the intense pleasure of his mouth on the part of her aching so much. He held her thighs as he ran his tongue along her heat—up and down, over and over again—before he circled her swollen flesh and sucked hard.

She screamed as an orgasm ripped through her, but he gave her no mercy, his lips and tongue sweeping across her sensitive flesh. She could barely breathe the feelings were so intense, but he didn't stop, didn't give her mercy.

"Finn, I'm going to fall," she choked out, her legs too shaky to hold her.

He just gripped her tighter as he pressed her into the wall and continued sucking and licking her swollen flesh. And much to her surprise another strong orgasm ripped through her as she tugged on his hair and screamed out her pleasure. He swept his tongue along her heat one last time before he carefully stood, making sure to keep her in his arms. She would've fallen if he didn't.

"I want so much more," he told her before gently rubbing his lips against hers. The taste and scent of sex and pleasure consumed her. It was a chaste kiss, though, because too soon he pulled back; then he was cradling her in his arms as he moved with purpose through her house.

"You're mine all night," he said as he gently laid her on the bed, then stood over her, looking at her shaking body from head to toe. She still had her shirt on, but her pants were long gone. She felt a bit self-conscious as he stood gazing at her. But the heat in his eyes told her he wanted her, so she pushed those thoughts aside.

Then all thoughts evaporated as he began taking off his clothes, revealing one beautiful inch after another of his golden skin. There was a black tattoo on his shoulder and upper arm, and it was sexy as hell. She couldn't wait to run her fingers over it, see exactly what it was. But at the moment she wasn't even capable of words.

There were also scars adding more character to the man. She wanted to know the story behind them, wanted to know so much more about him. Not at this moment. Now she wanted more pleasure, wanted him to have pleasure, too.

When his pants came off, a rush of air escaped her starving lungs. He was beautiful—absolute perfection. Long and thick, and she wanted him buried deep inside of her. She wanted that right now.

"Take off your shirt for me. I want to watch as you show me your body. I want to savor the moment," he said, his voice low and filled with barely controlled need.

She didn't hesitate to obey him. She was his to command—at least right now.

She pulled off her T-shirt, then undid the clip of her pink bra and pulled it away. Her breasts spilled out, and he stepped forward. He didn't lie down right away. Instead he stood over her and placed a hand at her throat and smiled when he felt her out-of-control heart rate. Then he ran his hand down, gently brushing both breasts, making her nipples throb, before leaving too soon and tracing her stomach.

He did this several times, making her back arch off the bed as she became more and more needy. She had to feel the weight of his body on top of hers, needed to be filled by him.

"Please, Finn, please," she begged, too turned on to care.

"Please what?" he asked as he cupped her breast before pinching a nipple and making her cry out as her core heated even more.

"Please. I need to feel you inside me," she pleaded.

His eyes met hers, and that's when she realized he was barely in control. He might seem more in control than her, but he was holding on by a thin thread.

"Take me," she said again, her hips arching, her legs spreading.

"I haven't been with anyone in a long time. I'm clean, and I really want to feel flesh on flesh," he said. She noticed a slight shake to his voice.

She was too excited to be embarrassed by his words.

"It's been a really long time for me, too. And so am I, and I'm on birth control," she told him.

Now there was no more waiting. He climbed onto the bed, his body hovering over hers but not touching. She reached for him, grabbing his neck, needing them to be pressed together.

Finally, he kissed her again, taking her bottom lip between his teeth and gently biting down before his tongue soothed the ache and dove into her mouth, consuming her. His hand drifted down her side and reached for her butt as he pressed his thickness against her.

She pushed her hips upward, her core empty and wanting. But he wouldn't connect them. She growled against his mouth, and he pulled back and smiled at her.

"Something wrong?" he wickedly asked.

"Yes!" she yelled. "I want you."

"Soon. Very, very soon," he assured her. "But I have to taste you some more. I can't get enough of you."

She tried holding him to her, but he was stronger, was the one in control. He moved his lips across her jaw and sucked on her neck before going lower. He circled her swollen nipples with his tongue before latching on and sucking, making wetness saturate her.

Then he moved lower, his tongue tasting its way across her belly as he pushed her legs wide apart and ran his tongue over her hips. Then his mouth was on her silken folds again, and he tasted every inch of her before latching once more onto her swollen nerves and sucking hard.

She twisted beneath him as he pleasured her over and over again, this time pushing his fingers deep inside her. He was a large man, and she knew it was better to be prepared for him, but she didn't want to wait anymore.

Finally, when she didn't think she could possibly take any more, he began making his way back up her body, his tongue doing things to her she wanted to feel over and over again.

"Open your eyes," he told her.

It felt like there were ten-pound weights on her lids, but she slanted them open as he hovered over her.

"Damn, you are so beautiful," he said in awe.

She felt tears come to her eyes, but she desperately tried pushing them away. This was just sex. It was just sex. It was nothing more than sex, she told herself repeatedly.

But then the head of him was at her entrance, and all thoughts vanished from her mind. He paused as she pressed against him. Then he slowly pushed forward. Now there was no trouble keeping her eyes open. He was so big, so thick, she felt every centimeter of him.

With a final hard push he sank fully inside of her, making Brooke gasp in pleasure and a bit of pain.

"Wait," she begged as she tried to adjust to him. He leaned down and kissed her again, his lips and tongue working magic on her mouth.

It didn't take long for her body to soften around him, and then he began to move, slowly at first, building and building the pleasure inside her. He gripped her hips as he pushed in and out of her.

Their bodies were covered in a damp sheen, making them slide together in perfect rhythm. She cried out as he picked up speed and intensity.

"So good, so tight," he growled as his body slammed against hers.

Brooke wrapped her legs tightly around him as she held him close.

With an explosion rivaling the pleasure he'd already given her, Brooke completely let go and focused on the intense pleasure of the strongest orgasm she'd ever had. He gasped as he kept moving. But then his cries joined hers as she felt him pulse deep inside of her.

Heat filled her as she shook beneath him. After several long, beautiful moments, he sagged against her, his chest pressed against hers, his hardness buried deep. She kept herself wrapped around him, not wanting to let go—not ever wanting to let go.

Too soon he was pulling out of her, and she whimpered her disapproval, but then he slipped onto his back and pulled her against him, his strong arm wrapped around her back, her head cradled against his chest.

She ran her fingers across his chest, her eyes closed, her body sated—at least for the moment. They didn't speak as his hand rubbed along her back. But unbelievably she felt arousal stir in her again. Her nipples tightened, and her core began to pulse.

"More," he said. And she didn't argue as he pulled her over him. She gladly sank onto his hardness. She didn't think she ever wanted to stop.

She might be in trouble where this man was concerned, but she was too satisfied at the moment to care. She'd save that for another day.

CHAPTER TWENTY

The smile Brooke was wearing instantly made Finn suspicious. What had he agreed to? He tried to assure himself he was a soldier—or at least he used to be a soldier. He'd been in just about every dangerous situation known to man. There was nothing this woman could throw at him that would be nearly as scary as anything he'd already been through.

But that smile worried him.

"Are you ready?" she asked with far too much glee in her voice.

"What are we doing?" he asked. He was desperately trying to act nonchalant. He had a feeling he was failing.

"Oh, darling Finn, it's tit for tat. You wouldn't tell me, so I can't tell you," she said with a laugh. He was worried, definitely worried.

"But you had a blast," he reminded her. She didn't seem to be a cruel person, but . . .

"Yes, best nondate I've ever been on." She seemed like she was pulling teeth to admit that. He couldn't help but laugh, some of his worries relieved.

"When will you admit it was an actual date and so is this one?" he asked.

"Never. My stubbornness knows no bounds," she reminded him.

"And my persistence is never ending," he fired back.

"Well then, isn't this the beginning to a perfect . . . friendship." She hesitated with the last word.

"Oh, Brooke, this is so much more than a friendship," he told her before pulling her into his arms and kissing away any argument she might have.

By the time he let her go, she was swaying on her feet, exactly what he liked to see. She might have a hell of a time admitting what was between the two of them, but he had no problem reminding her over and over again. He wasn't normally a patient man, but when it came to her, he'd be willing to wait. Hell, he'd be willing to drop to his knees for her. And that had never happened in his life.

Damn, were his brothers going to have a field day when they saw the two of them together. Finn knew he was a goner. He didn't really care. That's how much he liked this woman. He was absolutely shameless.

"Okay, no more distracting me. It's time to go," she told him.

"I'm your willing slave," he said as he held out an arm. She took it without hesitation, and his heart thumped an extra beat.

One thing Finn wasn't comfortable with was being a passenger in a car, but Brooke had insisted on driving. She said this was her night, which meant she was the driver. He had to suck it up and climb into her roomy SUV. And though he wouldn't tell her as she jumped on the freeway going a bit too fast, his entire body was tense.

He didn't take in a full breath until they arrived. It wasn't that he was worried about her driving skills; it was that most people weren't aware of the drivers around them, and other drivers were careless. They texted, did makeup, ate sloppy food, dropped things, played with the buttons, and generally only gave 50 percent of their attention to actually driving. Finn was a very defensive driver—most people weren't.

Brooke pulled up to a small outdoor mall, and Finn reminded himself that he didn't care what they did as long as he was with her. There was no way this date could top what he'd planned, but they could go sit on the pier and fish, and he'd be happy as long as she was at his side.

"Sit," he told her. She gave him a weird look as she began undoing her seat belt. He rushed from the car and made it to her door before she could open it.

"What is that?" she asked.

"Just because you're driving doesn't mean I'm not a gentleman," he said as he helped her from the vehicle.

"I don't need a gentleman," she said, but she did smile.

"Well, then, you're out of luck because my mother taught me how to treat a lady."

Her smile fell as she looked away from him. He wasn't allowing that at all.

"What's wrong?" he asked, his finger under her chin, forcing her to look at him.

"Nothing. It's nothing," she said, but there was a slight scratch in her voice.

"Come on, Brooke. There's something," he said, shocked at the slight sheen in her eyes.

"There are times you really remind me of my brother. We didn't have good parents, but my brother was still a really good man. He always told me to never spend time with a man who didn't treat me like a lady. He told me that when I was five years old. I miss him so much."

She choked on her last words, and her eyes filled, spilling over.

"I'm so sorry," she said as she tried to pull back from him.

"Please don't apologize. I wish I'd have been able to meet your brother. I'm sure he was an incredible man, and I'm glad he was always there for you," he told her.

"But he's not anymore. He left me," she said, more tears falling.

"Oh, Brooke. He didn't leave willingly. You aren't a woman anyone walks away from without regret or pain," he told her before pulling her against him.

She was tense for only a moment before her arms wrapped around his waist, and she snuggled her head against his chest. He wrapped one hand against the back of her neck, gently massaging the area. The other kept her tightly pulled against him as she pulled herself together.

"I'm sorry," she mumbled again.

I love you was on the tip of his tongue, but he somehow managed to hold it in. Seeing this woman strong and stubborn was a beautiful thing. Seeing her raw and emotional was a true gift.

"Me too, Brooke. I'm so sorry for your loss. I'd take on your pain if I could."

"I think you mean that. I think you're that guy who needs to save the world. But I don't need saved, Finn. I need only this right now," she told him.

"Well then, it's a start."

"It's a start," she agreed as she pulled her arms away. He was reluctant to release her, but when she pulled back her face was more composed. Her cheeks were flushed, but there was a wobbly smile on her pink lips. "Now, let's go. Tonight is supposed to be fun."

"We can go somewhere and talk instead, if you want," he suggested.

She shook her head. "No. I can't cry anymore. I did nothing but cry for months. I wanted to give up, wanted to throw it all in. I couldn't imagine living in a world without my brother. But I have zero doubt of how much he loved me, and every time he deployed he told me if anything ever happened to him, he'd haunt me forever if I didn't live my life. I was tempted to do just that so he *would* haunt me, but I promised him I wouldn't ever give up. And I keep my promises, even when it feels like the hardest thing I'll ever do."

"You're so incredible, Brooke," he said, feeling in utter awe of this woman.

"I'm just a normal girl with normal emotions. Yes, there are times I feel messed up, and I know I'm in no way perfect, but I try to live my life as if the world is watching. That way I can still look in the mirror and not feel like a failure."

"You're doing a damn fine job of it."

"You have to say that," she told him. He was relieved to hear the slight giggle escape her.

"I don't have to say anything. I speak the truth," he told her.

"You scare me, Finn," she admitted.

"Why is that?" he asked. Frightening her was the very last thing he wanted to do.

"Because I like you," she said.

"And that's a bad thing?" he asked with a laugh.

"It could be," she told him.

"Let's just play this day by day," he offered. That wasn't what he wanted, but it was what she needed, so he was willing to do just that.

"Thank you," she said, as if she knew it was hard for him to offer just that. They understood each other so much more than she realized.

"Anytime."

"Are you ready?" she asked. Her eyes were dry, and the next smile was genuine.

"I'm a soldier. Bring it on," he told her.

She grinned . . . big.

Yep, he was done. It was over.

Hook.

Line.

Sinker.

Over.

Chapter Twenty-One

It was truly an odd feeling to go from incredible grief to beautiful joy in such a short period of time. But Brooke was finding that the more time she spent with Finn, the more she felt. It wasn't one emotion—it was a myriad of them.

She was so used to being in control of her life and her surroundings that she didn't know how to deal with Finn. He was a force of nature that didn't slow down. He could be kind and gentle, but he was also fierce and determined. He was a lot like her brother, but she certainly didn't feel chaste with him.

No. She felt lust and joy and need so deep it was threatening to pull her under. She wanted to run as far and fast from him as she possibly could, but she couldn't. He had pushed his way into her life, and she didn't want him going anywhere. That should send her scurrying for the hills, but she kept walking toward him.

Maybe it would end soon. Maybe she'd wake up. Maybe this was all part of her breakdown over losing her brother. She wasn't exactly sure what it was. She just knew she needed to figure it out before she went crazy.

"You're bringing me to a pottery store?" Finn asked with skepticism as she stopped in front of the double doors with painted ceramics on them.

"Yep, we're sculpting something amazing. Then we have to come back and paint it later," she told him with a big smile.

"Really? A pottery class?" he asked as he held out his huge hands. "Do you honestly think I can build something delicate?"

She really, *really* liked his hands. They were big and strong and felt unbelievably good all over her body . . . and inside of it.

"Chicken?" she taunted. She knew how to stiffen his spine. And that's exactly what happened.

"I'm not afraid of anything," he told her as he stepped forward and opened the door.

"Good. I think you're going to have fun, even if you won't admit to it."

"I'm with you, so I have no doubt I'll have fun," he told her, making her heart give a little hitch.

"Quit saying things like that," she muttered.

"Why?"

She refused to look at him. "Because it's . . . it's . . ." She couldn't seem to find the words. "You should just stop saying things like that." She couldn't fall for him, though she feared it might already be too late.

"You just need to get used to the idea of me liking you, Brooke. It's not changing, and I'm not going away."

She was saved from answering him when the shop owner approached.

"Hello, Brooke. So nice to have you back in here." She turned to Finn. "You must be Finn. I'm Hannah. You guys are set up in the blue room. Follow me."

Brooke practically ran away as she trailed Hannah to the back of the store. She was liking her idea of a pottery class a little less when they stepped into the blue room, which was small and intimate, with only two pottery wheels set up. She'd been thinking they'd be surrounded by other people.

"I thought we were taking a class," she told Hannah.

"You know how to do pottery. You can teach your date. That's all part of the fun," Hannah said with a wink. "I'll just go over the basics with you."

"Thank you," Finn told her.

Brooke stood by as Hannah told them how to start the machines and the basics of what they needed to do, and then she left, shutting the door behind her, leaving her in there all alone with Finn.

"Okay, I'm liking this," he said as he came up behind her and wrapped his hands around her stomach, pulling her back against him and nuzzling her neck. The heat of his breath on her sensitive flesh made a shiver travel through her.

"We haven't done anything," she said a bit nervously.

"Doesn't matter," he told her before sucking on that sensitive place where her neck met her shoulder.

"We're not going to get anything done if you don't stop," she warned as she gave in and reached up, wrapping her arms around the back of his neck, stretching out her torso and exposing herself to him.

His hand ran from her neck, over the curve of her breast and the flatness of her stomach, before whispering across the front of her jeans and then back up again.

"I'm more than willing to mold you," he whispered in her ear before nipping the lobe.

She was instant jelly in his arms, grateful for him holding her up.

"Then we've wasted our nondate," she said with a sigh.

He laughed as he released her. She was incredibly disappointed as she turned and looked at him. Her body was on fire, and there was so much more from him she needed than a few gropes and kisses on her neck.

"We can't waste a nondate," he said with a chuckle. "Now, when we have a real date, that's okay to waste."

She glared at him. Good. When he irritated her, it was easier to focus on anything other than the constant burn in her body while with this man.

"Shall we start?" she asked.

"What are you making?" he asked as he moved over and chose his clay.

"A vase," she said.

"That's boring," he told her.

"There's nothing boring about it. It's practical," she said.

"Sometimes it's more fun to go for the adventure than to be practical," he said.

"Well, that's just not who I am. You can walk out the door anytime you feel like accepting that."

His smile fell away as he faced her. He closed the gap between them and looked at her, waiting for her to focus on him. She hated when he did that. She felt so damn vulnerable, and she didn't like it.

"I don't want to change a single thing about you, Brooke. You're perfect as you are. I just want to walk by your side. And now that I've had a taste of you, I want more and more. It will never be enough."

Her heart thundered as she looked into his beautiful blue eyes, feeling as if she were sinking into a deep abyss. She didn't even have it in her to remind him to not say things like that to her.

As if he knew she was panicking, he leaned in, gave her a quick kiss on the lips, then turned her body and smacked her on the ass.

"Let's get to work, woman."

That pulled her out of her panic. She turned her head and glared at him before grabbing the first clay she came to and sitting at her pottery wheel.

"You know I don't like being told what to do," she said.

"I think you do. I think you love the fact that you can't intimidate me," he said with a smile that made her want to throw her clay at him.

"What makes you think you know me so well?" she challenged.

"Because I can't resist you, which means I study every single thing about you," he said. Before she could reply to that, he asked her a question. "Tell me something you like about me."

She was so stunned by the question she wasn't quite sure what to say. "Are you fishing for compliments?" she asked.

"I have a psychologist brother who gives me advice. I'm more than happy to tell you everything I like about you," he added with a wink as they both continued sculpting their projects.

She thought about his request and realized it wouldn't hurt anything to share with him. She also might be able to torture him a bit with her words. She smiled as innocently as she could.

"I love the way you kiss," she finally said. "It's soft and naughty at the same time and makes my insides all warm and gooey."

She nearly laughed as his fingers clenched the clay he was molding, making his project go lopsided for a moment. Her words certainly affected him. She sort of loved how powerful that made her feel.

"Are you trying to get me to take you right here and now?" he finally asked.

She did chuckle at that but couldn't deny that it also made her insides clench with a need so great she had to press her thighs together as heat filled her.

"We're trying to work here," she said with her best school principal face.

"Well, I'm a heart-on-my-sleeves kind of guy, so when you tell me you like something, I'm inclined to act on it," he warned. "But being this man, I at least get to enjoy my life and not live in fear like so many people do."

"I actually really like that about you," she told him. "But you were the one fishing for compliments, so you can deal with the consequences of that with zero action."

He chuckled at this before he began fixing his project. He seemed to be enjoying himself, which made her quite happy. A guy willing to bend for the woman he proclaimed to have feelings for was pretty great.

"How can you be this guy?" she asked.

"What guy?" he questioned.

"You've been through the worst of hell, and yet you're still sweet and humble. I mean, you can be a total ass, too, but I think that part of you is more the act. How can you still be this giving after all you've been through?"

He looked at the clay he was molding and thought about her question for long moments; then when he glanced up, his gaze was intent. She found it difficult to breathe as she waited to hear what he had to say.

"It's the men who will show you their scars that are real men. They are the ones tough enough to earn the scars but tender enough to show you their past wounds. Yes, for other people I wouldn't be willing to do that—but for you—for you I don't think there's anything I wouldn't give, including the worst of me."

She was floored by his words, utterly floored. This man was so much more than a typical anything. He had depth and soul, and she might be falling a little in love with him. That was terrifying but awe inspiring at the same time.

"How do you not have bitterness after all you've been through?" she asked.

He looked at his project, surprising her that he wasn't looking her in the eyes, but when he did finally glance up, she noticed right away there were no shadows in his eyes. He truly was okay.

"It was a different world, and we all have ways of processing it. I was lucky to not come home with issues, but I was also very protected. I have amazing guardian angels who looked out for me," he told her. He was incredibly serious. She was such a goner with this man.

"You know, you're pretty unique," she admitted.

"I'm just a guy," he said with a shrug. "But I have no problem with saying what I think or telling a person I care about how I feel."

She felt a sting of tears in her eyes and realized this was way too personal. She was falling down a rabbit hole, and she wasn't sure she wanted to be rescued.

She was glad when Finn smiled, and the topic lightened. It was growing too intense, and she was afraid he was going to break down the rest of her carefully built walls. If that happened, she wasn't sure what would come next. But for now she wanted to have fun and live in the moment. Too many people forgot how to do just that.

The next hour passed with laughter, some thrown clay, and Brooke realizing she was falling harder and harder for a man she didn't want to even like. But that didn't matter. It was too late. It was far too late.

CHAPTER TWENTY-TWO

There was a knock on Brooke's door again far too early on a Saturday morning. Her eyes narrowed, thinking it could be no other than Finn. Yes, she was enjoying him, and yes, she wanted to see him far too often, but if she allowed him to come anytime he wanted, then she'd start to really need him. And that wasn't something she could allow to happen.

She opened the door, ready to give him her full fury, though she was also ignoring the hint of excitement she was feeling in her stomach. A nice morning round of sweaty sex sounded better than yelling.

But her mouth dropped open when she saw a well-dressed woman standing at her door with her two best friends. And beyond them at the curb was a long black stretch limo.

"Um . . . hello?" she said as she gazed first at Sarah, then Chloe, and then the perfectly groomed woman.

"Hello," the woman said. "I know this might seem strange, but my name is Bree Anderson. I didn't change my name because I'm a daddy's girl, through and through, though I'm head over heels in love with my husband." She paused and laughed. "And I'm giving you far too much information you don't want. But family means the world to me, and I hear you're the future bride of my newest cousin, so I'm being nosy and wanted to meet you. I met your friends this morning at a planning meeting for the veterans facility, and I insisted we come over."

Brooke's jaw dropped. She couldn't help it. She looked like a cartoon character. She was sure of it, but she couldn't help it. This woman was beautiful, confident, and not shy at all. She was probably wearing clothes as expensive as Brooke's car, but she seemed completely at ease on the doorstep of Brooke's modest home.

"Are you going to let us in or stand there gaping like a fish?" Sarah asked with a laugh. "Trust me, I know how you're feeling. I don't think I said two words today at the meeting, but that's something I'll tell you all about later."

"What meeting?" Brooke finally managed to ask.

Chloe was practically bouncing on her feet as she grinned at Brooke. "You'll never believe what happened!" she practically squealed. "But we're coming in to tell you the story."

With that Chloe moved forward, followed by Sarah and Bree Anderson. It wasn't until the door was closed that the opening part of Bree's statement processed through Brooke's brain.

"Wait!" she said, her voice a bit too high. All three women turned and looked at her, none of them saying a thing. "Did you say the person marrying your cousin?" There'd been so much information delivered in a single monologue Brooke was sure she'd heard wrong.

"Yep," Bree said as she moved with ease into Brooke's kitchen. "Do you mind if I have a cup of coffee?"

"Of course. I just made it," Brooke said as she moved to her cupboard and pulled out three more mugs, then moved to the fridge and pulled out a pan of brownies she'd made the night before. She didn't do a lot of cooking, but she had a major sweet tooth at least once a month. And that had happened the night before.

"What do you mean by getting married?" Brooke asked, a little thrown off kilter still but not letting go of that remark.

They all made their coffees, grabbed brownies, and sat at her break-fast bar. Brooke was far too edgy to sit anywhere. She stood in front of them, feeling as if she were in a lineup as she held tightly to her coffee mug. There was no way she could choke down a brownie.

"Hey, these are pretty good," Chloe said, which was a huge compli-ment from her bestie, considering the woman was a phenomenal chef.

"You're just being sweet. They're from a box," Brooke said with a smile.

"Yeah, but I can tell you added nutmeg and fresh chocolate. You're learning," Chloe told her.

"Well, when your bestie's a chef . . . ," Brooke said with a laugh.

"When *one* of your besties is a chef. The other one is a soon-to-be world-renowned architect," Sarah said.

"Yeah, yeah, you're both my besties. Now, about the marriage," Brooke insisted.

"But it's so fun to listen to you three talk. I'm having a great time," Bree said with a giggle.

Brooke felt as if her head were about to spin off her shoulders. There were so many things being fired at her at once, and she couldn't seem to keep up. She paused and downed the rest of her coffee, poured another cup, then started a new pot while Bree chatted with Chloe and Sarah.

She was a nurse practitioner and used to chaos. Hell, she'd been a medic with the military in dangerous situations, and she felt more out of control in her own kitchen at this very moment than she'd ever felt at work.

After her coffee was done, and she'd taken a fresh sip, she turned and glared at the three women, who slowly stopped talking.

"What marriage?" she said, her eyes narrow, her words fierce.

Bree giggled again. "Your wedding to Finn," she said with a wave of her hand.

"I'm not marrying Finn," Brooke said. "Whatever gave you that idea?"

"He told his brothers, who have told everyone they know, including our entire family. There's nothing more my uncle Joseph likes than a family wedding. He thinks we don't know about his meddling, but we're all very aware. He's just lucky we love him as much as we do," she said. "And that we love our spouses."

"I'm completely lost here. Yes, I'm *friends* with Finn." Her cheeks went red as she said this.

"Just friends?" Chloe said with a giggle.

"Well, yes, just friends, if even that. We've been on a few nondates, and we, well, we . . ." She took a long pause. "Never mind. That doesn't matter. I'm never getting married, for one thing, and for another, I barely know him." She let out a frustrated sigh.

"Well, honey, doesn't matter—when it's love, it's love," Bree assured her.

"But it's not love. You can't fall in love with someone you don't know," she insisted.

"Yeah, trust me; that's what I thought. When I met Chad I wanted nothing to do with him. He was hired by my dad to be my bodyguard. I was independent and offended at the thought of my dad and brothers thinking I needed a babysitter."

"Did you need one?" Chloe asked.

"Well, yeah, I did, but that wasn't the point. I was stubborn as hell. But thank goodness, Chad was more stubborn than me, because I'm so in love with that man there's nothing I wouldn't do for him," she added with a sigh.

"Well, I think he's being dang presumptuous to say he's gonna marry me," Brooke said. But even as she said the words, she felt a bit of warmth seep through her. It was stupid and silly to even imagine she'd be with him forever. It wasn't something she'd ever wanted before . . . well, before meeting Finn.

It didn't matter that he was the last thing she thought about before falling asleep and the first thing she thought about when waking up. That was infatuation. It had nothing to do with love.

"I know that look in your eyes," Chloe said with a huge smile. "You've totally had sex with him. I want a tell-all."

If Bree hadn't been there, Brooke wouldn't have been as mortified at her friend's words as she was. She glared at Chloe.

"Oh, honey, we're going to be family, and I love a good sex story," Bree said with that warm smile that was already growing on Brooke.

"You Andersons are quite overwhelming, aren't you?" Brooke asked.

Bree laughed as she reached for her third brownie. The woman didn't even hesitate to take a bite. Her body was flawless. Brooke wondered how she could consume whatever she wanted.

"Yes, we're a force to be reckoned with. And not because of the money, but because we were raised believing there was nothing in life we couldn't have if we wanted it bad enough. We were taught to work hard, but that work has its rewards. And now I'm married to one of the strongest men I've ever known, and that's saying a lot, considering I have four very alpha brothers and a lot of cousins. But in life if you want something, you don't hesitate to go after it."

"I've always felt that way. I had an older brother who taught me I could be or do anything I want."

"I miss him, too," Sarah said with a sympathetic smile.

"Yeah, we all do," Chloe added.

"I'm sorry for your loss," Bree said, her smile fading. "I don't know how I'd survive the loss of one of my brothers. They might be a pain in my ass most of the time, but I know they'd die for me and vice versa. And one thing for sure is that we love each other. Yes, we lost that for a while, but it wasn't gone—it was buried. Life can be messy sometimes, but when we take the time to pick up the pieces, those who are truly meant to be in our lives will always be there, will always forgive us."

"I can't talk about him right now. If I do, I'll fall apart, and I don't have time to fall apart anymore," Brooke said, her tone pleading.

"That's right. There's no time to fall apart. We're going to the spa to celebrate," Chloe said, her smile a little forced as she tried to push away the melancholy mood.

"The spa? What?" Again the topic was switching so fast Brooke's sleepy brain wasn't able to keep up.

"Yep, we've been hired to work on the veterans project with the Anderson Corporation. Bree's a big part of it. That's why we're all together."

"And we're becoming lifelong friends," Bree said with her easy smile back in place.

"Wait. I'm so lost right now," Brooke said.

"Well, go get dressed, and we'll tell you all about it in the limo—yep, the limo," Chloe said with a giggle.

They weren't the type of girls who rode around in stretch limos. They were perfectly acceptable used-Toyota kind of girls. With the Andersons blowing into their small town, the world was shifting under their feet.

"Okay, give me twenty minutes. Finish the brownies, and have another cup of coffee," Brooke said. She needed a shower to clear her head. She needed ten minutes to try to process the last half hour of conversation.

So much had been said with so few words. Of course the most prevalent was marriage. Why was Finn telling people they were getting married? It had to be a joke. But no matter how much she tried pushing it from her brain, she wasn't able to.

She wasn't the marrying kind of girl. She never had been, never would be. She was strong, stubborn, and independent. She didn't need a man in her life to define who she was, who she was meant to be. She was happy on her own. It was okay to date once in a while, but even that failed her.

Well, that was until she'd met Finn. The last few weeks with him had been the most exciting of her life. But that didn't mean she was even remotely close to thinking about marriage. No. That was ridiculous.

But even as she had those thoughts, she couldn't push the idea from her mind. It wasn't what she wanted, she assured herself. But there was a small part of her that also couldn't imagine never seeing him again, never talking to him again, and especially never being held tightly in his arms again while he was buried deep within her.

She had problems, definite problems, and she didn't have a chance of not talking them out while her besties were in the house. And Bree Anderson seemed like the type of girl capable of digging into a person's deepest, darkest secrets.

It was probably too late to plead sickness . . .

CHAPTER
TWENTY-THREE

After a relaxing day at the spa, Brooke felt better than she had in a very long time. There was nothing on this planet that could alter her mood in a bad way. She had friends she adored, a man she couldn't chase away no matter how hard she tried to do just that, and a life a lot of people would envy.

That didn't mean she didn't have inner demons she battled with on a constant basis; it just meant she was getting better each and every day. She had a good life, and she could be proud of what she'd done in her years and proud of who she'd become.

She just wasn't sure what that meant while she was moving forward. Maybe it meant she needed to let go of some of her carefully guarded control. Finn seemed to be a man who loved to live in the moment. What would it be like for her if she chose to do that same thing? Would she be happier? Did she want to be happier?

That was something to really think about. The happier you were, the harder you fell when things went wrong. Wasn't it somehow easier to live a more sedate life where you didn't get overly excited? Sure, the highs were never enough, but the lows couldn't drop you to your knees.

She wasn't sure what to do.

She opened her door and moved into her kitchen, where she found a gift basket sitting on her table. There weren't many people who had a key to her house, so she was hesitant as she moved to her table to look at the basket.

She'd been a soldier too long to not be suspicious of an unwarranted package—especially one that had made it past her locked door. The pretty purple bow on the top of it made it appear innocent enough, but some of the most dangerous things were wrapped in a pretty little package before they exploded and took lives.

A large note that wasn't wrapped hung down from the ribbon, and she looked at the signature before looking at anything else. She had to smile as she read the words coming from her two best friends. They must've had someone drop off the gift while she'd been at the spa. She rolled her eyes a bit as she undid the bow and looked inside before reading what her friends had to say.

Though Brooke was a medical professional, she found herself blushing as she pulled out a box containing a vibrator. She'd owned some in her life. She'd spent a lot of time single, and owning a vibrator was almost mandatory. Since she didn't want to go around sleeping with random men, it was a wise investment. She could honestly say she'd never been given one as a gift, though.

Next to the vibrator was a tube of lubrication, a candle that actually smelled pretty phenomenal, and a book. She pulled out the book, which had a sexy pair of legs in cowboy boots on the front cover. It was called *Taken, Not Spurred*, by author Ruth Cardello.

What the heck? Was this a romance book? She didn't read romance books. She didn't believe in romance, so when she tried to read the books, she found herself rolling her eyes instead of enjoying the books.

But she found herself looking at the cover, finding it pretty cute. What in the heck were her friends up to? Maybe it was time to find out. She set the stuff down and read the note.

Okay, your choice on where you go next in life. You can either read this book and use this toy while sitting in a tub with a candle going and some soft music playing. Or you can grab the bull by the horns and ride that delicious man who can't get enough of you. This book has both options in it. There's a wicked hot bathtub scene where the girl finds some good pleasure on her own. There's also some even hotter scenes where the cowboy takes her to heaven. Have fun and truly enjoy. Love you, woman.

   Kisses,

   Chloe and Sarah

She picked the book back up, completely intrigued. Damn her friends and their meddling. They liked Finn. They obviously liked him a lot. They were pushing her to make a decision where he was concerned.

She decided to draw a bath and do some of what they'd suggested. She left the vibrator in the basket. There was no way she was giving them the satisfaction of using the dang thing. But she might want to remember to hide it later, or it could be pretty embarrassing if someone showed up and walked into her kitchen.

An hour later Brooke found herself clenching her thighs together as she read the bath scene her friends had been talking about. Hot damn, she was tempted to call Finn right then and there to relieve the ache. She kept on reading.

Sarah wanted to tell him that he'd violated her privacy when his tongue flicked at the spot just behind her ear, and she moaned in pleasure instead. His other hand shifted from her hip to cup her ass and lift her more fully against him. Her nipples hardened and pushed at the material that separated them from the rock-hard chest rubbing against her.

I'll tell him later.

Once again he was whispering in her ear. "I want to teach you to come until you can't think, until you can't move, until nothing else matters but having me deep inside you again."

Okay.

Adrenaline and desire swirled within Sarah. It's one thing to fantasize about having that experience with a man you hardly know, and it's another to receive the offer. And, oh . . . what an offer.

Brooke closed the book, breathing heavily. She climbed from the tub, put on her robe, and headed for her phone. She sent one message.

I need you.

The reply took less than three seconds.

On my way.

Yeah, Brooke didn't care. She didn't care at all. She wanted him, and she was going to have him—and have him right now.

Chapter Twenty-Four

Finn made it to her house in record time, and Brooke opened the door and devoured him with her eyes. It didn't matter how much time they spent together; she wanted him with a vengeance that bordered on insanity.

"Do you want a drink?" she asked.

He didn't say anything, making her body shiver. She wanted to attack him but somehow managed not to. Instead she turned and moved into her kitchen, trying to remember what she was doing. That's right, she'd offered a drink. Not that she wanted to take the time to mix one.

"What would you like to—"

She didn't get to finish her sentence. Finn stepped up to her, put his hand on the back of her neck, his thumb on her cheek, and leaned down, his lips cutting off her words. She stood there in a daze as his firm mouth molded to hers, moving ever so slightly in the most intoxicating way.

She sighed as her mind shut off and her body came alive. Her mouth opened to his as he traced his tongue over her lips, dipping inside in a teasing manner that had her body trembling. It didn't matter how many times they were together. She always wanted more.

She reached up, wrapping her arms around his strong shoulders, caressing the back of his neck as she pushed toward him, wanting more, needing everything he was offering. Her body was on fire, and he'd only just begun this dance the two of them were sharing.

One hand cupped the back of her neck as he deepened the kiss, making her sigh into his mouth. The other began rubbing down the center of her back as he pulled her closer. He was so hard against her softness, making her body mold to his muscles.

His hand came up the side of her, sending shivers down her spine. She squirmed in his arms, not able to get close enough, wanting the clothes between them to evaporate.

His hand left her neck as he moved both arms lower, sliding them over the curve of her butt and touching her trembling thighs. Then his mouth broke away from hers as he trailed his lips across her jaw and sucked the skin where her pulse beat out of control.

Her knees grew weak as his lips traced the V of her shirt, kissing the top of her breasts. And then her breath was taken away as he suddenly lifted her up and stepped forward, setting her on the counter, then pushing against her as he ran his lips back up her neck and kissed her again—this time harder and with more purpose.

She clung to him, all thoughts evaporated from her brain—all thoughts except to have him buried deep inside her. She clung to him as he ran his hands up the front of her shirt and cupped the weight of her breasts in his calloused fingers, his lips putting her in a trance.

When he broke away this time, she grumbled her protest. Her mind was in a fog, and she wanted this man with a desperation she'd never felt before. There was a pulse in her core that nobody else could possibly tame. Only Finn. She feared it would be him from this moment on. It really had been from the first moment his lips had touched hers.

Finn tugged on her shirt as his lips lowered, teasing her breasts but not giving her what she wanted to demand from him. She could do nothing more than hang on and pray she made it through the storm.

"Still want to have drinks?" he asked in his wickedly confident voice.

"No," she admitted, her voice husky and needy.

He stepped back, his eyes on fire. She tried to gain back some of the control she'd lost as she hopped down from the counter and turned on wobbly legs, making her way toward her bedroom. She could feel his hot breath on the back of her neck.

The slight pause in them not touching was making her wonder if she should slow this down. Should she have sent the text? It was the first time she'd initiated. But before she could even think about that thought, he was pulling her back into his arms, his mouth once more on hers.

She was his—there was no doubt about it.

He pushed her onto the bed and climbed on top of her as he once more molded his mouth to hers. His hands traced her body as she reached beneath his shirt and ran her fingers up his smooth, hard back.

He sat up, pulling her with him, and she was utter putty in his hands as he lifted her arms, tracing his fingers down the length of them before reaching for the hem of her shirt. He pulled it over her head and tossed it aside before reaching for her bra and sliding it down her arms.

Then he laid her back down and kissed her again before moving across her neck. His fingers molded her heavy breasts as his tongue drew closer to her aching nipples. When his lips finally latched on to one, her back arched off the bed as a groan escaped her.

He sucked and nibbled on the peaked tips, taking his time, building the pressure that threatened to explode within her. She could barely do more than hold on as he lavished attention on her aching body.

She reached for his shirt, but her fingers were shaking too badly to do anything other than plead with him to remove it. He did so in record time, then lay against her, flesh to flesh. The heat and hardness of his body against hers was pure heaven.

He trailed his lips across her breasts, then lower over her shaking stomach as his fingers reached into the waistband of her pants. His lips never stopped moving as he pulled them down her legs, leaving her panties in place.

Then those magical lips of his traced over the silk of her panties, his hot breath lighting her on fire. He pushed her thighs apart as he ran his tongue along her barely covered flesh. Then he slid her panties aside, and his tongue swept up the length of her heat, and she saw stars dance before her hooded lids. It was so intense she wasn't sure she'd survive it.

He spread her heat and licked and sucked, bringing her closer and closer to the pleasure only this one man could bring her. She sucked in a breath as his magical tongue swept across her trembling nerves, and then light exploded before her eyes as her body convulsed in a raw release so intense she nearly lost consciousness. He didn't stop licking her, drawing every pulse of pleasure from her body.

She went limp, begging him to stop. He looked up and smiled. She could barely open her eyes. Her skin was flushed, hot, and damp. But as he traced his fingers along her thighs, up over her shaking stomach and the mounds of her breasts, circling her sensitive nipples, she was shocked to feel that burning need start to build again.

He climbed up her body, and the sight of his solid chest, his beautiful shoulders, and his muscled arms made her stomach stir. She wanted more. He'd made her so greedy—and she didn't even care.

He sat up on his knees as he undid his pants. She sat up and pushed his hands aside as she pulled them down and gazed at the beauty of his solid manhood, the tip wet with his excitement. That was all for her. At least on this night he belonged to her and nobody else.

She leaned in and ran her tongue over his stomach, smiling as he trembled before her. Then she leaned down and tasted the tip of him as his fingers reached into her hair and tugged.

She circled her lips over him, sighing at the taste. Musk and salt and heat. It was delicious. She licked her lips, getting them nice and wet before circling him and lowering herself, taking him deep into her mouth. He groaned as she sucked him, moving her head up and down, tasting his pleasure as her tongue circled his sensitive flesh.

His fingers tightened in her hair as he pulsed in her mouth. She squeezed him with her fingers as she tightened her mouth around him, greedy for more.

"Enough," he growled, tugging hard on her hair. She held on for a second longer before letting him go.

He was no longer gentle as he pushed her back on the bed, his beautiful body looming over hers. She enjoyed the show as he ripped off the rest of his clothing.

And then he was finally climbing over her. He positioned himself at her entrance and waited, making her arch her hips; she needed him buried deep inside her. Though his eyes were on fire, he still held on to control, smiling down at her.

His lips claimed hers again as he surged forward, burying his thickness deep within her. She lost her breath at the intensity of belonging to him. Her arms wrapped around his back, and she held on tight as he began to move, slowly at first, building and building and building the pressure.

His chest rubbed against the ache in her breasts as he reached behind her and gripped her ass. He moved faster and harder, slamming against her body in the most delicious way.

She wrapped her legs tightly around him and held on as new stars danced before her eyes. His hand caressed her ass before pulling back and slapping it. And then she was lost. He surged forward, and she exploded, the orgasm so intense she couldn't stop herself from shaking in his arms.

He pounded in and out of her, his hot breath on her neck as her pleasure went on and on and on. And then he groaned as his body tensed, and she felt him pulse within her, his heat filling her up and causing another wave of pleasure to surge through her. Their ragged breaths were all that could be heard for several long moments as she clung tightly to him.

And then she let go, her body going limp as his weight comforted her.

No words were spoken. What could either of them say? All she knew was she wasn't willing to let him go—not quite yet. He rested inside her, and she felt utterly complete. She knew she'd never get enough of him—and the scariest part of all was that she wasn't afraid.

CHAPTER TWENTY-FIVE

The week began in an unusual way. Of course, maybe the new normal in Brooke's life was abnormal. Since getting to know Finn more, she couldn't deny she liked how he was turning her perfectly ordered life upside down.

She might not be willing to admit that out loud, but he brought her excitement, challenged her, and made her want to live outside the proverbial box. She'd always been tough. It was why she'd chosen the career she'd gone into, and why she fought for the underdog. But he made her want to be free. He made her see the world in a new light.

Monday morning she received a bouquet of flowers, but not just any bouquet. No, that would be too ordinary for Finn. It was stunning with yellow, orange, red, and green, in a thicket of beautiful weeds with a note that asked, *Where do you think we're going next?*

She had no idea. He didn't call her, and it took everything within her to not call him. He liked his games, his dances with her. And she liked them, too. If the surprise was given up too quickly, they'd both be disappointed.

On Tuesday she got an envelope with a map in it. She studied it for quite some time, but she still didn't know what he was up to. It appeared to be a maze in the woods. Were they searching for treasure?

Tuesday night he texted, telling her he was out of town meeting with people, but he missed her. She hated how much joy it brought her that he was thinking about her, hated the amount of power the man had with a simple message. Her day could be brightened or dimmed on whether he talked to her or not. That was a definite problem and something she should try to control.

On Wednesday she received a heavy package with a big smile drawn on top of it. Her fingers trembled as she cut through the tape and opened the lid. Inside were several different packages of paintball ammunition.

This time she couldn't help but smile. The game was over. Now she understood the weed bouquet and map. She'd never been paintballing before, but she was more than excited to give it a try.

On Thursday she received a long box. Inside was the coolest paintball gun she could imagine, with a scope, extra clips, and safety equipment. There was a new note with this package.

> *I'll be home tomorrow. Will pick you up at five. Be in*
> *full gear, because I won't show you mercy. Miss you more*
> *each day.*

There was no hesitation as Brooke picked up her phone and dialed. Maybe he was busy, but she needed to hear his voice. Maybe that had been his plan all along: to make her ache for him. Well, she didn't care if she was the loser in this situation. She liked him whether she wanted to or not, and she was done fighting herself on it.

He answered after the first ring.

"Good afternoon, beautiful," he said in that perfectly amazing deep tone.

"Hello, sexy," she replied, not even giving herself a second to think about it.

"Hmm, you find me sexy?" he said with a deep chuckle.

"You know I do," she said with a roll of her eyes he couldn't see.

"I miss you," he told her. That thumping in her heart increased as tingles ran down her stomach.

"I . . . yeah, I miss you, too," she admitted, though she might have preferred a dental visit than telling him. Maybe him staying away from her after being on her heels for so long was another strategy, because she really did miss him.

"We're going to have fun tomorrow," he told her.

"I've never done it before. I'm actually excited."

"I like taking you to do new things."

"Well, you've certainly done that. How's your work going?"

He sighed. "It's good. I'm at a veterans facility in Montana. It's definitely not the way we'll do ours, but what's nice is they're giving us valuable information, and in turn, they're listening to our ideas. I think we can spread this information around all the states, and maybe we can truly save lives. Depression and PTSD are very real for veterans, and if there are better resources out there, and more people who understand what they're going through, then maybe we can make a real change."

"I agree. I really want to be involved in the project more than just providing my services when it's done. I'd love to come to some of the planning meetings," she told him.

"Then I'll give you the schedule. The more people involved who truly care, the better off we're going to be."

"I fully agree," she said.

"So next week we'll have a meeting, and you'll come. But right now I want you to get some practice in. It's only fun to beat you when you can't claim I cheated," he said with a chuckle.

"Oh, I can totally beat you with zero practice. It's no different than shooting a real gun."

He laughed again. "Yeah, it's a bit different than shooting a real gun, but you can take a day to think you'll win. My victory will be all that much better."

Now it was Brooke's turn to laugh. And before she knew it, an hour passed with her lying on her bed, smiling and laughing and feeling better than she had all week. She was becoming infatuated with him. That should scare her a lot more than it did. But she pushed those thoughts aside. For now, she felt joy and excitement. That was so much better than the pain and sorrow she'd been feeling since her brother's loss. She'd take the joy anytime.

And that's exactly what Finn was bringing her.

CHAPTER TWENTY-SIX

Finn had been in the military his entire adult life . . . until the explosion that had forced him out. He hadn't dealt with that very well, but he was beginning to see that everything happened for a reason. Had he still been in another country, he never would've met Brooke.

Just the thought of not knowing this spectacular woman caused him sorrow. In a short amount of time she'd changed his life—for the better. She was as important to him now as his family was. He didn't want a single hour to go by without seeing her, let alone days, weeks, or months.

Love was a funny thing. He'd never really believed in romantic love. Why settle down with one person for the rest of your life when there were a myriad of women to choose from weekly? That had always been his philosophy. But the second his vision had been filled with a feisty female who'd taken him to the ground, his intentions had shifted dramatically.

He now didn't understand how he'd lived as long as he had with such emptiness. She was his world now, and he wanted to be hers. He knew she cared about him. He could read it in her eyes. He just had to make her trust herself enough to accept what he was so willing to give.

"Come out, come out, wherever you are."

Finn smiled as Brooke's whispered words came through his earpiece. The two of them might be slight adrenaline junkies, because they sure as hell were doing very active dates.

He was currently hiding behind a shed at the massive paintball course he'd found about an hour outside of Seattle. Not only did he have this day of fun and shooting with Brooke, but he got to drive with her at his side, smelling her sweet perfume and enjoying her husky voice as she told him about her week.

"Better be careful, Brooke, or I'm going to find you," he whispered back as he looked through his scope.

He loved that she wasn't an easy target, loved how much she challenged him. He hadn't believed a woman like her had existed before he'd met her. And each day he spent with her only confirmed what he'd known from that first sight of her—she was the one, the only one.

"You've grown too confident in your years as a soldier," she said, a husky chuckle in her voice. "I'm closing in on you. I can feel it." Even the smugness in her voice turned him on. He'd definitely take her down, but her utter confidence in herself had him shifting where he knelt as his pants tightened.

"Be careful, Brooke. You aren't playing with a little boy; you're challenging a man," he said, knowing his words would fire her up. The gasp made him smile.

"Oh, all men are truly little boys," she said. He could practically feel her breath on his ear as her words whispered over the pod. "And I'll greatly enjoy taking you down again and again and again . . ."

Finn had to force himself not to laugh out loud. He didn't know if she was five feet away or a hundred yards. But his spider senses assured him she was near. He took a moment before responding to her taunt.

"You can take me down anytime you want, sexy lady. Especially if you squeeze those knees of yours tightly against my thighs as you straddle me."

This time the gasp he heard coming across the line wasn't annoyance or anger. She might try to fight what she was feeling, but Brooke was a bomb waiting to explode, and the moment their skin connected they both went up in flames. He suddenly lost interest in their game of cat and mouse. He wanted her now—needed her with a desperation that bordered on insanity.

"Brooke?" he said. She was silent. The hair on the back of his neck stood up a second too late as he felt a pellet slam into the back of his arm, then another round of fire hitting him on the helmet, back, and side as he shifted.

"Gotcha," she said. He only caught a brief glance of her before she dropped out of sight. He was in total awe. "Mmm, is the Navy SEAL losing his tracking abilities?" she taunted.

"You have me so messed up I think I've lost all my senses," he admitted.

Sure, she was a soldier, but he was the elite of the elite, and she was repeatedly surprising him. And it only made him love her that much more. But now was time for victory. He couldn't give her too many wins.

Finn quickly left his location and stopped talking as he tracked her. She was good, damn good, in fact, but she wasn't a match for him. Once he put his mind to something, he needed to be the best at it. Injuries or not, Finn was still proud and determined, and he wanted to be the man taking care of her the rest of her life. He felt he needed to prove to her that he was capable of doing just that.

They were fairly matched with him injured. She sneaked up on him one more time, but at the end of the day, if he'd been counting points, he could consider himself victorious. But even if he didn't win the game, it didn't matter. He was with her, and she was laughing and living her life. That was a victory he'd celebrate every single day for the rest of their lives together.

He wondered how soon he could get away with proposing to her. He'd do it right there on the paintball course if he thought she'd accept, but he could be patient. What was a few more weeks or even months in the scheme of things? The two of them had a lifetime left together.

Besides, he'd once heard that patience was a virtue. He'd laughed at the time, thinking he didn't need to wait for anything. But he was truly getting to enjoy that statement now. He was growing as a person. Hell, if he could give himself a hard pat on the back, he might just do that.

Of course, with the number of paintballs that had hit him there, a pat might sting. But pain was a person's best friend. If you felt pain, you weren't dead. That was always a good thing in his line of work.

Love and pain went hand in hand. You couldn't love a person with everything you had without utter devastation at losing them.

CHAPTER TWENTY-SEVEN

Brooke was daydreaming. She was having an actual end-of-the-day fantasy that totally involved one very sexy ex-soldier with very few clothes on, pressed up against her. It took her assistant three tries to get her attention. Brooke didn't daydream—not ever—not when the earth was spinning on its normal axis.

"Your last patient's in room three," Rose said so loudly Brooke couldn't help but hear her this time.

"Sorry, Rose," Brooke said as she snapped out of her trance. What in the world was wrong with her? What had Finn Anderson done to her normally cool demeanor? She wasn't sure she could even recognize herself anymore, even while looking in the mirror.

She wasn't some dreamy teenager with nothing better to do than think about a man morning, noon, and night. But that seemed to be what she was doing. She wished she could say it was just about the sex. That would make it easier for her to understand.

After all, it was the best sex she'd ever experienced in her life. Not that she'd had a lot of partners, but still, he was unbelievable in bed, or on the ground, or in the tub, and *definitely* in the car. She was sure she'd never be able to look at another man again and feel desire, not after being with Finn. He was *that* good.

But it wasn't always sex she thought about when it came to him. She thought about weekend trips, lazy Sunday mornings, and laughing while the two of them challenged each other. She thought about cooking together, sleeping together while wrapped in each other's arms. She thought about an aisle filled with rose petals.

That final thought was enough to snap her to full attention. This daydreaming had to stop, and it needed to stop yesterday. But no matter how much she seemed to lecture herself, she couldn't seem to stop the thoughts or fantasies. She couldn't seem to shake this obsession she had with one certain man.

"Which room?" she asked, hating that knowing smirk on Rose's face.

"Room three. Are you sure you aren't the one who needs to see a doctor?" Rose asked with a laugh.

"I'm just fine. It's Friday, and I haven't slept a lot this week. That's all," Brooke said as she stood and straightened out her lab coat.

"Yeah, I believe that as much as I believe in time-shares and global warming," Rose said.

"Global warming is real," Brooke told the woman.

"Yeah, yeah, I'm too old to care," Rose said with a laugh. "I'm going to take a cigarette break."

"You're adding to the problem," Brooke called out to her.

Rose held up a hand. "Too old to care," she repeated.

Brooke couldn't even bring up future generations, because Rose had never married and didn't have kids or grandkids. That thought stopped Brooke from walking out the door of her office.

She'd never put that into perspective before. Rose was an amazing woman—truly incredible, actually. She was stubborn and independent and didn't care what anyone thought about her—sort of like Brooke . . . and she was all alone . . . just like Brooke.

Brooke had been determined her entire life to not get married, to not give in to the illusion of love and happily ever after. But did she really want to be in her seventies, going home alone to an empty house? Did she want to spend holidays on her own with no one to cook for? Did she want to have no one to turn to when she needed someone?

Did she really want to keep her independence so much that it was worth having nothing in the end? Bracing her hand against the jamb of the door, Brooke felt her pulse speed up as mild panic filled her.

Why hadn't she thought of this before? Probably because she was twenty-nine, and mortality wasn't something she'd ever really thought about. Come to think of it, even when she'd been in war-torn countries, she hadn't taken the time to think about her own death. It was something she didn't consider.

And then she'd lost the only family that had ever mattered. And she'd been so full of grief over the loss of her brother she still hadn't been thinking about herself ten years down the line, or twenty, or fifty. But now—now that the thought had appeared in her mind—she was afraid she'd think about it a lot.

But how did someone pick another person to spend your life with? What if it all went wrong? What if they tried to change you? What if they cheated? Lied? Married you and then showed their true colors? What if kids were involved?

She hadn't been shown good examples of love and happiness. Her mother was a druggie, and her father had disappeared long ago. So she had no examples. Even her besties had been through relationships, but they'd never married.

People too easily told one another how much they were in love, and maybe they were when they said it. But love didn't last forever. That she was sure of. So what was the worse of the two risks? Was it scarier to be in a loveless relationship or to be alone? She wasn't sure.

"Your patient's still waiting and not getting any younger," Rose called from down the hallway.

"On my way," Brooke called back. "Bossy woman," she added under her breath, praying Rose didn't hear her.

She shook her head to clear it as she made her way to room three. It wasn't far from her office. She opened the door and froze.

"Good afternoon, young lady," a booming voice said. She was surprised the pictures on the wall didn't fall. His voice was as big as his body.

Joseph Anderson.

She'd never met him in person before, but she knew exactly who he was. There wasn't a chance of residing in the Seattle area without knowing the man who did so much good in the world. He was a giant of a man, but his acts of kindness were known near and far. She smiled as she looked at him.

"What is someone like you doing in my small town and in my clinic?" she asked as she stepped forward. She was slightly suspicious of him being there, as he was the honorary uncle to the man she was seeing, and Bree had said he *was* a meddler.

"I was visiting the site for the veterans facility and felt pain in my chest," Joseph replied, suddenly suspiciously quiet as he tried to appear meek and fragile. The look and sound weren't deceiving her at all.

"I see," she murmured as she stepped up to him. "Anything to do with the heart isn't a laughing matter. I should call the helicopter and have you rushed to the hospital. Don't you have surgeons in your family? I can't imagine you don't," she said as she pulled out her stethoscope. She didn't believe he was having any heart problems, but there were too many years of training in her experience to completely dismiss what he was saying. If something were to happen to him, she'd never forgive herself for not giving him proper care.

"No, no. That's utter nonsense. You're a fine medical person," Joseph said with a wave of his hand. "I'm happy to have you helping." The man just couldn't help it—his voice rose the more he spoke. She was sure he hadn't been meek or humble a day in his life.

"I'll need to have you lie back," she told him.

"Not a problem," he said as he lay down on the table, making the thing disappear beneath him, with his legs dangling off the end.

She listened to his heart, had him breathe in and out, and took his pulse. He was healthier than her, she was sure. But she gave him a full exam anyway, just to be sure. He was Joseph Anderson, after all. She wouldn't be the person responsible if anything were to happen to him.

"I'd say it was probably heartburn," she told him after a few minutes, not willing to accuse him of faking it to get into her office. "And I'd recommend you tell your wife as soon as you get home and schedule an appointment with your doctor."

She turned to add notes in her computer. She began counting in her head, because she knew it wouldn't take long for Joseph to come up with the real reason he was in her office. She was turned away from him, so when he next spoke, she didn't try to hold back her knowing smile. She did, however, have to force herself not to laugh.

"So how are things going with you and Finn? I thought I'd ask since I'm here anyway," he said. He didn't do the casual voice any better than he did the meek one.

"Who?" she said, very proud of her casual question. She kept typing on her computer, though she really had no idea what she was entering. For all she knew she could be prescribing the man Valium and recommending a space shuttle trip to Mars.

"Did you ask *who*?" Joseph asked, his voice back to normal in his bafflement. She composed her features before turning.

"Sorry. What did you say?" she asked.

His eyes widened. She was 100 percent positive he wasn't used to having to repeat himself. When he spoke a room stood at attention, and his voice was loud enough to hear in the next county, so she was truly enjoying the perplexity of his expression.

"I asked how things are going with my nephew Finn, the man you're *dating*," he said, his eyes narrowing as if he was picking up on the fact she was messing with him. He was much too smart for her to outwit.

"Oh, sorry, we're not dating. I've seen him a few times, but that's all," she said with a shrug. She was praying her cheeks weren't flushing. She could tell herself all day long they weren't dating, but they were together all the time, and when they weren't he was pretty much all she thought about, so to say they weren't dating was an absolute lie. And Brooke really didn't like lying.

"Mm-hmm," Joseph said with a knowing smile that made her have to look away. The man was smart—way too smart for her.

"I'm going to recommend again that you see your primary care doctor. I think we're done for now, though," Brooke said, deciding it was far safer for her to end this conversation quickly.

"I asked a question. It's impolite not to answer," Joseph said, sitting on the table, appearing as if he had all day. He did. She didn't. Finn was supposed to pick her up from work at any moment, and she absolutely didn't want Joseph there to see it happen.

"I did answer. We aren't dating, so there's nothing to tell."

And right on cue, there was a tap on the door before it opened, and Rose called in. "Finn just got here. I told him Joseph was in exam room three, and he said no problem; Joseph wouldn't mind him coming in."

Brooke sighed in frustration.

"Well, send the boy in. It's good he's worried about his fragile uncle," Joseph called out. If Finn were on the street in front of the building, he'd have heard.

The door widened, and in strode Finn, looking far too beautiful and put together. Brooke felt frumpy and uncertain in the room with the two larger-than-life men.

"I didn't say I was worried; I said you wouldn't mind me coming back," Finn said. Finn gave a once-over of Joseph, and Brooke could see the man was trying to look as if he didn't care if his uncle was on the exam table, but there was slight concern in Finn's eyes. He might not want to like Joseph—he might not even trust the man—but he did care, even if he wasn't admitting it to himself.

"Well, even though you aren't asking, I'm doing just great, thanks to this beautiful woman," Joseph said with a bit of a growl.

"I didn't do anything other than give you an exam," Brooke pointed out.

"But you ruled out a heart attack. That's certainly something," Joseph said.

"Heart attack?" Finn said, again trying not to look concerned.

"I think he just had heartburn," Brooke said. She didn't want to say Joseph was faking his way into her exam room, but she also didn't want Finn unnecessarily worried. It seemed the Andersons liked to push in when they weren't invited, considering she had two of them in a room she wanted to escape from.

"Hmm," Finn mumbled.

"What's that supposed to mean?" Joseph said, looking a little defensive.

"I think I should take you to the hospital. They should run tests," Finn replied, mischief in his eyes. Brooke knew Finn was guarded with Joseph, so she was pleased by this turn of events. She didn't like the meddling he was trying to do in her life, but she hoped he and Finn could have a real relationship. She'd love to have family she could count on.

"Nonsense, boy. You didn't come here to see me. I'm sure you have better ways to spend your evening than babysitting an old man."

That nearly made Brooke chuckle. Sure, he had white hair and the beard to match, but there was far too much life in Joseph's eyes for anyone to ever assume he was too old.

"I think it's a great idea," Brooke told Joseph. "Finn and I didn't have anything special planned. I'm okay with him taking you."

Joseph's grin fell away. "I'm perfectly capable of getting places on my own," he told them as he hopped down from the exam table. "You can walk me out," he added as he looked at Finn.

"Sure thing. Where are you parked?" Finn asked as he stepped over to the door and pulled it open.

"The helicopter is on the school grounds," Joseph said. They used the wide expanse of lawn to land helicopters when there were emergencies in their town. Brooke wasn't surprised they'd let Joseph land there.

Brooke let out a sigh of relief as Joseph's and Finn's voices faded away as they left her building. If Joseph truly did want to meddle in her life, she realized there wasn't a thing she could do to stop it. She didn't think a wrecking ball could stop Joseph from something he wanted.

She just wondered why she wasn't more upset about the situation. Maybe because she wanted to be with Finn—and maybe because she just didn't want to admit that to herself or to the man.

CHAPTER TWENTY-EIGHT

"Tell me why you're so jittery," Sarah asked Brooke as she sat on the couch, eating way too much ice cream.

"I don't want to go to this party," Brooke said with a sigh. "You know I'm uncomfortable with a lot of people surrounding me."

Sarah laughed, making Brooke take an extrabig spoonful of ice cream and regret it instantly when she got a painful brain freeze. She tried not to show her discomfort, but Sarah smirked.

"You've always been surrounded by people, so that excuse isn't working one little bit on me. What's the real reason?" Sarah pushed.

Brooke sighed. There were people you could lie to and those who'd never allow you to get away with it. Her two best friends could always call her out on her crap. She knew this already. It wasn't as if she truly expected she'd be able to get away with it.

"Considering the entire family is planning our wedding, I'm not looking forward to going. They might have a dress waiting for me," Brooke said with a shudder.

Sarah laughed. "I don't think that will happen." She didn't seem so sure. Brooke might be saying it as a joke, but with the Andersons that was a very real possibility.

"And there's the fact that I'm getting far too attached to Finn, and spending an evening with his family doesn't seem to be the smartest thing for me to do when I'm not even sure what there is between us," Brooke added. "I need some distance to figure it all out."

"I don't understand why you need to put any distance. He's a great guy. You're more than available. Why don't you see where this'll lead?" Sarah asked.

"I don't think I'm in a place in my life I can give a real relationship a chance. So what if I fall in love with him, and it all goes to hell?" Brooke asked.

"What if it does?"

"Huh?"

"We can't always be in control, and we can't predict every single outcome. So I'm beginning to learn that sometimes it's just better to go with the flow. I'm also learning that it's better to try and fail than to never try at all."

"Are you reading self-help books again?" Brooke asked with a smile. "Whenever you do, we get lots of zen quotes."

Sarah laughed, not at all offended. "I always read self-help books. When we aren't trying to improve ourselves, we begin to wither. Maybe you should try it sometime."

"I'm plenty happy with how my life's going," Brooke assured her. Sarah raised an eyebrow but didn't call her on her false words. "Okay, I'm ninety-eight percent happy."

"It's okay to live your life and be happy," Sarah said as she reached out a hand and patted Brooke's leg. The gesture instantly brought tears to Brooke's eyes, which frustrated her.

"I'm such a strong person I hate feeling so dang moody," Brooke admitted.

"We all hate being anything other than our best," Sarah reminded her.

"I can't stand the chaos that's become my life."

"Well, maybe you just need to live each day by the hour. Quit trying to see into the future," Sarah said.

"I have nothing to wear to the party," Brooke told her friend. "I can't go there in jeans and a T-shirt, not to the Anderson mansion." That was a real reason to not go. She was quite proud to have come up with it.

"Well, it's a good thing there are these convenient places called malls where you can buy things like clothes," Sarah said with another chuckle. "And there's nothing I'd love to do more this afternoon than some good old-fashioned shopping. I want a new dress for the party, too."

"I'm not getting out of this, am I?" Brooke said.

"Not a chance. I've been hired to help create this massive veterans facility, and the last thing I want to do is no-show a birthday party for Katherine Anderson. Besides the fact it would look bad, I'm more than flattered to be invited. And I can't go without you, because then I wouldn't have a good time, and I'd be worried about you all night."

"Fine. I'm proud of you for getting the contract," Brooke said.

"I don't know how it happened, but I'm not looking a gift horse in the mouth. It's too amazing."

Brooke really was happy for Sarah. It was a dream come true to work on any Anderson project. This would truly help launch Sarah's career beyond anything else she could ever do.

"Then I guess we're heading to the mall," Brooke told her.

"Yahoo. Go get dressed." Sarah took the ice cream from Brooke and took a bite, sighing in bliss. Brooke slowly walked toward her room, feeling as if she was going to regret all of this, but beginning to not care so much.

Even though she took her time getting ready, it wasn't long before she and Sarah were in the car, driving to the mall in Seattle. Of course there wasn't good shopping in their tiny town. But that's just one more reason she loved where she lived.

Brooke definitely wanted the convenience of shopping within a couple of hours of her, but she also loved small-town living, where she could feel safer and have a quieter existence. That was more than important to her after her years of being in the military, where there was no such thing as quiet or privacy.

She hadn't minded any of that in her years of service. Maybe she was getting too old, too soon. Maybe it would be good for her to live a little more freely—more like her two best friends.

It didn't take long for them to arrive at the mall, and Sarah was instantly in shopping mode. That wasn't anything new. Brooke wasn't nearly as big a fan of shopping as her best friend was, but she liked having someone along who knew what they were doing. It made it a little less painful.

"Okay, we're going to find the perfect dresses, then get our hair and makeup done. It's a full day of beauty for a great night out," Sarah told her.

"We better call Chloe, or we're both toast," Brooke told her.

"Don't worry; I'm on it," Sarah assured her. "She'll be here in two hours. She's in a meeting right now."

The girls talked as they wandered through the stores, and when Brooke put on the red dress and stepped from the changing room, she had no doubt this was the one for her. Sarah's eyes widened before she smiled, her eyes lighting up.

"Yes, yes, yes," Sarah said as she clapped, making Brooke blush as she glanced around the area.

"It's a bit clingy," Brooke told her friend. She wasn't normally a girl to wear something so revealing, but she knew she was in shape, so it wasn't that she was trying to hide anything—it was just that she didn't feel a woman should reveal all her secrets with formfitting clothes.

"It's perfectly clingy and hugs you in all the right places. You're going to knock Finn's socks right off," Sarah assured her.

"It doesn't take much to do that," Brooke said with a laugh.

"I don't care what it takes; you're getting that dress. It was made for you," Sarah insisted.

"I don't think I have shoes that'll go with it," Brooke told her.

"That's even better. I'm always happy to shop for shoes. Go change, and meet me in the heel section."

With that Sarah turned and walked away, the deal set in stone. Brooke took her time admiring the dress in the privacy of her changing room. She did feel pretty great in the silky thing. It was nice to feel like a woman—a desirable one at that. It wasn't something she often felt because of her job and life in general.

Shoe shopping took much longer than finding the dress. It was difficult to find a perfect pair of heels that looked great, made your legs look even better, and didn't destroy your feet before the night was over. If men only understood what women went through for a two-second compliment, maybe they'd be a little more appreciative.

Chloe met them at the mall just in time for them to all do their hair and makeup together. Brooke didn't normally put on much of a mask, but she was letting her friends run the show on this night.

They were going to the famous Anderson place, after all, and her friends had more experience than she did when it came to sophisticated lifestyles. It wasn't that Brooke was broke or anything. She made decent money. It was just that she'd lived a frugal life for as long as she could remember, and she didn't see a point in overspending when she could enjoy herself for so much less money and have an even better time than going out to some hoity-toity place.

"Let's do this," Sarah said with a smile.

"We're going to walk into that party looking like a million bucks," Chloe added.

"Or I'll trip in the entrance and land on my face first thing," Brooke told them.

"Nah, you're going to be making one sexy man do that," Sarah assured her.

"I don't know if I want to flirt too much," Brooke said, making Sarah and Chloe laugh.

"Honey, it's far too late for that," Chloe told her.

"It's never too late for anything," Brooke reminded both her friends. That was something her brother had always said to her. Even if a person didn't like where their life was headed or what road they'd taken at an earlier turn, they could always change it up the next time. *Never* wasn't a word her brother had liked.

"Let's finish this day so I can have some wine and calm my nerves," Brooke said.

"Oh, we don't have to wait," Sarah said. "They serve wine here."

"And my day just improved," Brooke said as she picked up a menu.

It was time to have her Cinderella moment. Maybe she'd feel like a princess in search of her very own Prince Charming. Or maybe she'd trip in the doorway. She certainly wasn't going to find out until she stepped out of her comfort zone. And maybe it was far past time for her to do just that.

CHAPTER TWENTY-NINE

Finn wondered if he'd ever get used to being one of the Andersons. Sure, he had the name, and yes, he certainly had the confidence, but to be part of a family belonging to Joseph Anderson would be overwhelming to the most secure of people.

There was a loyalty and respect among his new family that was both awing and humbling. And Finn felt like a new man. He felt anchored in a world that had once been spinning. He'd been finding the walls around his guarded heart crumbling more and more as time passed, but he wasn't ready to let Joseph in.

He could admit the man wasn't a monster. But Finn had never had a father and didn't want one now. He'd never had uncles, either, and hadn't been searching for any. Now, having cousins was pretty amazing. He didn't find himself guarded with them.

So much had changed in a very short period, and Finn felt comfortable with that, secure, and he knew beyond a shadow of a doubt he was right where he needed to be, right where he belonged.

He had a plan. He was going to marry Brooke and accept this new life he'd been given—and he was doing it with grace and the usual confidence he'd been born with.

Walking into the huge ballroom, Finn took a moment to appreciate the crowd dressed to the nines. No, he hadn't hung out at a lot of formal events, but it didn't matter. Finn was comfortable wherever he might end up.

Laughter and music rolled over him, and he smiled as he spotted his youngest brother flirting with a young blonde woman in the corner of the room. The rest of his siblings were mingling with their cousins, and of course Joseph Anderson was the center of attention among a sea of people.

The larger-than-life man currently was in the middle of the dance floor, his lovely wife securely tucked against his chest as Joseph held one of her delicate hands and gently swayed to the music.

Finn moved closer, drawn to the powerful couple, finding that he wanted to know more about the man who wouldn't let him be. People stared at both of them. Some even tried to interrupt the intimate dance, but Joseph couldn't be distracted. He had eyes for only one woman—his bride of over forty years.

Feeling a bit like an eavesdropper, Finn listened as Joseph leaned down and whispered in Katherine's ear.

"Happy birthday, my darling wife. No other woman ever has or will ever compare to your beauty, grace, and sophistication. You've been mine from the very first moment I laid eyes on you," Joseph said.

"I can't even imagine my life without you, Joseph. Thank you for another beautiful birthday," Katherine replied.

"How about we sneak away now?" Joseph said with a seductive chuckle.

"Oh, you are insatiable, dear," Katherine said with a blush that took twenty years off her face.

"Because I'm holding you in my arms," Joseph told her.

"And every year you throw me this beautiful party, and then you try to escape it with me. And I love you all the more because of it,"

Katherine said as she reached her arms up and clasped her fingers behind his neck.

He leaned down and gently kissed her pink lips. That's when Finn turned away, knowing he was intruding on an intimate moment. As he searched the room for Brooke, he hoped the two of them would be saying similar things to each other after so many years together.

It was so odd that he was having those thoughts. He'd never pictured himself as a man to settle down, but now it consumed him. There was no future in his mind if Brooke wasn't by his side. When the right woman came along, there was no chance he'd let her go.

It didn't take long for Finn to find her. She was spectacular in a red gown that emphasized her luscious curves and had him shifting on his feet. He couldn't get enough of her—her beauty, smile, laughter, sparkle, and energy. Her body was amazing, but it was the entire package she made up that had him utterly drawn to her.

She was standing with her two best friends, the women who'd given him a chance to get to know her a little, the two women he appreciated and was glad she had in her life. Their laughter could be heard across the room, and he began moving toward them.

She turned as he approached, and their eyes met. He could see she felt the pull between them as strongly as he did. She just fought it like hell, and he'd accepted it from the very first moment. It was odd because he'd always run from anything even remotely resembling commitment—before Brooke.

He wasn't running anymore—not ever again.

"I've missed you today, Brooke," he told her.

"I don't think it's even been ten hours," she replied, her voice low and husky. He couldn't help but reach for her, already missing how she felt in his arms.

"That's ten hours too long," he said.

She didn't fight it as she melted against him. All was right in the world as her soft curves pressed against him. This was right where she belonged and right where he wanted to be. It didn't matter where they were as long as they were together.

"Sorry to interrupt this seduction, but have you tried the bacon-wrapped scallops? They're amazing."

Finn turned to look at his little brother. "You have impeccable timing, Brandon," he said.

"It's a party with people all around. I was watching your slow walk to the girl of your dreams and wondering if I needed to get the fire hose and douse you. I thought this was smarter," Brandon replied, looking highly amused.

"The only one needing hosed off is you," Finn said.

Brooke shifted as if she was going to pull away, but that wouldn't do. Finn simply tucked her in at his side, his arm wrapped snuggly behind her back, his hand resting on the sweet curve of her hip.

Brandon lost all interest in Finn and Brooke as his eyes zeroed in on Chloe. The instant spark of attraction in his little brother's eyes amused Finn enough to not be upset over the interruption.

"I'm Brandon," he replied as he moved past Finn and stepped in front of Chloe, holding out his hand.

Finn watched as Chloe's shoulders went back. She appeared nervous, which was something Finn had yet to see in either of Brooke's best friends. This was very interesting.

Almost as if she was in a trance, Chloe shook her head before pasting a smile onto her delicate pink lips.

"Chloe Hitman," she said.

Sparks practically exploded between the two of them as their hands connected. Finn was even more amused as Chloe jerked her palm from Brandon's.

"Brandon Anderson. Can I buy you a drink?" he asked.

"The drinks are free," Chloe pointed out.

"Then can I escort you to the nearest waiter?" Brandon persisted.

"I'm good; thank you," Chloe said as she turned away from Brandon.

"I want to dance with you, and then I need to take you home," Finn whispered in Brooke's ear. As amusing as it was to watch his brother strike out, Finn was far more interested in being alone with his woman.

"I don't dance in public," Brooke told him.

"Make an exception," Finn said as he released her long enough to take her hand.

"Finn, no. I can't dance," Brooke said as she tugged against him. He knew she didn't like to make a scene, so he had no doubt he'd get her into his arms.

The song changed as they reached the dance floor, and Brooke stopped fighting. Then he had her exactly where he needed her to be. But it didn't take long for him to want her all to himself.

When their eyes met, she didn't say a word. She simply nodded. And the two of them left without goodbyes and without a glance backward.

CHAPTER THIRTY

The flames of the fire cast light and shadow over the two of them. Finn couldn't imagine feeling more than he was right then. Brooke was curled up against his side as he gazed up at the perfectly clear night, the stars bright, the moon dim.

He knew no matter how much time he spent with her, it wouldn't be enough; no matter how many times they made love, he'd crave more; and no matter how far apart they were, he'd feel her.

What he felt for this woman was indescribable. He'd known from the moment she stepped into his life that he'd never let her go. It took everything within him to take things slow, to allow her to come to the same conclusion he had months before.

"Thank you for an incredible day," she said as she snuggled a little closer.

"Ah, my sweet Brooke, I'm the one who should be thanking you. I haven't felt this much peace in a very long time," he told her as he squeezed his arm tighter around her.

"I know of many ways you can thank me," she said in her sexy, sassy voice that instantly had him hard and wanting.

She slowly untangled herself from him, and he instantly felt cold, though the night was warm and cozy. But it was well worth it when she smiled down at him as she sat up and straddled his hips and pressed down. He wanted their clothes gone.

She circled her hips over his increasingly growing arousal, and he moaned as her head tilted back and she laughed.

"You're a tease," he told her.

"Mmm, you're easy to tease," she said as she reached for the hem of her shirt and slowly pulled it over her head, tossing it aside. She wasn't wearing a bra, and her breasts were absolute perfection.

He reached for her, cupping their luscious weight in his hands. Her smile fell away as she moaned while he squeezed and molded them. She reached down and ran her fingernails across his naked chest, scraping his nipples and making him groan.

"We have too many clothes on," he told her.

"What are we going to do about that?" she asked before he grabbed her back and pulled her toward him.

He swept his tongue over her hard nipple before gently biting down, making her cry out her approval. His hands ran up and down her silky back while he took his time pleasuring one breast and then the other.

The fire crackled next to them, and the waves from the ocean were the perfect backdrop for this magical night. He couldn't taste her or touch her enough. He had to have her over and over again.

Finn pulled her face to his and finally got a taste of her sweet lips. He wasn't in a hurry. He took his time as he traced the fullness of her mouth before dipping his tongue inside and memorizing her all over again.

Her fingers reached up, tangling in his hair as she wiggled her hips against his, pressing into his erection again and again and again until he was ready to explode.

"You turn me on so much," he told her.

"I've never felt anything like this before," she admitted.

He felt like he could soar at her words. She was everything to him. The word *love* popped into his head, but he knew it wasn't the right moment. Not yet. She wasn't ready. So instead of blurting something out that would make her run, he tugged on her hair and took her lips in a passionate kiss that had both of them panting.

He needed to be inside her, but the anticipation was too damn good to go too quickly. She was so responsive to everything he did. He could make love to her all day and night and do it forever, and he feared it still wouldn't be enough. He flipped them over. Now it was his turn to hover over her.

The firelight lit her face, and he took a moment to gaze down at her, taking a screenshot in his mind of this exact moment.

"So beautiful. You are so beautiful," he said in awe.

"You make me feel that way," she said, a suspicious sheen in her eyes.

"If only you could see yourself the way I see you." He was shocked she couldn't.

"I need you inside me, Finn. I feel empty," she told him.

"Yes," he said. But he wanted to take his time. He wanted this night to last forever. He kissed his way down her throat and worshiped her breasts while he ran his hands across her stomach and hips.

Then he moved lower, undoing her shorts and slowly pulling them away from her golden thighs, kissing his way down her legs as he went. She wiggled beneath him, her hips arching off the blanket.

He stripped away his clothes in record time; then he made his way back up her legs, taking his time on the inside of her spread thighs. Perfection. She was utter perfection. And she opened to him, trusting, wanting, needing.

He ran his tongue along the seam of her heat, and she screamed into the night, her voice crashing with the sound of the waves such a short distance away. But he wanted more.

"Please," she begged. He smiled. They had all night.

His arousal pulsed as he latched his mouth to her heat and licked and sucked. It didn't take long for the first orgasm to take her. She cried out as he continued pleasuring her, waiting for the next wave to hit.

She was so damn responsive, so gorgeous as she came. And he wanted to do that for her all night long. He wanted to give her the world.

"Enough," she begged as another orgasm washed through her. "It's my turn to taste you."

She sat up, and he didn't fight her as she turned him onto his back. She straddled him as her gaze caressed his body. It was almost as good as a touch. The heat from the fire was no match to the heat of their bodies aligned.

She bent down and ran her tongue over his lips but didn't allow him to deepen the kiss. Much too soon she was moving, her lips caressing his jaw before moving to his neck. His pulse was beating out of control as she licked and sucked her way over his shoulder and across his chest while her fingers rubbed up and down his sides.

She scraped her teeth over his nipple, making his hips arch up as he sought her heat.

"Not yet," she whispered before running her tongue down his abs. It was his turn to shake as she stroked her fingers across his hips, not touching him where he wanted her to the most.

But finally she moved lower. Finally her fingers circled his throbbing arousal and stroked it up and down. Then she bent and traced her tongue over him before her beautiful lips circled him and tightened, her tongue flicking that sensitive spot just below the head, making him groan in pleasure and agony.

He nearly exploded with the first suck of her luscious lips. And the things she did with her tongue were absolutely devilish. She sucked him deeper and deeper, and he reached down, tangling his fingers in her dark hair as he fought against the pleasure building. He didn't want to let go this way. He wanted to be buried deep within her tight walls.

He tried to pull her away, and her lips popped off him.

"I want you," he said, his voice barely recognizable.

"I want to taste you," she replied. He shook his head. Her firelit face gazed up at him, pleading in her eyes. "Please."

And he was a goner. He didn't fight her as her lips circled him again, and she moved up and down his erection. He didn't fight the pleasure, either, just watched her beautiful face as his pleasure built.

"I'm going to come," he warned, and she tightened her mouth around him.

The explosion ripped through his entire body as he released inside her mouth. She moaned against his arousal and sucked until there wasn't a drop left. Then she let go and licked up and down the length of him. He shook beneath her. And he didn't even care how vulnerable she made him feel.

Slowly she climbed back up his body until she was straddling him. "Do you have more in you?" she asked with a devilish smile.

"Oh, I have plenty left in me, you little minx," he assured her before lifting her up and settling her down on his hardness.

She gasped at the pleasure of their bodies together. It was a perfect fit, as if they'd been made for each other and no one else. And he believed they had been.

Thoughts vanished from his mind, though, as soon as she began to move up and down on him, slowly at first, and then with increasing speed. The next orgasm they did together, her head thrown back, his hands gripping her hips, and their cries carried away into the night sky.

She collapsed against him, and he knew this wouldn't end. He knew nothing would tear them apart. He wouldn't allow that. If he wasn't with her, he'd lose an essential part of his very being.

He bit his lip to keep from blurting this out to her. She wasn't ready. But soon . . . soon she'd be ready. For now, he'd give her what she was willing to take—for now.

CHAPTER
THIRTY-ONE

They'd be breaking ground soon on the first building for the veterans facility. Finn felt so much peace at this beautiful place. His life wasn't perfect, but it was so close he wasn't sure what perfection actually looked like.

He had security in life, knew the direction he was headed, had a family he could rely on, and, of course, he had the love of his life, who was falling more and more in love with him. She might not be willing to admit that to herself or to him, but he could see it in her eyes.

Finn had been a man to not put off to tomorrow what he could do today, but he also knew how to be patient. Some people needed more time than others to come up with answers that seemed so obvious to the rest of the world.

"You spend a lot of time here."

Finn didn't even try to stop the smile at the soft words spoken by Katherine Anderson. She was close to seventy years old and didn't look a day over fifty. Maybe it was the glow in her cheeks, or maybe it was the gentle smile that seemed to always have her lips turned up. But there was no way Finn could keep guarded with this woman.

As he had that thought, he wondered if maybe he was being a little too harsh with Joseph. If the man had inspired a deep love with this gentle soul, he certainly couldn't be a monster, could he? That thought confused Finn more than he already was about his newly discovered relative.

"From the moment I stepped foot on this land, I knew it was where I was needed," Finn told her.

"Walk with me," Katherine said as she wrapped her delicate arm through his.

"I'd be honored," he told her, meaning it.

"You've had a great burden put on you, Finn. I know I haven't been your family for very long, and I hope you won't take this as condescending, but I'm very proud of you. I truly wish I'd been there to see you grow up. Finding your siblings and you has brought great joy to my heart."

Finn took in a long slow breath as he fought the emotion her words brought. He'd been raised by a beautiful, kind, and loving mother. He had no doubt if she and Katherine had been in the same room, they'd have been immediate friends. Their souls were so much alike.

"I wish I'd known you while growing up, too," he said.

She chuckled. "And what about my bear of a husband?" she asked.

He had to force his body not to stiffen. There was nothing he wanted to say to hurt this woman, but he still had his reservations about Joseph.

"My dad wasn't a good man," he finally said. "I don't have a lot of faith in father figures."

"I understand that, and I appreciate your honesty. I know Joseph can seem a little overwhelming. He's larger than life, and to some people that's too much to take. But I will tell you, sweet man, that he's a good person. He loves you, and he'll do anything for the people who mean that much to him. I hope you'll give him a real chance." He tried to say something, but she held up her free hand. "I don't expect it to happen overnight. I'm just asking you to keep a piece of your heart open and see what it tells you."

They moved slowly across the land, where stakes had been placed in the ground, showing where various buildings would be lined out. His brother and Sarah were working furiously to finish the plans, and Hudson was itching to get started building. This was all going to fit together like a perfect orchestra performing a masterpiece.

"I can try," Finn said, not willing to lie to this woman.

"That's all I ask," she said, her sweet expression never changing. "Why don't I stop making you so uncomfortable and have you tell me about your girl?"

Finn really did relax at those words as they took their time walking the path that had been worn in the ground from the many visits through the huge parcel of land.

"Brooke is unlike any woman I've ever known. She's strong and beautiful, kind and independent, and she has so much love to offer. She's been hurt, and I understand her reluctance to risk more pain, but I'm confident she'll understand soon that I don't give up on the people I love. When she knows that, she'll let me in."

"I think she's truly lucky to have you, and I think you're very lucky to have her. Lost souls are meant to find one another, and nothing can keep you apart when it's meant to be," Katherine assured him.

"How did you know Joseph was the one?" he asked.

Finn would almost swear under oath he could see a slight halo circling Katherine's beautiful white hair. She practically floated when her thoughts turned to her husband. It gave Finn a lot to think about.

"I didn't know at first, and of course I fought what I was feeling. But in the end love conquered all," she said. "He's my world, my dream come true, and the love of my life. The only thing better than finding him and knowing I hold his heart as much as he holds mine is the love we've created in our family. We've only grown stronger as the years have passed. I don't know what I'd do if something were to happen to him."

"I fell in love with Brooke the moment I met her. I never believed in love at first sight before, but my feelings have only grown stronger from that moment. They've never swayed, never changed, and they never will. I do believe in love now. Up until Brooke, I'd felt love for my family. But being in love with my soul mate is something I'd never have been able to describe before."

"No. It's not possible to describe something you've never seen or felt. You can try to share it with others, but they won't understand until they experience it. I'm glad for you that you haven't fought it and that you're comfortable with who you are and what you want."

"Losing my mother took me to my knees. But getting to know you has truly helped. I'm glad you're in my life," Finn said as he stopped and leaned down, kissing the delicate skin of Katherine's cheek.

"As I am with you, Finn. I'll have you walk me back to the car now. If I'm gone too long, my overprotective husband will come searching for me," she said with a chuckle.

"Of course he will. Once you hold a beautiful woman in your arms, it's unbearable to go too long without her," Finn said.

Katherine beamed at him as he walked her back to her waiting vehicle and assisted her into the back seat. When she pulled away he stayed awhile, watching as the sunset splashed brilliant colors against the mountains.

This truly was a magical place, and they were going to do great things on this land. Finn wasn't sure what was going to happen in his personal life over the next few months, but he'd made a promise to

Katherine, and he kept his promises. He had a lot to think about where Joseph was concerned.

As for how he felt about Brooke, there was nothing to think about. She was the love of his life, and he didn't care if it took years for her to give him her heart. He wouldn't ever give up on her. That would be giving up on himself, and that wasn't something Finn was ever willing to do.

CHAPTER THIRTY-TWO

Before Brooke realized what was happening, she and Finn settled into a routine. He never asked for her to be his, and she never acknowledged that they were actually dating—well, more like a newlywed couple, if she was being honest with herself.

She spent nearly every night with the man—and made love to him at least once a day, normally a couple of times. She couldn't keep her hands off him. She could practically orgasm from doing something as simple as running her fingers down the hard planes of his chest.

Her new favorite song was "Something Just like This," by the Chainsmokers. She was falling for him, for everything about him, and she realized she might find him close to perfect, but she also wasn't seeking a superhero, though he might very well be one.

When her doorbell rang, she felt her heart thump. It didn't matter how many times she saw the man; she still felt excitement at knowing he was on the other side of her door. She was a goner. She just didn't want to admit that thought out loud. Maybe if she didn't, she could save herself.

The smile Finn wore as she opened the door took her breath away. He looked at her as if he were seeing her for the first time. It was hard not to feel special when she was with this man. Maybe that was another reason she'd stopped fighting what she was feeling for him.

"Do you want a drink before we go out?" she asked, her voice a bit breathless. She wondered if the butterflies were ever going to dim in his presence. Part of her wanted them to go away, and part of her hoped it lasted forever.

"I'll settle for a drink, even though I really just want to sip on you," he said with a wink.

She was instantly wet—just like that.

They made it to the kitchen island before she felt his hot breath on her neck. That was the only warning she got before she was spun around, and he was pulling her tightly against him.

"Sixteen hours of not seeing you is too long," he said. Then his lips were pressing against hers in a scorching kiss that had her forgetting all about a drink.

She pushed her hips into his, rubbing against his hardness and sighing at how wonderful it felt. His fingers tangled in her hair and pulled as he deepened their kiss and pushed her against the island, their bodies as close as they could be with clothes still on.

He pulled back just enough to allow them to begin removing each other's clothes; then he lifted her onto the island, lining their bodies up perfectly.

"No foreplay. I need you buried deep," she demanded. She undid his pants and squeezed him tight, loving the groan escaping him.

"I'm yours to command," he told her.

That brought a smile to her swollen lips. Finn wasn't a man to be controlled by anyone, but she did feel powerful with him, did feel as if he would do anything for her. That was a humbling feeling with a man as strong as he was.

Finn spread her thighs wide and slipped a finger deep inside her, making her lean back on her elbows as he wiggled inside her pulsing body.

"I'm ready for you, Finn. I'm always ready for you," she said.

"I know you are, baby. That's what makes me so damn hard," he told her as his finger slipped out, and he positioned himself in front of her.

He didn't ease into her, just pushed forward, knocking her body back as she took his full length deep inside. She nearly came at that one movement. Her walls clenched around him, making both of them groan.

She fell apart in seconds once he began to move. Months of sex with this man, and he still pushed her over the edge so dang fast. She'd never been so responsive with anyone before him. She came once more with him as he sank deep within her, and his heat filled her.

"I can't seem to control myself when it comes to you," he told her as his fingers ran in circles on her chest and stomach. She clenched him again as he rested inside her, and he chuckled. "You're going to be the death of me."

"Won't it be a pleasurable death?" she asked.

"You're totally worth dying for," he said with a smile. But there was a glint in his eyes that made her wonder how serious he was with those casually spoken words. It scared her a little. Their connection was too deep.

She shifted, and he looked a bit sad as he pulled from her and stepped back. She couldn't look him in the eyes as she sat up and hopped down from the counter.

"Let me clean up so we can get out of here," she told him.

He grabbed her before she walked past him. "Someday you'll quit running from me when it gets a little emotional," he told her. He didn't give her a chance to respond, just gave her one hard kiss, then turned her and slapped her behind as she began walking away.

She turned and glared at him but didn't quit moving. If she touched him again they'd never leave the house, and though right now it felt as if they could live on sex alone, they needed fuel in their bodies to keep going the way they'd been going.

She knew she was hurting him with her inability to tell him how she was feeling, but she wasn't quite sure. She knew she was attracted to him, knew she couldn't imagine him not being in her life. She had zero doubt she was falling completely for him. But he wanted the forever kind of love—and she just wasn't sure she was capable of giving that to him.

She might not be capable of giving it to anyone.

CHAPTER
THIRTY-THREE

"You're coming on a double date with me."

It had been a long day at work, but even though she was tired, Brooke couldn't help but smile as Sarah stood in her office with a scowl on her face.

"You don't seem to be too pleased about this date," Brooke told her.

"I'm not at all pleased about it," Sarah said with a sigh before she moved over to the chair in the corner and plopped herself down.

"Then why are you going on the date, let alone dragging me with you?" Brooke asked.

Sarah rolled her eyes. "Because I'm working with the guy, and whether I want to or not, I've been so turned on by him I can't even think straight, which is then messing up my work, which really ticks me off," Sarah said.

"I'm so lost I don't even know what to ask next," Brooke told her.

Sarah threw her hands in the air as she jumped to her feet and began pacing in and out of the room. Brooke wasn't sure if she should try to follow her friend or sit there and wait. She decided to wait. She sort of knew how Sarah was feeling, since she wasn't sure what was up or down anymore thanks to Finn.

"I guess I should ask who this is," Brooke finally said when Sarah didn't add anything more to the conversation.

"Noah Anderson, of course. Who else could possibly have my organs turning inside out right now?" Sarah said. "It's so ridiculous. I date all the time—okay, maybe not *all* the time, but certainly more than you or Chloe. I don't have any deep-set emotional fears of dating. I just like to feel in control. And right now I'm feeling anything but that."

"You like Noah?" Brooke said. This could be complicated. What if something happened with her and Finn, or something happened with Sarah and Noah? Their friendship was far too strong to ever let a man come between them, so if there was a bad breakup and the other was with one of the brothers, it could be very complicated. But there was no way Brooke was going to say that right then.

"No. I absolutely, positively don't like the pompous butthead. But my body hasn't gotten the message that he's a waste of time," Sarah told her.

"So you don't like him, but you want to have sex with him?" Brooke said. This she understood a lot more.

"Exactly," Sarah said with a little fist pump. "I figure if I just sleep with the guy, it will be terrible, and then I'll be over it. He'll be over it, too, and then we can get some actual work done. This project is a dream come true for me, and I don't want to mess it up."

"What if the sex is good?" Brooke asked.

Sarah stopped pacing and gave Brooke her full attention—with a glare.

"Don't even put that out there in the universe," she warned.

"Well, I know sex with Finn is the best I've ever had," Brooke told her.

"You aren't helping me out right now. Do you know how long it's been since I've had sex, let alone *good* sex?" Sarah asked. Before Brooke could say anything she continued talking. "You'd think sex would be easy, natural, and no problem. And sure, it's easy to get sex, but to get sex with someone you actually want to have it with isn't such an easy thing. And to get sex with someone you like and can laugh with seems utterly impossible. By the time I get to the stage of thinking about sex with someone, they've utterly turned me off. I'm beginning to see why people take vows of chastity or become nuns."

"I wouldn't take it *that* far," Brooke said with a shudder. "To give up sex for life would be utterly depressing."

"But it consumes us," Sarah said with a pout. "When we think about sex, that's all we seem to think about. It's hard to work, to play, to do anything when you're needy as hell. And yeah, there are ways to find satisfaction yourself, but it's just not the same. There's nothing like the feel of your body being filled by someone, of hands caressing you, of lips on yours . . ." She sighed as she gazed at the ceiling.

Though Brooke had been getting more than enough sex lately, at Sarah's words, she immediately began thinking of the night before with Finn.

"Yeah, you're right. When it's good, it's all-consuming," Brooke said.

"I wouldn't know. It's been *that* long since it's been good," Sarah told her.

"Well, then, I fully support your decision to have sex with Noah. Maybe it'll be good, maybe bad, but at least you won't be torturing yourself as you think about it all the time," Brooke pointed out.

"What if it makes it worse, though?" Sarah asked.

It was incredibly rare for her strong friend to show such vulnerability, and Brooke wasn't exactly sure how to answer her.

"I can't tell you everything will be perfect or awful, because I have no answers like that. But I've known you since middle school, and what I can tell you is I've never seen you ever back down from a challenge. Just remember how amazing you are and what an honor it is for this guy to get to spend time with you, and then you're going to remember who you are and what you want and, more importantly, what you deserve."

Sarah smiled at her before she moved across the room and threw her arms around her.

"I love you. Who needs dating when I have two of the best friends a girl could ever want? Of course you're right. I'm a badass with a great job and good personality. I have to quit stressing about this. I'll figure it out and then smack myself in the forehead for ever being such an emotional wreck."

"Dang straight you will," Brooke said as she hugged her friend back.

"And for now, we'll have a girls' night and then figure out this double date."

"That sounds perfect. We have to make an ice cream stop. I'm all out," Brooke warned.

"That's a tragedy that definitely needs fixed," Sarah said, as if this was a crisis of utmost importance. It was, if they really thought about it.

"At least there's one problem we can get fixed tonight," Brooke assured her friend.

"Oh, we'll get them all fixed—that's for sure. And in a few weeks I'll seriously be laughing about this. Tonight, it's wine, ice cream, and lots of chocolate."

"Mmm, you *are* the perfect date," Brooke told her.

"I know. If it wasn't for that pesky thing called sex, we wouldn't need to ever date," Sarah said.

"Yeah, sex," Brooke said with a sigh. "I really, *really* like sex."

"Sing it, sister," Sarah said with a laugh.

Or cry it out, Brooke thought with a chuckle. She cried out a heck of a lot when it came to Finn Anderson. She wanted to cry out a hell of a lot more. And she had zero doubt she'd be doing just that—over and over and over and over . . .

CHAPTER THIRTY-FOUR

A quick knock on the door was the only warning Brooke got before it was opened, and in walked two of Finn's brothers. Panic rose in her, which didn't happen too often, but she was standing in Finn's kitchen in nothing but one of his T-shirts, and it rested pretty high up on her thighs.

"Good morning," Brandon said with a wink that had her blushing.

"You're a sight better in that shirt than my brother," Noah added as they moved to the coffeepot she'd yet to take a cup from, as it had just finished brewing.

"What are you guys doing here?" Finn asked as he moved into the room, wearing nothing but a pair of loose sweats. He didn't appear at all embarrassed by both of their lack of clothing. Of course, it was his brothers, and for all she knew this was a common scene in his life—the only difference being which girl was standing in the kitchen in one of his soft T-shirts.

"We haven't seen you in a while and wanted to make sure you were still alive," Noah said as he sat down and sipped on his coffee.

Finn moved to the counter and poured his own cup before grabbing a muffin. He leaned right there and ate while his eyes slowly moved up and down Brooke's body, making her flush in a whole lot of other places than her face.

"I've been busy," Finn said.

"Yeah, I'd rather hang with her, too," Brandon said with a sultry smile.

"Don't flirt with my girl," Finn told his brother with a glare.

"Maybe she's bored with you and wants an upgrade," Brandon told him.

"I assure you she's not," Finn said.

"I don't think I've ever been in a room with a conversation like this," Brooke said. She found herself smiling even though she was slightly mortified. It was hard not to enjoy the interaction between the brothers. They obviously loved one another and had zero trouble flicking crap.

"Ah, baby, you better get used to it if you keep this one around," Noah said. "Finn has thought he's the boss of the family his entire life since he's the oldest. We're really enjoying this sappy side of him."

"Sappy side?" Brooke said as she focused on Noah. "I want to hear more about this."

"There's nothing to hear," Finn said. She was surprised when he shifted on his feet, as if he was nervous about what his brothers might say.

"Oh, there's plenty to hear. He's been writing poetry since meeting you," Brandon said with a wicked grin.

"Oh, I'd love to hear a poem," Brooke said, becoming completely at ease even though she was in less than great clothing. But men goofing around was something she was used to. Not only had she been around it with her brother and his friends but also in her life in the military. She felt peace with Finn and his brothers—so much so she was letting down her guard a little too much.

"Well . . . ," Brandon began.

"There's no damn poetry," Finn said as he sent a look at his brother she was surprised didn't make the man wilt. "But I'm about to write a sonnet about the murder of my siblings."

"Ah, you're just a teddy bear; admit it," Noah said with a laugh, not intimidated at all.

"I definitely can't wait to hear more, but I'm getting dressed," Brooke said with a laugh.

"That's a tragedy. You look just fine," Brandon told her with another wink.

"You might want to leave the room for a minute," Finn told her. "It's about to get bloody in here."

The brothers continued to banter as she walked from the room, chuckling. Her mortification at literally being caught with her pants down had quickly evaporated. If she wanted to create distance between her and Finn, hanging with his brothers wasn't going to help her do that.

Brooke took her time taking a shower and getting dressed. She figured she'd give the brothers some male time. Though she hadn't realized it was happening, she really had been monopolizing Finn's time.

She'd heard of relationships where the rest of the world fell away, but she'd never been so obsessed about a person before that she'd allowed that to happen. She'd been too strong for that. And she'd always had her brother in her life to tell her no one was good enough for her. She smiled, wondering if he'd think Finn was the right one. She was afraid he'd really like Finn.

Jack had always been protective of Brooke, even though at the same time he'd told her she was strong, beautiful, and amazing and didn't need protecting. Her heart clenched at the thought of never hearing those words from him again.

She knew that no matter how much time passed, she'd never get over the pain of losing her brother. But she also knew that she'd think of him and smile as well, because they had truly loved one another, and she had memories to last a lifetime with him. She just felt angry that she hadn't gotten to make more.

What was worse was the more serious she became with Finn, the more she thought of her future. Would she have kids? Did she want them? Did she want to be married and live a Norman Rockwell kind of life? She hadn't thought that was what she wanted, but her attitude was changing.

And she couldn't picture taking those next steps without talking to her brother first. She couldn't imagine having a child and him not being there to hold his niece or nephew. The world truly was a worse place without him in it.

Meeting and falling for Finn, though, was helping her heal in ways she didn't think she'd ever heal. Maybe, just maybe, her brother was still with her. And maybe he'd brought Finn into her life. That was a humbling thought. And that scared her more than any other she'd had.

CHAPTER THIRTY-FIVE

Finn wondered how much time he had to wait to propose to Brooke. If he could have his way, he'd take her to the closest city hall and make her his wife. There was no question in his mind she'd be his for the rest of his life, so he didn't see a reason to wait any longer.

The more time the two of them were together, the more he watched her walls crumble. She might've fought this thing between them from the moment their eyes had met, but she was falling as in love with him as he was with her.

But if he spooked her, she might not trust what she was feeling, and he might have her fleeing for the hills. And he didn't want to spend time apart from her. So if he couldn't get her down the closest aisle, then he was going to make sure she was such a part of his life she couldn't imagine not being with him. Therefore, it was time for a family dinner.

From the moment Finn had met Joseph Anderson, he'd been suspicious, but the man had a way of wearing a person down. Finn was trusting him more and more, and they'd come to an agreement. Finn didn't mind spending time with the Anderson clan—matter of fact, he enjoyed it.

There was a part of Finn that really wished his mother would've allowed them to know their family so much sooner, but he understood why she'd done what she had. His mom's life had never been easy, and his father had been a terrible man.

Finn didn't like to live in the past, anyway. He'd been through some hell in his life, and if he focused on that instead of the good in front of him, then he might miss something important. And he wasn't willing to do that.

He pulled up in front of Brooke's house and smiled as she stepped out her front door. They'd been apart the entire day, and she seemed to be just as eager to see him as he was to see her. She wasn't trying to play it cool anymore, and he loved her all the more for it.

He barely had time to jump from his truck and reach the passenger side before she was there, reaching for the handle.

"Mmm, you look delicious," he told her, taking her hand and tugging her against him.

"Aren't we running late?" she asked. But that didn't stop her from wrapping her arms behind his shoulders as she pressed into him.

"There's always time for a hello kiss," he assured her before he took her lips.

No matter how many times he kissed her, she still stole his breath. And the way she sighed as her lips molded against his made him melt. It took a lot of willpower to finally pull back. But if he didn't do it quickly, they might not make it to the dinner. And though the sex was phenomenal between them, he wanted her to know there was so much more between them than just great sex.

"Your carriage awaits, darling," he said as he stepped back. The sweet smile she gave him had his heart thumping all over again.

He opened the door, and she brushed her body against his as she stepped up into the truck. The next expression she wore told him she knew exactly what she was doing.

"Mmm, I might have to give you payback for that later, you little tease," he told her as he leaned in close and ran his lips across her neck, sending a shudder through her body.

"I'm looking forward to it," she told him with a wink. He shut the door. She completely won that round. It was going to be a very uncomfortable ride for him with his pants far too tight. As he climbed into the truck and her scent surrounded him, the discomfort only became worse.

He was utterly okay with it, though. He loved how she made him feel. It was as if he was a teenager again, but this time he was man enough to know what he wanted and to go after it and keep it. He wasn't letting such a good thing go.

He reached over and clasped her hand as they drove, and they fell into a comfortable conversation on the hour-long drive to Joseph's mansion. He'd been there several times, but he was still awed by it all.

"I don't know if I'll ever get used to all of this," he said quietly.

"It's got to feel a little surreal," she said as she squeezed his fingers.

"Yeah. My mom always worked hard after my father was gone. She wanted us to have a normal life and retain values that were important to her. My father was selfish right up until the very end."

"Did that hurt you?" she asked.

"No. Maybe when I was younger I wanted his approval, but by the end I couldn't stand him. I knew that wasn't the kind of man I wanted to be. Stepping up for my family gave me character. I was the oldest, and it was my job to take care of my mom and siblings."

"That's a lot of weight for a kid to have. What did your mom say about it?" she asked. There wasn't judgment in her tone. He was incredibly protective of his mom, but he knew Brooke was asking because she wanted to know more about him, not because she was faulting the life he'd lived.

"I respected, loved, and trusted my mother. She told me it was my job to be a kid. I told her I wouldn't know how to be a man if I didn't help her. I know my mother could've carried three times the weight on her shoulders than she already carried, but for me to let her do that would've made me a terrible human being."

"Was it hard to leave for the military when the time came?" she asked.

"Yes and no. I knew my family was fine, and it was time for me to see what the world was like without having the security of them around me. My youngest brother cried when I left, but don't ever tell him I told you, or I might get a black eye. That little bastard is quick now," he said with a chuckle that had Brooke laughing as well. Damn, he loved her laugh—he really loved when he was the one bringing her joy.

"It was tough for a while, but it did get easier. But as time goes on, we've all gravitated back toward each other. We've always been close, and we always will be. Now that we have more family, it's that much better."

"Family isn't always blood," she told him. "But I wish I had something like what you have."

There was such vulnerability in her voice at those words he was glad they were pulling up to Joseph's place. He pulled her to his side and held her tightly.

"I'll give you my family," he said as he kissed the top of her head.

She chuckled, but it sounded as if there were tears in the sound. She wouldn't lift her face from his chest, and he let her hide. She needed a moment. It was something he understood. When he'd lost men out in the field, he'd needed some moments, too.

"I'll take them," she finally said.

A marriage proposal was on the tip of his tongue, but this wasn't the right time or place. When he asked her to be his wife, he wanted it to be in happiness, not sorrow, and right now she was hurting.

"I'm sorry you lost your brother. I can't imagine how hard this is on you," he told her.

She shuddered in his arms. "Some days are worse than others. I miss him all the time, but I try to take it in moments. I feel guilty when I feel real joy, as if I'm forgetting him."

He pulled back and lifted her chin so she had to look at him. "If something ever happened to me, I'd want my siblings to be happy. I'd want them to get married and have a dozen nieces and nephews. I believe in an afterlife. I have to believe that because I've watched too many good men and women die. I believe our loved ones stick around and find joy in our lives, find joy in our happiness. So don't ever feel guilty about living. Feel guilty if you give up. Because from what I know about your brother, he loved you very much, and your happiness mattered to him more than his own."

The tears that had been building in her eyes spilled over, and she tried to turn away, but he didn't let her. He leaned down and gently kissed her lips, then rested his forehead against hers. He could sit there all day if that's what she needed.

"Thank you, Finn. That's exactly what he would've said to me," she told him.

"I'll get to know him through you," he promised her. "And that keeps him alive as well."

"When I'm stronger I'd love to show you his life. It was an adventurous one."

"Just let me know when," he said.

She was silent a few more moments, and this time when she pulled back, he let her go. She looked in the mirror and fixed the makeup under her eyes, applied a fresh coat of lipstick to her already beautiful lips, then gave him a wobbly smile.

"I'm ready now. Thank you for sharing more of your life with me."

"I want to share it all, Brooke," he told her.

For the first time, her eyes didn't shudder at his words. She looked at him and smiled. And his heart leapt because he had no doubt her walls were almost all the way down. She was going to be his wife, and they were going to live happily ever after. He couldn't think of anything he wanted more.

CHAPTER THIRTY-SIX

There were calls you couldn't wait to answer and other calls that drained the color from your face and nearly made you pass out. The call Brooke got as she was leaving the Anderson mansion was one of the bad ones—the really bad ones.

She could hear Finn's voice trying to reach her, but it sounded so far away. She'd never actually fainted, but she wondered if that was what was about to happen. She couldn't tell. Nothing was making sense at the moment.

"Brooke! Answer me, dammit!"

This time Finn's voice came through loud and clear. She felt his fingers on her cheeks, wiping away the tears she hadn't known were falling. She shook her head to try to clear it. She didn't need to panic. There was no need for that . . . not yet. She had to remain calm. She was a medical professional, and she knew the worst thing to do in this moment would be to give in to the unbearable fear and agony.

"Sarah was in an accident," she choked out.

His eyes widened, and the color in his own face drained. She hadn't expected that reaction from him. Yes, he was a good guy and cared about people, but he barely knew Sarah.

"She's out with Noah. What did they say?" he finally asked.

Now they both looked like ghosts. Before he was able to make a call, his phone rang. It was Joseph. It was impressive that he'd already become the head of their family in such a short time. But that was exactly who Joseph Anderson was.

They were given the hospital information, and Finn took a few deep breaths before he continued driving. He assured her there was no way he was adding to the problem by getting her injured on the way to the hospital. She was shaky and scared as hell but still appreciated how much he was taking care of her even though he was scared to death, too.

It took them about thirty minutes to get through traffic and pull up to the ER. They didn't talk at all. Both of them were scared, and there wasn't much they could say to each other in a moment like this.

They arrived before the ambulance, which was impressive. Finn leaned against the wall, too restless to sit, but Brooke appreciated him so much as he pulled her back against his chest and held her tight.

"Have you heard anything?"

They both turned to see Hudson and Brandon approaching.

"The ambulance just arrived. They're bringing them in. But they haven't told us anything else," Finn said.

"What in the hell is wrong with them if they don't give us information?" Brandon thundered. It was so rare to see Brandon do anything but smile. He was by far the happiest of the brothers, always cracking a joke. This showed how stressed he was.

"They're doing their job. I hate saying that, and I hate giving standard answers to worried family members, but they're doing their job," Brooke said as a few tears slipped down her cheeks.

"I'm sorry, Brooke. I'm sure Sarah is fine," Brandon said, his tone immediately lightening.

"Thank you, Brandon. I'm scared," Brooke admitted.

"Brooke!" Chloe yelled as she ran inside and rushed to them. "Have you heard anything? Why aren't you back there?"

Finn released her so Chloe could throw her arms around Brooke. She held tightly to her friend, and the two of them sobbed before Brooke could respond.

"They won't let loved ones back there until they know what's going on," Brooke told her.

"But you're a doctor," Chloe shouted.

"I'm a nurse practitioner, but I don't have privileges here," Brooke told her.

"I don't care. Someone needs to be with Sarah right now," Chloe said before she choked up again and sobbed in Brooke's arms. They were far more sisters than best friends. It would destroy either of them if something happened to the other.

It seemed like hours, but in reality it couldn't have been more than another fifteen minutes, before a doctor walked through the ER doors and approached the ever-growing crowd of people.

"Are you with Sarah and Noah?" he asked. A chorus of voices confirmed this.

The doctor smiled, though it was obvious he was trying to keep his professional mask on. Brooke knew that look well, and it sent a tremor of fear down her spine. She wasn't able to say a word as she waited for what he was going to say next.

"Noah warned me there'd be a lot of people out here trying to intimidate me," the doctor said. "I'm Dr. Simpson, and I've assessed them both. Noah has some bruises and scrapes, but he's fine," he began. Brooke grew even more quiet as a sigh of relief settled around her from the Anderson clan. It was never good when the conversation started this way. He wanted to give them good news before bad.

"What about Sarah?" Chloe asked.

The doctor turned to her, and Brooke couldn't look him in the eyes. She was too afraid of what he was going to say.

"Sarah's side of the vehicle was impacted, and she's been taken into surgery. We'll know more when she comes out," he said.

Brooke wasn't sure when Finn had come back up to her, but he was the only reason she was able to remain on her feet. Her knees gave out as flashes of light sparkled around her eyes. The next words spoken seemed to be coming through a tunnel.

"Brooke, it's okay. Take some deep breaths," Finn was saying against her ear. "It's okay. We're going to know more soon. Come on, baby, take some air in."

She felt herself being lifted into his arms as he tried to keep her awake. She shook her head, and her vision began clearing. He sat down and cradled her in his lap, gently rocking as he kept speaking soothing words in her ears. She needed to check on Chloe, but she didn't even have the energy to do that. She was so damn scared.

The next two hours dragged by in horrific slowness. Noah came out and joined them, a few bandages on his face and arms, and his face as white as theirs, but other than that he was deemed okay to go home.

Not one of the Andersons left.

She told them they could, and they looked at her as if she was truly insane and needed to be checked into the mental ward. If something happened to Sarah, she might just need that. She and Chloe both would.

She appreciated that they didn't try to tell her everything would be okay. She didn't need to hear empty words as she waited to see how her best friend was doing. She just needed Finn's arms around her and needed the support of this amazing family. She was grateful they didn't leave.

Every fifteen minutes or so Noah began cursing at someone as he demanded answers. But even as powerful as the Andersons were, they couldn't make a surgery go any faster. Finally, about two hours later, a doctor came out and told them there was some internal bleeding, but they were making good progress.

That was all the information they were given before they were left alone again. Brooke knew how bad internal bleeding could be. She knew everything wasn't perfectly fine yet.

It wasn't for another two hours that the doctor came out. Brooke finally let out her first relieved sigh. She knew that look well. She knew her friend was okay . . . at least for now.

"Thank you for your patience. Sarah has come through surgery remarkably well. She's in the recovery room and will be moved within the hour. She's groggy and doesn't understand yet what's happening, so when she does get to her room, we need to keep the visitors down to two at a time," he told them.

"Of course," Chloe said. "Thank you. Thank you so much." Chloe ran to the doctor and threw her arms around him. He stood there for a moment before giving her a slight hug back, then pulling away. Brooke actually smiled a tiny bit. She'd been hugged by many grateful family members when delivering good news. And it was sometimes a bit awkward.

This time the next hour actually went by quickly. Someone had handed her a coffee that she gratefully sipped on while waiting to go back and see Sarah. There was no doubt it would be her and Chloe as the first ones, though she knew Noah really wanted to be there. He also knew the best friends needed to assure themselves she was fine before they'd have any peace of mind. It gave her great respect for him that he didn't try to argue with them.

She and Chloe held hands as they walked down the cold corridor leading to their friend's room. When they pushed open the door, new tears sprang to Brooke's eyes at the sight of her friend. She was covered in bandages and had an IV hooked to her arm. There was a cast on her leg and cuts and scrapes on her left arm.

"Oh, sweetie, I'm so sorry," Brooke said as she approached the bed.

"I'm okay, Brooke. You can stop worrying," Sarah said, her voice hoarse.

"No, you're not, but we'll be here to take care of you every single minute of the day," Chloe said as she sat down next to the bed and gently laid her hand on top of Sarah's.

"I was afraid of that," Sarah said, attempting a joke. "But really, I'm okay. I guess it was a drunk driver, and they got him."

"Good. I hope he fries," Chloe said, tears falling down her face.

"I don't get why people do that," Sarah said. "They have no regard for anyone. I'm glad it was us hit and not a family with kids."

"Honey, no one should've been hit," Brooke said.

"No, you're right," Sarah agreed. "But I'll be okay. I'm going to hurt for a while, but it gives me an excuse to work from bed. I guess I have to slow down for a couple weeks."

"And we really will take care of you," Brooke insisted.

"I'm not worried about that. We always take care of each other," Sarah said.

The girls sat with Sarah until her meds kicked in and she fell asleep; then Brooke left Chloe with her and went out to tell Noah he could take a turn. He gave her a quick hug and thanks, then rushed off to see her.

"I think my brother has fallen in love," Finn said as he pulled her close to him.

"You might be right," Brooke agreed in wonder. "I think Sarah might like him, too."

"That's a beautiful thing," Finn told her.

"Maybe," she said.

Nothing seemed sure right now. All she knew was there were people in her life who meant the world to her. And Finn was now one of them. She couldn't afford to go through another trauma right now. She'd fall down and never stand again.

It might be too late for her, though. She might have already fallen, and she just hadn't realized the full impact of that yet.

CHAPTER THIRTY-SEVEN

Hospitals weren't normally the most fun places to hang out. But that wasn't the case for Brooke. She loved the places. Well, she did when she wasn't worried she was going to lose her best friend. But now that everything seemed to be good, she could relax and enjoy being there.

She loved the smells and sounds, loved the staff and talking to them. There wasn't much she didn't like about it. She wouldn't admit this to anyone, but she even loved the food. There was comfort in it from her years of being a student and scarfing down whatever she had time for.

"I can't believe they've had me stuck in this bed for an entire week," Sarah said as she leaned back on her pillow and moaned. "I'm so sick of being here."

"What happened to loving being in bed and working?" Brooke asked.

"Ugh. It's not quite as fun as I'd envisioned. I want to get up and move," Sarah said. "I'm sick of this damn bed."

"Now, now, quit being a brat, or they're going to order an enema," Brooke warned.

Sarah glared at her, not at all amused. "Isn't it Chloe's turn to baby-sit me? At least I get some pleasure out of the fact that she hates being here as much as I do. You act like a kid in the candy store every time you walk in my room. It's downright depressing how much you like it. It's strange, too. I'm surprised Finn hasn't seen the look and run before you grab a glove and tell him to bend over."

Brooke laughed at the image of that. Finn wouldn't be a willing participant, but it would be damn funny to see his face if he heard Sarah's words. She giggled even more thinking about it.

"You're rotten—rotten to the core," Sarah said. "Isn't it lunchtime? Can you order pizza? I'm so sick of mush."

"You know they have you on a special diet. They don't mess around with internal bleeding. Be a good girl," Brooke told her.

"I'm not a dang dog," Sarah said as she leaned forward so she could flop backward again, just so Brooke would know how miserable she truly was.

"I'm making excellent progress on my blanket, so this downtime is great," Brooke said as she held up the crocheted blanket she'd been working on. "I haven't pulled out my yarn in forever."

"That's because you're always in bed with a sexy man, something I haven't gotten to do in a week," Sarah said with a perfect pout.

"Mm-hmm. I heard he crawled in with you a couple days ago and got in trouble," Brooke said with another chuckle.

"He wasn't trying to do anything," Sarah said. "And I didn't invite him. I was sleeping."

"Not when the nurse came in. You were practically on top of him from what I heard," Brooke corrected.

"I can't be held liable for my behavior when on drugs," Sarah said. "I don't even like him."

"Yeah, I'm not believing that at all," Brooke told her.

"Why don't we talk about you and Finn?" Sarah said, perking right up when turning the tables on her friend.

"Since I've been with you far more than him this week, there's nothing new to tell," Brooke said.

"But are you finally admitting you're falling for him?" Sarah pushed.

"You look a bit paler than you did yesterday," Brooke pointed out as she looked at the machines. "Your blood pressure is up, too." Suddenly she wasn't smiling anymore.

"I know. I know. I haven't been feeling well today. But it'll pass. The staff is keeping an eye on me. Here, you're my friend, *not* my doctor," Sarah told her. "And quit trying to get out of talking about Finn. I like him."

"Wow, that's a big compliment from you, since you rarely like any of the guys I date," Brooke said. She was trying not to worry about her friend, but she really didn't like the numbers on the monitors.

"So spill," Sarah insisted.

When her friend had her mind set on something, there wasn't much that would change it. She sighed as she put her blanket down. She would miss a stitch anyway if she was talking about Finn.

"I honestly don't know what to say. I admit we're in a relationship. I just don't know what that means. I don't think I'm in a place in life I can run off into the sunset with him."

"Why not?" Sarah asked.

"I just can't," Brooke said.

"I don't see why not. You're a grown adult. The guy is head over heels for you. You like him, possibly love him, so what's the problem?"

"It's not that simple," Brooke said.

"Why can't it be? Why do we have to make everything in our lives so complicated?"

"I don't know," Brooke admitted. "I just . . . I don't know."

"Well, maybe you should just go with what you're feeling and stop analyzing it so much. He's a good man, and he's so into you it's nauseating. So let him love you. You deserve to be loved like the princess you are."

"You have to say that as my best friend," Brooke pointed out.

"No, because I'm your best friend I can say anything to you. I'd never sugarcoat it or lie. We made that oath to each other a million years ago."

"I love you, Sarah. You better never scare me like this again," Brooke insisted.

"I love you, too. Now, just let yourself love Finn."

"You are sure bratty and pushy today," Brooke said.

"And you keep trying to change the subject," Sarah said.

"I was hoping you wouldn't notice that."

Sarah laughed, which then made her cough. When she kept coughing, Brooke jumped up.

"Okay, I'm calling the nurse. That doesn't sound good," Brooke said as she pushed the button. Sarah tried telling her she was okay, but that just made her cough more.

The coughing became more violent as the nurse rushed into the room, and then blood came from her friend's mouth as she went deathly white. The nurse pushed another button, and within thirty seconds several people were rushing into the room, asking Brooke to stand aside.

She knew better than to ask what was happening. They didn't know what was going on. That's why they were there. Suddenly Sarah's body began shaking, and Brooke's tears fell in rivers down her cheeks.

Sarah stopped shaking, but they were suddenly doing CPR on her as they placed an oxygen mask over her face and spoke. Brooke wished she didn't understand what they were saying.

"Call a code," a nurse shouted.

"We need to get a blood pressure and oxygen saturation right now," another shouted.

"Get the Ambu bag!"

"I want you to start bagging her."

The doctor rushed into the room as all hands on deck were working quickly and efficiently. Brooke couldn't fault a single thing they were doing, but this was her best friend, and she'd never felt more helpless in her life.

"Her stats are eighty-two percent, and her heart rate is at one thirty," the doctor said.

Brooke's heart thudded.

"It's really hard to bag her," the nurse said.

The doctor leaned over, listening to her heart sounds. "There's no lung sound on her right side. We're going to need to needle decompress her. I think she's got a spontaneous pneumothorax. I need a needle decompressor right now!"

A kit was quickly opened, and within seconds there was a whoosh of air, allowing Sarah to take a breath. Brooke took her own for the first time in probably a full minute. Her lungs burned as oxygen flooded them.

"Oxygen saturation is at ninety-six percent. Her color's improving. We need to put in a chest tube."

They worked quickly, doing just that, keeping her lungs expanded. Brooke didn't move from her position pasted against the back wall.

"All right, I want a chest X-ray. She's stable. Let's get her to ICU, and I want hourly updates," the doctor said.

They rushed her out of the room. Tears flowed down Brooke's face as she stumbled over to a chair and fell into it. There was only one person she wanted to call. She lifted her phone, and he answered on the first ring.

"I need you, Finn. I'm at the hospital in Sarah's room. Please call Chloe and tell her to come."

"I'll be there in ten minutes, and I will," he said.

She was grateful as she hung up the phone. He hadn't asked any questions, didn't need details. She'd told him she needed him, and that's all he needed to know. Maybe she was a fool to fight this. Maybe she would be so broken by the end of this, though, that she wouldn't be lovable. She wasn't sure of anything anymore.

CHAPTER THIRTY-EIGHT

Brooke felt as if she was only partially conscious over the next five hours. Once again all the Andersons showed up at the hospital. She wasn't sure exactly what was going on between Noah and Sarah, but something was, because the Andersons were concerned about her best friend. They were also there for her.

They tried forcing her to eat, to drink, to get up and move a little. She felt as if she was on autopilot as she did as they asked—well, demanded, really. You weren't really able to say no, especially when Joseph Anderson was the one doling out the instructions.

After an hour, the doctor did come out and say some of the stitching in her lungs had come undone. Noah's head had about blown off as he'd asked what kind of medical personnel they had who couldn't do the job right the first time.

Then some bigwig doctor had been brought in and finished the surgery. They were waiting for him to come out and tell them how it had all gone. Brooke was awed by the amount of power money afforded people.

There was nothing out of touch for the Anderson family. But in this moment she was more than grateful for their reach. Because of them she wasn't shaking in fear that her best friend wasn't going to wake up. Because of their generosity and love she might be able to sleep when this was all over.

When the doors opened up and the doctor walked out, the full waiting room was unusually quiet. They all waited as the man walked forward. Brooke was an utter mess, but she was surprised to note that the man moving toward them looked more like he belonged on an episode of *Grey's Anatomy* than in a real hospital setting. If he knew the Andersons, of course that was the case.

"I'm sorry to keep you waiting," he said. "Who should I be addressing?"

"Well, any of us, boy," Joseph said, his voice echoing off the walls.

The doctor laughed as he looked at Joseph. "It's good to see you, old man. I hate that it keeps being under these circumstances."

"Well, if you'd come to a birthday party once in a while," Joseph grumbled. "But none of that right now. How's our girl?"

"You can talk to Chloe and Brooke," Finn said as he placed a hand on each of their backs and parted the crowd.

"Thank you," the doctor said as he turned his full attention on both of them. "I'm Dr. Kian Forbes, and Sarah came through surgery beautifully. She'll make a full recovery, but she needs to be on total bed rest for two weeks. From what the staff has been saying, that won't be too easy, so I'm placing that on you."

"Yes, we'll tie her to the bed if we need to," Chloe said. "But you promise she'll be okay?"

The smile he gave them surely had melted many hearts in his lifetime. Brooke waited. She didn't even feel as if she could speak right then.

"I promise you I'm the best at what I do, and I checked every inch of her. That's why the surgery took so long. When Joseph Anderson demands your presence, you drop everything else you're doing," he told them before winking at Joseph.

"Thank you," Chloe said before throwing her arms around him. He gave her a hug, then opened his arms for a hug from Brooke. She took a step forward, and Finn stopped her.

"We're all good on hugs," Finn said with a possessive look.

Dr. Forbes laughed. "I see someone has caught you," he said. "You have excellent taste," he added with a wink that made Brooke blush.

"Can we see her now?" Chloe asked.

"You can in about an hour," he assured them. "Now, I have a very pregnant wife I need to get home to," he told them. "I might be getting checked in to the ER myself if I'm not there for her to hold on to as she goes through labor."

"Congrats, my boy. I'll be there to hold the wee one as soon as she comes out."

"I didn't say if it's a girl or boy," he replied.

"Ah, I feel it's a girl," Joseph said with confidence.

If Joseph was predicting a girl, it most likely was. She hoped the cute doctor wanted a daughter. After he left, the mood lightened for most of the family. Noah was consistently pacing the room, and Chloe and Brooke kept their arms wrapped around each other as they waited for the nurse to escort them to Sarah's room. Finn didn't say much but made sure she knew he was there.

When the nurse finally came out, they rushed behind her to Sarah's room. "I'm getting sick of seeing her looking like this. It's so wrong," Chloe said.

"I know. She's so strong. I never imagined anything could happen to her. Just like I can't imagine it happening to you," Brooke replied.

"Aren't you two sick of being here?" Sarah asked. They turned and looked at her half-opened eyes.

"We never get sick of being with you," Chloe said as she leaned in and kissed Sarah on the forehead. "But if you could stop scaring the crap out of us, I'd really appreciate it."

"You know I live for excitement," Sarah said. "Besides, when I woke up in recovery, there was a hell of a cute doctor standing over me, so it was worth almost dying for."

"Only you can make a joke when you've come so close to dying," Brooke said with a frown.

"If we're not laughing, then we're not living," Sarah said.

"You are on mandatory bed rest for the next two weeks. Those are direct orders from the hot doctor," Brooke said.

Sarah rolled her eyes. "It's so much sexier if he says it."

"I don't think I like hearing you call another man sexy." They all turned to see Noah smiling in the doorway. "Not that I'm worried. I'm hands down hotter than him."

"Someone has too much confidence," Sarah said with a weak laugh.

"I agree with your friends. You need to quit scaring us," Noah said. "I don't want to interrupt, but I bribed the nurse to let me come in. I needed to see you were okay."

"What did you bribe her with?" Sarah asked.

Noah flushed. "I gave her a kiss on the cheek," he mumbled.

"What?" all three girls asked in unison.

"Yep, and it was worth breaking the rules for," a woman who appeared at least seventy said from the doorway. "But you only have five minutes. There really are only two people allowed in at a time."

She walked away, and they could hear her chuckling quietly as she moved down the hallway.

"I see you like older women," Chloe said with a chuckle. Brooke joined her. It felt so dang good to laugh when she'd been stressed out for hours on end.

Noah left, and the girls sat with Sarah until she went to sleep again; then they went out to let Noah know he could go back in. He gave them each a hug before rushing to the girl.

"Let me take you home to eat and shower," Finn said to Brooke.

"I don't want to leave. What if something happens?" she asked.

He smiled. "The whole clan is here to watch out for her. They won't let anything happen on their watch. You look like you're about to fall over any second," he said.

"Okay," she finally agreed.

She leaned on him as he walked her from the hospital. She really was exhausted, but she didn't want to leave Sarah alone too long. No, she wouldn't exactly be alone, but if something did happen, and Brooke wasn't there, she'd never forgive herself. She should've noticed sooner something was wrong.

That's why they didn't let friends or family be worked on by medical staff. When you knew a person, you couldn't be properly objective. Well, Brooke was going to watch her friend like a hawk from then on out. There'd be nothing else she didn't notice.

They went home together, and Finn helped her shower, fed her, and then took her back to the hospital, all without a single complaint. She wasn't sure she could go through any of this without him. She was also pretty dang sure she was in love with him.

She just didn't know what she was going to do about that.

CHAPTER THIRTY-NINE

Two weeks came and went in the blink of an eye—for Brooke. Not so much for Sarah, who got increasingly grumpy until they released her. Brooke was pretty sure the hospital staff was going to throw a bon voyage party for Sarah they'd be so happy when she was gone. She didn't make the best patient.

Brooke found it highly amusing once she knew her friend was out of danger. But now she was getting payback, because she woke up feeling sick. She lay in bed for a few minutes, praying it would go away. She didn't often get sick, and she might be a worse patient than her best friend.

As she slowly sat up in bed, her head spun, and she knew she was in trouble. Was it the fish she'd eaten the night before? It had to be. Slowly she got to her feet, then gagged. Nope. There was no avoiding it. She ran for the bathroom and heaved out the contents of her stomach.

She sat there with her head against the cool porcelain, and then her eyes widened as she felt the sickness begin to dissipate. She didn't move for a while as she waited for the second go-round. It didn't come.

This wasn't good—it wasn't good at all.

Turning, she looked at her shelf, where an unopened box of tampons sat. A box she should've been using by now. With all the stress of the last few weeks, she hadn't even thought about it. When had her last period been? Oh my gosh, she couldn't remember. A month ago? Six weeks ago?

But they were always safe, she tried to assure herself. Always. She was protected. There was no way she could be pregnant. It couldn't be that. She had to just be scared right now. That's all this was—irrational fear.

When she could stumble to her feet, she moved out to her bedroom and grabbed the calendar. There was no doubt about it. She'd completely missed her period. As a medically trained person she was shocked at her stupidity in not noticing such an important thing.

She took her time getting ready for work, finding herself on the verge of tears as she gave herself a quick exam. Yes, her breasts were tender; yes, her hormones had been all over the place; and yes, she'd missed that ever-important monthly event. But stress could cause all the same symptoms. She wasn't going to panic—not yet at least.

She got to the office before anyone else, and though she was terrified, she grabbed a pregnancy test and went into the bathroom. She knew she needed to do a blood test, and that certainly would come next, but for now she needed instant relief.

When both lines on the test turned blue, she felt anything but relief. She took three more tests just to be sure of the results. She wanted to be in denial, but she was too smart to ignore the facts. She drew her blood and bagged it to go to the lab on a rush order. But even without those results she knew what her body was telling her.

She was pregnant.

And there was only one possibility of who the father was.

How could she have been so foolish? She'd always told women that even with protection, there was a chance of pregnancy. And she and Finn had a lot of sex—great sex, but still, a lot of sex.

How in the world was she going to tell Finn she was pregnant? She wasn't worried he'd be upset. She was more worried he was going to insist on marrying her. She knew he cared about her, but they were so new together. And now all the fun and dating would disappear. Now it would be about the baby growing inside her.

Would he grow resentful? He might not think he would, but it was a lot of responsibility for a lifelong bachelor to take on. He might be happy at first, might even stay that way until her third trimester. But then, when she wasn't able to have sex very easily, the passion would dim.

Then, after the baby came, and she was sore and exhausted and fat, how would he feel? They were too new to have to think about these sorts of things. Many young couples wanted a baby so badly, but they didn't realize the reality of children. They were exhausting and demanding—and they were perfect, but they did consume the parents.

She'd watched many marriages break up because the couples were so resentful of the other for a lack of attention, or the body going to hell, or the crabbiness from no sleep. She'd watched people in the military cheat over and over again while their spouse was home with those babies. Then her own father had left. Had it been because he'd resented being a father? Too many people couldn't handle the responsibility. They might think they wanted a child, but in the end it was too much for them to handle.

She couldn't end up like that. She could admit to herself she cared about Finn, cared about him more than she'd ever imagined she could. But would all that change with a baby in the mix? Maybe it would for her *and* for him. This was a reason she'd never wanted to get married. It was a reason she'd always run from commitment of any sort.

But she didn't believe in abortion. She wasn't ready for a child, but that didn't mean that child wasn't ready for her. She couldn't act as if the life growing inside her meant nothing—as if it was disposable. She realized already that she'd love this baby.

She was scared—had no idea what the future was going to bring her. But this child *would* be loved by her. And maybe Finn would love it, too—even if that meant every other weekend. It was a devastating thought. But she needed to rip off the bandage. A part of her didn't want to tell him she was pregnant—at least not yet. A lot could happen in the first trimester. But there was no way she'd be able to bury her emotions for the next month or two. And she estimated she was about six weeks along right now.

She was too emotional to call him, so she sent a text. **Meet me for lunch at the diner.**

He answered quickly. **See you there, beautiful.**

She set down her phone and cried.

Her life was about to change again. There had been so many changes in the last few months, but this would be the biggest change of all. What didn't kill her would make her stronger. She had to remember that.

She closed the office early for lunch. Thankfully she only had a couple of easy patients before she had to meet with Finn. But she always had been a rip-the-bandage-off kind of girl. With her head held high she made her way to her favorite café.

Maybe if she was in public, she'd be conscious of the people around and not fall apart. And maybe they'd be settling on Mars any day now. It didn't matter. She could see him through the window, wearing a smile as he watched her walk by.

She took a breath and stepped inside.

Chapter Forty

Finn had been having one of those days where everything that could go wrong did. He was fighting with the city on permits for a project he was working on, arguing with a delivery driver on getting his new appliances to his house on time, and butting heads with the new designer, who didn't agree with his vision for the backyard.

Why he'd hired a designer, he didn't know. His brother had told him it was a good idea. He was beginning to think Brandon had done it to be a smart-ass and sent him a guy with a flair for pink flamingos to get a good laugh out of the situation.

Finn had Brooke in mind for every decision he'd made for the new house. He wanted it to be her home, too, and he had a lot of work to do on it before it was ready to bring her there. And the sooner it was done, the happier he'd be. He was ready to marry her yesterday.

When she walked into the café, he felt instantly better. She had a way of bringing sunshine out even through the fog. How he'd lived his life without her for so many years, he'd never know.

"You look stressed," Brooke said as she sat across from him. He frowned. Something was off.

"I'd be much happier if you'd give me a kiss and sit next to me," he told her. He'd chosen their usual back-corner booth so she'd do just that.

"I want to see your face," she said.

"And that means no kiss?" he pushed. But he reached for her and took her hand. It was cold, and her face was pale. "Are you sick?" he asked, worried.

"Sort of. My stomach has been giving me trouble all morning," she said with a slightly stunned expression that had him confused.

"Being with you is worth taking the risk of getting sick. You can kiss me anyway," he told her. "Besides, I have a perfect immune system. I don't get sick. I take my vitamins *and* eat my Wheaties." She didn't laugh. That wasn't a good sign.

"This isn't exactly something you can catch," she said with a humorless chuckle.

"Okay, you're worrying me, Brooke. Just tell me whatever it is. I'll help you get through it," he promised, envisioning cancer. He'd hire the best medical people in the country. Hell, he'd find the damn cure for it himself before he'd let anything happen to her. He had her in his life now, and there was no way he could lose her.

"I'm pregnant," she said.

She was looking him in the face as she said the words. She didn't add anything, didn't tell him how she felt about it. She just spit the words out and waited while he let them process.

He felt the grin on his face growing but couldn't focus on that, either. He was in total shock, but it wasn't a bad thing. A baby. Brooke's baby. Their baby. It was humbling and beautiful.

"Are you insane?" she asked a moment later, confusing him.

"What?" he said, his voice sounding odd even to himself. He was in awe right now.

"You're grinning like a loon," she said. "Did you hear me? I'm pregnant. And just in case you have any doubt, there's none. It's your child." She was now scowling.

Her words were processing in his brain but at a much slower rate than he was used to. She was pregnant. He was in love with her. This was probably the best day of his life. Scratch that. It *was* the best day of his life.

He stood up and noted the confused look on her face.

Then he dropped to his knee in front of her, enjoying the flush in her sexy cheeks. The café went deadly silent as all eyes turned toward them. He didn't care. He had eyes for only this one woman—this one woman he refused to live without.

"Finn, stop. What are you doing?" Brooke whispered as she looked over his shoulder at the crowded café.

"Brooke, I know you aren't ready to hear this, but I love you more than I thought it ever possible to love anyone. I see you're scared. I know this isn't something you were looking for. And I can give you the time you need to come to terms with it all. But I've carried this ring around from the first week I met you. I knew you'd be my wife. This is sooner than I'd planned to spring it all on you, but marry me. Let's do this together. We'll let the pieces fall wherever they might. But I promise to love you, cherish you, help you, and hold you every single day. Be my wife and the mother of my children," he said, his throat tightening in an unfamiliar way.

He pulled out the black box that was a bit worn from rubbing inside his pocket for weeks. He opened it, and she gasped as she looked at the sparkling diamond inside.

Her eyes filled with tears as she looked him in the eye and tried to get control over whatever it was she was feeling. He wasn't sure, but he knew she loved him. She just had to come to terms with that.

"You don't have to marry me because of a baby. This isn't the eighteenth century," she told him.

"I *need* to marry you," he whispered. "It's beyond a desire. You've infiltrated my soul, and I can't breathe without you."

Never did he think he'd ever make himself so vulnerable with a woman, but he couldn't have stopped himself even if he'd wanted to. It was as if the words just poured out of him. He loved her. It truly was that simple.

"You're sure about this?" she questioned.

He couldn't stop the smile from splitting his cheeks.

"I can honestly say I've never been so sure of anything in my life."

She smiled through her tears as she gave him her shaking hand. "Yes, Finn. Let's do this together," she whispered.

A strange calm settled over him as he leaned forward, gripping the back of her neck. He gently kissed her before laying a hand over her stomach and thanking the fates for giving him this gift. Then he pulled back and placed the ring on her finger that showed the world she was his.

"I love you, Brooke." A slight panic filled her eyes, and he kissed her again. "You'll get used to me saying it," he assured her.

He rose to his feet and turned toward the silent room. "She said yes!" he shouted.

A thunderous applause filled the café, and Finn didn't think he was ever going to quit smiling. This truly was the best day of his life. He didn't think anything could ever get better from this moment on.

"Lunch is definitely on the house," the waitress said as she brought their usual orders. "Congratulations."

"Thank you," Finn told her before giving the woman a crushing hug.

He then pulled Brooke from her seat and lifted her into the air, spinning them around. Her face went white.

"Oh, I wouldn't do that," she warned.

He set her down and laughed. "Sorry. I'll have to remember to be more gentle. I'm going to enjoy you being all delicate and sweet," he added with a wink.

"Not too sweet," she threatened, making him laugh again.

"I can't wait to tell my brothers. This is going to be the most spoiled child who's ever lived."

"Not too spoiled," she warned. "I want him or her to have values, not think the world should be handed to them."

"Ah, but she'll be a princess," he said with a pout.

"And if it's a boy?" she asked.

"Nah, it's going to be a little girl who looks like your twin," he informed her.

"You can't special order a child," she told him.

"The fates have been kind to me," he said. He was confident.

"Thank you, Finn. I was terrified to tell you," she said.

"You never have to be afraid to tell me anything," he assured her.

"My dad left," she said, tears filling and spilling over her cheeks. Finn was stunned at the raw vulnerability in her expression.

"Oh, baby, I know he did," he said as he cradled her in his arms. "And my dad was a worthless piece of crap. But we don't have to repeat that cycle. I don't know how to be a dad, but I'm going to give it everything I have. And I can honestly say I love you so much I can't bear the thought of living in this world without you, and that love will be the same for anything you create. Give me a chance to prove to you that some men can be good fathers."

She sniffled against his chest, and he gave her time to process this new world she'd found herself in. He wanted to repeat the words, wanted to tell her it was all going to be okay, but he waited.

"My brother would've made a great father. He was my everything," she said. "You remind me a lot of him."

A warm glow filled Finn at her words. "I'm honored to be compared to such a great man," he told her.

She cried harder in his arms. "I don't know how I'm going to do this. I had a terrible mother and father. What if that rubs off on me?"

"Oh, Brooke, you're nothing like the people who gave you life. You've risen from the ashes of a burdened childhood, and you're beautiful and kind, and our children will know how very much you love and want them."

"I don't know. I just know I'm scared, but I also know I already love this baby."

"We'll figure it out together," he assured her. "I'll take care of you for the rest of our lives."

"I think I believe that," she said.

"Someday it will be easy for you to believe," he assured her.

Finn had thought his life was over just a few months earlier. He'd lost his career and had wandered, not knowing what would come next. And then this woman had magically appeared. He truly believed now that everything did happen for a reason.

CHAPTER FORTY-ONE

Finn took a deep breath as he paced in front of the huge Anderson mansion. He was scared—more scared than he'd ever been before. Yes, joy had filled him from the moment Brooke had told him she was carrying his child. But then she'd fallen asleep in his arms that night, and he'd lain there wide awake, wondering how he was going to be a dad.

He'd stepped up when his siblings had needed someone to be the head of the household. But that was so different from raising a child. He'd had no men in his life to tell him how to do it, had no one to guide him.

Except for Joseph.

The man hadn't given up on him once in the months since they'd met. Finn had tried to put distance between them, and Joseph hadn't backed down. He'd given as much space as a man like him could give, but he'd shown nothing but respect and love toward Finn and his siblings. Maybe it was time to have a real talk with the man. Finn didn't feel as if he had a choice anymore—not if he was going to be everything he'd promised Brooke he'd be.

When a solid twenty minutes had passed, Finn grew frustrated with himself and finally climbed the staircase and rang the bell. It was opened in less than ten seconds, when he found Joseph's favorite employee standing there with a smile.

"Mr. Anderson's in the den, waiting for you," he said.

Finn didn't ask how Joseph knew he was there. Of course, there were cameras everywhere. His uncle must've been watching him pace the entire time, wondering if he was going to come in. He had to give some props to Joseph for not coming to the door and demanding he enter.

Not allowing himself to stall any longer, Finn took long strides down the somewhat familiar hallways until he reached the den. Joseph sat in his favorite chair, his usual cigar in one hand and a glass of bourbon in the other.

"What has you so anxious, boy?" Joseph asked as he approached.

He was too nervous to sit. He also didn't want to draw this out. He'd learned early in life that it was best to simply spit it out.

"I'm going to be a dad," Finn said. His words were strong and filled with awe. It had been less than twenty-four hours since Brooke had shared that news with him. "And I'm scared."

Admitting any form of weakness wasn't easy for a man like Finn. He'd always been a leader, and even if he'd been scared sometimes, he never would've let anyone see that side of him. There'd been too many people in his life who had counted on him to be the strong one for him to show such a weak emotion.

Finally exhaustion flowed through him, and he plopped down on the couch in front of Joseph. He gazed at the floor for a few moments before looking up. Joseph was grinning, his cigar and drink forgotten.

"That's wonderful news, son," Joseph said, his voice filled with pride. "There's nothing like waiting for your first child."

"I already love her," Finn said.

"Ah, you're going to have a girl," Joseph said with a grin. "Jasmine was my first grandchild, and there's nothing like a baby girl in your arms." Joseph's expression went dreamy as he spoke of his eldest grandkid.

"But what if I screw this up?" Finn said. "I don't know how to be a father. I don't know what a good dad looks like."

"Oh, Finn, you know more than you realize," Joseph told him. "You've been taking care of others your entire life. This won't be easy for you, but it will bring you so much joy you won't know how to handle it. And if you let me, I'm more than willing to be at your side to help you along the way the best I know how."

"I've wanted to make you a monster because my dad was, but suddenly I don't have it in me to be guarded with you or to keep pushing you away," Finn told him. "I don't want any piece of anger or resentment flowing through my veins. I want this child to be born in a house filled with love and family. Brooke needs family, too. And there's nothing I won't give her."

"Your trust in yourself and in me is the most beautiful gift you can give me, Finn. You're family, and family always sticks together," Joseph assured him.

"Just like that, all is forgiven?" Finn asked. He'd never been a man to feel vulnerable, but at this moment that was exactly what he was feeling.

"There's nothing to be forgiven. We just needed time to know and trust one another. Now, we get to live out our lives as a family, and the bond will grow stronger each and every day."

"You really are this man the world has painted you as," Finn said in a bit of awe.

"I have no secrets, and I don't need to pretend to be anything I'm not," Joseph told him.

Finn finally smiled, feeling a weight lifting from his chest. Maybe with this man's help he could be a good father. Maybe with the burden of resentment lifted from his chest, he could be a better man.

"What do I do?" he asked.

Joseph laughed as he brought his cigar to his mouth and took a puff. There was a suspicious gleam in the billionaire's eyes that told Finn more than anything else what kind of man he was.

"This is the easy part. Your future wife has to do all the work. You just need to love her and have patience and understanding as she creates a family for you. When that child is born, you're going to know exactly what to do. The love you have for her will guide you."

Finn sat back and smiled. "I wouldn't mind a drink and cigar," he said. As if on cue a man walked in the room and handed both to Finn.

"Let's toast to new tomorrows," Joseph said.

They grinned as they clinked their glasses together and sipped the fine liquor. Finn really was going to be okay because he had people in his life to finally take the lead and let him become the man he'd always been meant to be. He didn't need to be the leader anymore. Now he just needed to follow his heart.

CHAPTER FORTY-TWO

Brooke shouldn't have been surprised with how quickly things moved in the Anderson universe. But she was. She found herself at one of their huge complexes, being whisked around as a personal shopper insisted on sticking by her side like glue while she was supposed to find the perfect wedding dress and everything that went along with that.

"I could so get used to this," Chloe said in awe as they sat in a huge changing area with perfect lighting, comfortable chairs, and champagne for the girls and sparkling cider for her.

"Seriously. You're being treated like royalty," Sarah said.

"Look who's talking," Chloe grumbled. They'd brought in a special chair with pillows for Sarah to make sure her leg was propped up at a perfect angle and no part of her still-healing body was the least uncomfortable.

"At least I'm not in the hospital anymore," Sarah said with a sigh. "This is so much better."

"I agree," Chloe said. "I think the smell of that place is permanently on my skin."

"I love the smells. You two are crazy," Brooke told them.

"You're the psycho," Sarah assured her.

"Medicine keeps people alive. Just remember that," Brooke said.

"Yeah, yeah, we've heard it a thousand times before," Chloe said.

"Here's the selection we think would suit you best. If you hate it, we'll start over," a woman said as she rolled in a rack with the most stunning gowns Brooke had ever seen.

"Those look a bit out of my price range," Brooke said with worry. They were white and lacy with sparkling beads and gems impeccably placed. They were the most stunning gowns she'd ever seen.

"This is a gift from Mr. Anderson. Don't worry about price," the woman said with a smile.

"I can't accept that," Brooke said.

The woman's smile fell. "Oh, he'd be so hurt if you didn't."

And that's how the woman won. Brooke would never want to hurt Joseph's feelings. He'd been nothing but kind to her through her friend's ordeal and while she was at his home. She couldn't insult him by refusing such a generous gift.

"I want a fashion show," Chloe said, clapping. "And don't you dare put us in terrible bridesmaid dresses. Just remember you're the first to get married, and payback will be swift and furious if you even think about it."

"We have a selection of gowns coming in for you as well in the colors Brooke suggested," the woman said.

"I guess we'll get started," Brooke said as she rose and walked to the rack, running her fingers across the satin and silk. She was in awe that she was picking out a gown that she'd wear down an aisle to marry the man she couldn't stop thinking about.

She'd asked for a simple justice of the peace, and Finn had looked at her as if she was insane. He'd told her he was proud to make her his wife, and he wanted the world to see it happen. He'd then pointed out how disappointed his family would be if they eloped. That had won him the argument. She liked his family.

She took her time choosing the first dress, and then the woman took it into the changing room. Brooke stepped inside, where she found the most luxurious white undergarments waiting.

"Put these on first, and then call me, and I'll help with the dress," the assistant said before stepping out. Even the dressing room was the size of a normal person's bedroom. As a matter of fact, it was *bigger* than her bedroom.

Brooke's fingers trembled as she stripped down and put on the corset. She wasn't going to be able to tighten it on her own and didn't want to go too tight. She wasn't showing yet, but she certainly didn't want to squish the baby.

"Can you strap me?" she asked the woman waiting on the outside of the room. She stepped inside and tied the back of the corset.

When Brooke looked in the mirror, her eyes filled with tears. She didn't normally feel like a delicate woman. But right in this moment she felt beautiful and sexy.

"You are going to knock his socks off on your wedding night," the attendant said. "Let's get you in the dress and complete the picture."

It took them a solid fifteen minutes to get the dress on and buttoned. It fit almost perfectly. The woman left, and Brooke stood there for a moment, gazing in the mirror. She felt like a princess.

"Hurry up," Chloe called. "We need to see."

"We aren't getting any younger," Sarah called out.

"Wait, it's not done until you have these on. They were sent over by Finn," the woman said as she stepped into the room with a pair of shoes that made Brooke gasp. They were Louboutin, white and sparkly, and probably worth more than her car. She was wondering if there were real diamonds on them, they shone so much.

"Oh, oh, these are pretty," she said.

"Yes, they are," the woman agreed, looking at the shoes with admiration and lust.

Brooke stood there as the woman slipped them on her feet and buckled them.

"Yes, your man has amazing taste," the woman said.

"Oh my, yes, he does," Brooke said with a sigh as she held out her foot and looked at the gorgeous shoe.

"Let's show your friends," she said.

Brooke stepped out, feeling as if she were walking on clouds. For once in their lives neither Chloe nor Sarah said a word as Brooke was helped onto a platform that slowly began to spin in a circle.

When she came back around and it stopped, there were tears streaming down both her best friends' faces. She felt her own tears fall. It was a good thing she wasn't wearing makeup. She wouldn't want any to drip on the gorgeous gown and ruin it.

"That's the one. You don't even need to try anything else on," Sarah said.

"I agree. It's perfect on you," Chloe told her.

The dress was tight from her bodice to just below her hips, where it flared out in multiple layers. There were stunning crystals woven throughout it and no sleeves. She felt sexy and innocent at the same time. She felt beautiful.

"Really?" Brooke said.

"Really!" Chloe and Sarah said in unison.

"I agree," she told them.

Chloe jumped up and launched herself onto the platform, throwing her arms around Brooke. Then she helped her down so they could go to Sarah and all three girls could hug.

"I can't believe you're getting married," Chloe said.

"And having a baby," Sarah added.

"And that I'm happy," Brooke told them.

"You deserve happiness," Sarah insisted.

"Yes, you do," Chloe agreed.

Brooke was sad to take the dress off, but since the wedding was being pushed quickly, she'd have it back on in two weeks. The tailor made quick work, coming in and placing a few pins. He'd insisted the dress had been made just for her, since there wasn't much modification needed.

"Try not to get fat in the next two weeks," Sarah told her with a gleeful laugh.

"Yeah, I'd stay away from the ice cream, preggo," Chloe told her.

"I'm allowed to get fat being pregnant," Brooke said with a laugh.

"*After* the wedding," Sarah and Chloe said together with a giggle.

"I do want to feel beautiful on my wedding day," Brooke admitted.

"Oh, honey, you could be wearing a paper bag and look beautiful on your wedding day," Chloe insisted.

"You have to say that, being my bestie."

"I *know* that because I am," Chloe said.

The attendant got the bridesmaid dresses right just as quickly as the wedding gown. Sarah and Chloe chose two shades of purple that complemented each other, and then they were leaving the shop, but not the facility.

Everything was there, and they got to laugh as they tasted wedding cake samples and appetizers. There were so many people helping them Brooke truly did feel like royalty. Before one thing was taken away, something new was placed in front of them.

They spent the entire day there, and just that easily a huge wedding was planned in an afternoon. They were having it at the Anderson mansion, and the flowers were chosen, the food checked off the list, and the decorations taken care of.

And it was all happening in two weeks—two weeks!

"I might panic," Brooke said as they stepped outside, exhausted but feeling accomplished.

A huge Hummer stretch limo was waiting at the curb for them, with a driver smiling as he pulled open the back door.

"What is this?" Brooke asked with a laugh.

"Mr. Anderson wanted to make sure you three girls get home safely," the driver said as he waved them inside.

"Tell Mr. Anderson thank you," Chloe said. They both helped Sarah inside before they joined her.

"I think I'm falling in love with your man," Chloe said with a sigh as she poured herself another glass of champagne.

"I'm afraid because I do love him," Brooke admitted.

"Oh, honey, you are in love, and that's beautiful. When you just accept it, your stress level will decrease dramatically," Sarah told her.

"But this has all been a fairy tale. What if the wicked witch casts a spell in the end, and it all disappears?" Brooke asked.

"There's not a chance of that happening. I've seen the way that man looks at you, and he's head over heels in love with you," Sarah said.

"Yeah, this is the fairy tale, and you're definitely the princess," Chloe told her.

"But I've never needed rescuing before," Brooke said.

"Oh, darling, we all need rescued. We just don't know from what until it happens," Sarah said with a sigh.

"I love you girls. Thank you so much for being here with me today," Brooke told them, crying again. "These stupid hormones are killing me."

The girls all laughed through their tears. "We don't even have hormones as an excuse," Sarah said as she wiped her face.

"But we love you, too. It's us for life, no matter what else is thrown at us," Chloe said.

And it was the three of them against the world. But maybe, just maybe, there was room for some men in their lives, too. It seemed to be working out well so far.

CHAPTER FORTY-THREE

It was only a few days before her wedding, and Brooke found she wasn't that nervous. She should be, but Finn was so dang attentive and so kind to her. They hadn't spent a single night apart, and she'd agreed to move into his house when it was ready. She'd miss her small place, but with a baby coming it made more sense to have a yard. Finn had already ordered a monster-size playground that was being delivered any day.

She was meeting him at the doctor's office. They were about to have their first ultrasound. She'd told him he didn't have to come, but he'd looked at her as if she'd sprouted two heads. He'd insisted on being there, seeing the first picture of his baby. She was so glad he was coming.

"How's my beautiful fiancée?" he asked as he approached.

She got that flutter in her stomach she always seemed to feel anytime he was near. She prayed that would never go away.

"I'm nervous. What if the baby has two heads?" she asked with a chuckle.

"That's just more brainpower," he told her as he leaned down and gave her a soft kiss. That was one more thing she loved about the man. He could be kind and gentle or rough and sexy. She liked all the sides of him.

"Ms. Garrison, we're ready for you now," a nurse said as she came through a doorway.

"We should put 'Anderson' on the forms now. It's only a few days away," Finn said with a frown.

"I didn't say I was changing my name," she said, making his face fall. "I'm just kidding. I'll take your name," she said as she rubbed his cheek.

"I want the world to know you're mine," he told her.

"Oh, Mr. Anderson, I won't be owned by anyone," she warned.

"You already own me," he told her with such raw love in his expression it was almost blinding.

"We need to go inside," she said, feeling overwhelmed.

He placed his hand on her back and walked with her through the doorway. She was a little mortified when they weighed her in front of him, but she had nothing to be concerned about, as she took care of herself, but over the next few months those numbers were definitely going to be climbing.

They followed the nurse into the ultrasound room, and Brooke climbed up on the table and pulled down her yoga pants. She was shaking a bit as she waited for the nurse to pull out the jelly and get the machine ready.

"It's going to be slightly cold, but you'll forget all about that in about five seconds," the woman said with a smile.

"You have a pretty amazing job," Finn told the woman.

"Yes, I do. I get to give the gift of your baby's first picture," she replied as she poured the goo on Brooke's stomach and placed the wand there. She wiggled it around for a while, and then the beautiful sound of their child's heartbeat could be heard loud and clear.

"Well . . . ," the nurse said, and Brooke's heart nearly stopped.

"Is everything okay?" she asked, trying to remember not to panic as she gazed at the screen, trying to see what the nurse was seeing.

"Everything looks healthy and well . . . with both babies," she said with a smile. "It appears as if you're going to be getting double the trouble."

Utter silence followed her words. Brooke couldn't take her eyes off the screen, where the nurse pointed out two blobs that looked like nothing. But the sound of their heartbeats was definitely more than clear.

"Two babies," Finn finally said, his voice awed and excited at the same time.

"Yes, you are definitely carrying twins," the nurse confirmed as she printed out some pictures.

"I was barely getting used to the idea of one," Brooke said.

"It's a little too early to tell the sex of the babies, but you appear healthy, as do the babies. In two more months, we can check the sex."

"Two," Brooke said again. She didn't know what else to say.

The nurse looked around awhile longer, took more pictures, then handed them over before wiping Brooke's stomach and telling them to take their time before she left the room.

Brooke looked at Finn, surprised by the sparkle in his eyes as he gazed at her belly and then the pics and then at her belly again. He moved closer and placed his hand on her still-flat stomach.

"Thank you for this gift, Brooke. Thank you so much," he told her as he looked up into her eyes. She gave him a wobbly smile, and he leaned down and kissed her. "I know you're a little overwhelmed right now, but just know I'll be with you every step of the way, even up at three in the morning, changing diapers and holding one of our babies while you feed the other."

"You can't possibly be real, Finn. You're far too perfect," she told him.

"I wasn't this man until I met you. You've changed me in so many good ways. I want to be a great man for you," he said.

"I want to be a better person for you, too," she told him.

"You can't fix perfect," he insisted.

She laughed. "Let's see if you're saying that in another few months when I'm begging you for tuna-and-peanut-butter sandwiches. I've heard horror stories of pregnancy hormones."

"Baby, if there's anything I can do to make this better for you, I will," he insisted.

"Oh, Finn, you make me so happy," she said.

"Good, because I feel joy every moment I'm with you," he told her.

The two of them walked from the clinic in a bit of a daze. A few months earlier, they'd both been single and content in their lives. Then they'd met, and it had been a perfect storm since that moment. Their lives were moving in fast-forward, and Brooke found that she didn't want to hit the rewind button.

"I wonder if they're identical or fraternal," she said as he helped her into his car. She'd taken a cab to the clinic, so she was glad to ride home with him.

"I hope fraternal. Maybe we'll get a girl and boy. But I'm also perfectly content with two little girls with your hair and eyes," he said.

"It could be twin boys with your mischievousness," she warned.

"They will be half you, so no matter what they'll be perfect," he told her.

"You're a little biased, I think," she said with a giggle. "Let's throw a dinner party and announce it to everyone," Brooke said. "That way we aren't repeating ourselves, and we get to see all the shocked faces."

"I like how you think, woman."

"Tonight. I can't stand waiting," she insisted.

"Definitely tonight."

When an Anderson wanted something done, it got done quickly. Before they even arrived home, the phone tree was going, and they were having dinner at the Anderson mansion. She'd meant a restaurant, but she wasn't complaining about visiting the huge place again. Her friends loved going there as well.

The next few hours went by in a whirl, and when they did announce the babies to the room, there was such an uproar of excitement and congratulations Brooke didn't know what to say.

So much love was in this huge mansion she could barely comprehend any of it. She was squeezed and kissed and loved on for so long she nearly felt faint. But in the end it was Finn's arms wrapping around her.

And that's the moment she wasn't afraid of loving him anymore. She was in love with the man she was about to marry. She was in love with the father of her children. And she was in love with being in love.

And she began to think that everything was going to be okay. Maybe it would truly work out. Maybe it really was her turn to have a fairy tale come true.

CHAPTER FORTY-FOUR

It was the night before her wedding. It was surreal to even think that. She was sitting in her house, missing Finn, which was insane since the two of them practically lived on top of each other on a daily basis. She could go one night without the man. She was determined to do just that.

"Stop thinking about him," Sarah insisted before taking a big bite of her Oreo ice cream.

"Who in the heck came up with these traditions, anyway? Why is it bad luck to see the groom before the wedding? I'd think it was good luck," Brooke said with a pout.

"Because the anticipation makes you actually want to walk down that aisle," Chloe said with a laugh. "I think you'll be fine going one night without the man."

"It's these damn hormones. I've always been perfectly content being on my own. I love being alone. Or I used to before Finn ruined me," Brooke said.

"If you're happy, then you definitely aren't ruined. And I've never seen you happier, so I love Finn," Sarah said.

"I love him, too," Brooke admitted for the first time out loud.

Both friends stopped and stared at her before smiling like loons. "It's about time you said it," Sarah said with a whoop.

"Yeehaw," Chloe added.

"Shut up, both of you. I do use the word *love*," Brooke said with a chuckle.

"Yeah, not so much," Chloe said. "But that's okay. It just means you don't freely give your love away. So it means something with Finn."

"I fought it, but I can't seem to go a single hour without thinking about him. And when he is here, I can't seem to get close enough. When we finish making love, I can't stand it when he pulls out of me. I want us connected, want him inside me. I've never felt this way with anyone."

"He's your lobster," Sarah said with a chuckle.

"Ha ha, can't have a prewedding night without at least one *Friends* reference," Chloe said.

"Pivot!" Sarah said with a laugh.

"Oh my gosh, we all need to get a life. We're way too easily amused," Brooke told them.

"Come on, Brooke, this doesn't end till you give a saying," Chloe warned.

Brooke chuckled again before smiling. "How you doin'?" she said in her best Joey voice.

They all laughed again. There had been many college nights they'd had chocolate and *Friends* marathons.

"We were on a break!" Sarah suddenly shouted, sending them into giggles again.

"We *are* easily entertained," Chloe admitted.

"Maybe it's time for a YouTube marathon. I'm up for 'Threw It on the Ground' or 'Jizz in My Pants,'" Sarah said.

"Oh my gosh, those are so not prewedding videos," Brooke told them.

"You're right. I guess it'll have to be 'The Creep,'" Chloe said as she clicked on the TV and did a search on YouTube.

They spent the next few hours eating way too much chocolate, chips, gummy bears, and soda. It was a sugar rush. But because Brooke was pregnant, they all decided sugar and salt were better than alcohol.

The night was winding down when Sarah turned to Brooke and grabbed her hand. Her eyes filled with tears as she smiled.

"I know we love to laugh, and I know we try to avoid mushy, but I do need to tell you how happy I am for you. Tomorrow is your wedding day, and you're going to be the most beautiful bride to ever exist. And I have to say this, too," she said with a wicked smile. "If he ever hurts you, I will cut him."

Because she said it so seriously, it gave Brooke the giggles again.

"I honestly don't know what my life would've been like without both of you in it. You're my everything. Finn is just a bonus," she told Sarah and Chloe.

"Well, don't think that means I'm putting out just because you love me more," Chloe said with a scowl that had them hurting they were laughing so hard.

"Seriously, I was so content with good friendship I didn't think I needed a man. But I'm glad he came into my life harder than a wrecking ball," Brooke said.

"There aren't many men out there who can combat your stubbornness. It had to be Finn," Sarah told her.

"I tried so hard to chase him away," Brooke said, a bit thunderstruck at herself for being so foolish.

"And he's still here, and you have twins on the way. So you failed at that mission . . . thankfully," Chloe told her.

"Yeah, I'm pretty thankful for that myself," Brooke said.

"Have your nerves dissipated at all?" Chloe asked.

Brooke thought about it for a minute. "I'm not sure. I might just be in a constant state of nervousness, so I don't really know how I'm feeling anymore, or I might actually be better. I know I love Finn, so that also helps. But I'm scared. Most people have so much more time before they bring a baby into the mix, and we're starting out with two of them. What if it's perfect now, but it all goes to hell in a few months?"

"We can't predict what tomorrow will bring, but we can alter the outcome by being negative. Just go into this being positive, and in the end what's supposed to happen will for sure," Chloe told her.

"Logically I know this. But emotionally I'm a wreck," Brooke admitted.

"That's me every single day," Chloe said with a laugh.

"Why don't we talk about Sarah and Noah for a while?" Brooke said. She was too emotional to think about her and Finn any further tonight.

"No, let's not talk about that," Sarah said with a scowl.

"Why is that?" Chloe asked.

"Let's just say the man drives me a little crazy," Sarah said.

"In a good or bad way?" Brooke asked.

"I have no idea. One second we're ripping each other's clothes off, and the next we're both running for the hills. I don't think we're going to get a fairy tale like you and Finn," Sarah said with a sigh.

"Do you want a fairy tale?" Brooke asked.

Sarah thought about it for a minute. "I've never been afraid of love," she finally said. "But I think I want to love someone new way too often. Maybe Noah scares me because he's not the kind of guy you love and leave."

"Maybe you've met your match," Chloe said with a laugh. "I want to see you taken down."

"Oh, Ms. Chloe, you'll be taken down before I am," Sarah said with an evil laugh.

"Want to make a bet on it?" Chloe challenged, and Sarah's eyes lit up.

"Bring it, girlie," Sarah said as she held out her hand.

"I'm soooooooo in on this bet," Brooke said as she stuck her hand in the mix. "I predict Sarah going down first."

"That's easy to guess since Chloe has been single, but you know how much I like to win. This will be easy pickings," Sarah said with confidence.

"Nope. I've discovered when love hits, nothing will stop it," Brooke said with a shrug.

"What's the bet?" Chloe asked.

"A weekend spa trip the first person to fall in love has to pay for," Brooke said.

"That would be you. When are we going?" Sarah asked.

"Okay, if it's Sarah, she pays. If it's Chloe, she pays. If it's at the same time, I pay. I'm changing my prediction," Brooke said.

They all thought about it. "This so isn't fair 'cause it certainly won't be both of us," Chloe said.

"My new prediction is it will be both of you marrying within six months of each other," Brooke said, feeling confident.

Both girls analyzed her.

"Deal," Chloe said.

"Deal," Sarah echoed.

"Deal," Brooke said as she leaned back. She had a new uncle-in-law who loved to matchmake. This one was in the bag for her.

"Okay, we need our beauty sleep to look our best tomorrow," Brooke said. "You have husbands to find."

"Not funny," Sarah said with a scowl.

"Agreed," Chloe echoed.

Brooke's phone dinged, and she couldn't stop the smile from lifting her lips.

"Hey! You were supposed to have that turned off," Sarah said with a laugh.

"I did most of the night," Brooke told them as she picked it up.

"What did he say?" Chloe asked.

"Oh, it's very nice," Brooke said, drawing out the moment. "He told me he won't sleep a wink tonight without me in his arms and can't wait for me to be his wife in twelve short hours that are drawing out to be the longest of his life."

"Oh, he's too good to be true," Sarah said.

She typed a reply to Finn: I can't wait to be Brooke Anderson. I love you. She hit send and held her breath. She'd never spoken those words to him before, and she wasn't sure what he was going to say back.

There wasn't a reply. She sat there, growing worried. He'd told her he loved her, so she'd think he'd be glad she was admitting she loved him back. But when seven minutes passed and there still wasn't a response, she grew really concerned.

"What did you say to him, and why are you looking as if the world is falling apart now?" Sarah asked.

"I told him I loved him," Brooke admitted. "And then he disappeared. What does that mean?"

"Maybe he fainted," Chloe said. "It did take you long enough."

"I don't know," Brooke said. But she didn't get the chance to say anything else. Suddenly her front door was pushed open, and Finn was striding toward them.

"You're not supposed to be here," Sarah said with a wicked smile.

"It's bad luck," Chloe echoed, though they both knew neither Finn nor Brooke even knew they were there anymore.

"There's not a chance you tell me you love me over text and for me to stay away from you. I'm going to make love to the love of my life now," he said as he moved forward with purpose.

"Yes, please," Brooke said.

He didn't even stop as he scooped her up in his arms and carried her to her room. Neither of them heard the giggles from her friends or the front door closing behind them.

CHAPTER FORTY-FIVE

She'd told him she loved him! The high Finn felt at this moment was unlike anything he'd ever felt in his life. Who needed drugs when a person had a beautiful, talented, confident woman who loved them? No one ever. He was so happy it felt almost like a crime to feel this good.

He carried her in his arms to her room, not caring that he was breaking the traditional rules of not seeing his bride the night before the wedding. He'd love her, hold her, and then slip away so she could wake up alone and anticipate seeing him at the head of that aisle. There wasn't a chance of him getting any sleep this night.

Finn slowly lowered Brooke to the bed and stepped back, taking his time looking at her luscious form in her sweet cotton pajama shirt. There was nothing she put on he didn't find sexy.

"You take my breath away," he said, feeling in awe that he was the only person allowed to touch her for the rest of his life. "I can't believe you're mine."

She smiled up at him, such a sweet loving smile it took his breath away. He quickly shed his clothes. He loved looking at her, could do it all day and night, but he also needed their naked flesh pressed together—and he needed it right now.

He climbed onto the bed and gently pulled her pajamas off. "It's better than unwrapping a present," he said as he leaned down and ran his lips across her jaw.

He wrapped his arms around her and moved slowly to her lips, connecting them together and loving her sweet taste.

"I should tell you this shouldn't happen," she said with a sigh as he licked her throat. "But there's no way I want you to stop." Her last words ended on a moan as he squeezed her nipple.

He kissed her again, smiling as their mouths connected. Then he trailed his lips down her slender neck, licking and kissing his way to the luscious mounds of her breasts. He wanted to build her hunger, her need. He took his time circling around her perky nipples until she was begging him to take one into his mouth.

By the time he did just that, her entire body was on fire, and she arched off the bed, crying out her pleasure, making him drip in anticipation of filling her tight body. He ran his tongue over her nipples, feeling himself pulse with each swipe of his tongue. Reaching down, he felt how wet she was and had to beg himself to slow it down.

He wanted to make love to her slow and easy, wanted to let her know how much it meant to him she was opening up, loving him, letting him into her world and her body.

"Oh, Finn, I'm yours tonight, tomorrow, forever," she said as he swept his tongue over to her other breast and latched on to her nipple, sucking it hard. She cried out again.

"Tell me again. I want to hear you say it," he demanded as he reached down and slipped a finger inside her tight heat.

With nothing more than her responding to him, his entire body was on fire. That's what this one woman did to him. Her cries of pleasure, her enthusiasm, her lust for him made him lose control. But her words of love sent him to another universe.

"I love you, Finn. I'm sorry it took so long to say it, but I love you," she said before moaning as he pumped his fingers inside her.

"Oh, Brooke, I love you so much it hurts," he told her.

He pushed against her body, letting her feel how aroused he was. That wasn't a surprise. From the moment he walked into a room, he was ready to take her—every single day, every moment.

Slowly he climbed back up her body, needing to feel her lips on his once more. He pulled back and looked at her. Slowly her eyes opened, and there was so much love and passion shining back at him he knew he had to take her, knew he couldn't spend another moment without them being one.

He climbed over her, bracing his weight on his elbows as he rested the head of his arousal against her heat. Then he paused, loving this torturous moment.

"Please, Finn, please take me," she begged as she lifted her hips, causing the tip of him to slip inside her. It was pure heaven.

"Yes, darling, anything you want," he said in total surrender. He needed to pleasure her, but he knew exactly how to do that.

He cupped her thigh in his hand, opening her fully to him; then he sank down, groaning as she gripped him, her body contracting at the sheer pleasure of them being connected.

Sweat broke out over his entire body at how good he felt and how much he was trying to control his movements. It didn't matter how many times they made love—it would never be enough. This desire he felt for her was insatiable.

Brooke gasped as he rested fully within her tight walls. When he didn't move, she pushed upward and twisted, making him call out her name in surrender. She knew how to drive him utterly insane.

He didn't need any further encouragement. He began to move, slowly at first, then picking up speed as the pleasure built for both of them.

"You take me to the edge so damn fast," he growled as he leaned down and licked her sweaty neck.

"Take me with you over it," she begged as her nails scraped down his back.

He lost it at her words. Letting go of her leg, he gripped her hips and began thrusting faster in and out of her tight heat. Her legs wrapped around his back as she held on, her cries the most beautiful sound he could imagine.

She suddenly cried out as her body clenched him over and over again, her nails digging deep in his back, her stomach trembling against his.

"Yes, baby, let go," he growled, barely holding back as she shook around him.

"Come with me; please come with me," she muttered as she continued squeezing him.

He couldn't deny her anything. This had gone too fast, but he'd slow it down, give her more pleasure the entire night. But not yet. Right now he was going to give her exactly what she was demanding.

He pulled back and thrust forward a couple more times, then cried out his pleasure as he let go, burying his seed deep within her walls.

They shook together for several long moments before he collapsed on top of her, with her limbs securely holding him in place. He needed to move, knew he was crushing her. But that had drained every ounce of energy from him.

"I'm sorry, Brooke. I wanted that to last so much longer than it did," he said.

She chuckled, her entire body shaking against him. "Mmm, make it up to me in five minutes," she said as her fingers loosened on his back, and she began caressing his hot skin.

When he could move again, he shifted, keeping her locked tightly to him as he rolled onto his back with her on top of him. She lay there, his arousal still inside her, still ready for more.

"Mmm," she purred against him as she wiggled her hips, making his thickness pulse with the need for more.

"Damn, I can't get enough of you," he said as he splayed his hands across her slick back.

She sat up, her skin flushed, her eyes bright, and her lips turned up in a satisfied smile.

"I ditto that," she said as she began moving up and down on him.

He watched in wonder as pleasure filled her face. She moved faster, and when she fell over the edge again, he was right there with her.

It was hours before either of them could even begin to think about stopping. It would be forever before they did.

CHAPTER FORTY-SIX

Before Brooke could even open her eyes, she stretched out her legs and groaned. Ouch! She was sore, more sore than any gym workout she'd ever done before. She moved her arms next and giggled.

She wasn't the best morning person in the world, but she had zero regrets about the night before. Their lovemaking had gone to an entirely new level, and she was a very satisfied woman.

Slowly her eyes opened, and she kept smiling as she looked toward her window. The sun was shining, the birds were chirping . . . and she was getting married . . . to a man she loved unconditionally.

She turned her head and then giggled when she saw the note and the perfect purple orchid on the pillow next to her. Reaching over, she lifted the flower and inhaled its sweet scent before picking up the note.

Leaving you in the early morning hours was like taking off a limb, but seeing you in a beautiful gown in a few hours will help me get through this time without you. I love you, my sweet bride.

"Oh, I love you, too, Finn Anderson," she whispered aloud.

"Yeah, yeah, you love him. Now get your lazy butt out of bed. We have a wedding to get to."

Brooke turned to find Chloe and Sarah in the doorway, grinning at her. One had a plate with goodies on it. The other held a cup of steaming coffee in her hand.

"These were left by your future husband. We already chowed down on lots of doughnuts," Chloe said with a giggle as she moved forward. Luckily, she was holding the plate of goodies, 'cause she bounced down on the bed, making a scone fall off.

"When did you come back?" Brooke asked, then was a bit horrified. "You did leave, right?" She hadn't even tried to be quiet the night before.

"Oh, yes, we rushed the hell out of here. There was no way we were going to listen to you screaming out your pleasure all night," Chloe said with a roll of her eyes.

"You would've definitely heard screaming," Brooke said, not at all embarrassed by it. "I have zero regrets."

"Even though you might have bad luck because of it?" Sarah asked.

"Not a chance will there be bad luck today," Brooke said, more sure of that than anything else she'd been sure of in her life.

"I think you're a hundred percent correct with that," Chloe said. "You are untouchable right now."

"Let's get you glamorous and then get you to the mansion on time," Sarah said as she handed over the cup of coffee.

Brooke took a grateful sip as she gripped the sheet to her chest. She took her time enjoying the goodies Finn had left and finishing her coffee. It was going to be a full day of beauty: hair and makeup and nails. Then she'd meet Finn at the end of an aisle at twilight. She couldn't imagine a more perfect way to spend a day.

She was also shocked that she was as calm as she was. For a girl who'd never wanted to be married before, she was taking this all in stride quite well. Maybe it was because she was so happy to be with this man. She was marrying a man she couldn't imagine living a single day without.

She felt like Cinderella as her hair was made up and makeup applied. Her friends were by her side every step of the way. There wasn't a chance she would do any of this without them. They'd saved each other when they were younger, and they'd save each other until the day they were no longer living.

By the time they arrived at the Anderson mansion, she was more than ready to take the next steps into her new life. She was ready to marry Finn, to be a wife and mother, and to have a family for the rest of her life. He'd given her this gift, and she appreciated him so much for it.

"It's almost time," Chloe told her as they stepped through a side door into the giant house.

"Unless you want to run," Sarah said.

She had to fight tears. "One thing I love about you both so much is that even if you think I'm wrong, you'd support me no matter what decision I make. That gives me confidence to do anything in life because I know you'll always be right there at my side," Brooke said.

"You know we'll always be there to help bury the body," Chloe said.

"And dispose of the evidence," Sarah added.

"I feel like I'm losing you today, but I also feel so happy. I want it all," Brooke said.

"Then take it all. We aren't going anywhere," Sarah assured her.

"For time and all eternity, we're together," Chloe agreed.

She hugged her friends as the music started.

"It's time to become Mrs. Anderson," Sarah said.

"I'm ready," Brooke told them.

She didn't have a father worthy of walking her down the aisle, so her two best friends were walking beside her instead of in front. It was the perfect way to take her journey to the man she was spending the rest of her life with.

The door opened, and she smiled.

CHAPTER FORTY-SEVEN

Two weeks in Bora-Bora was exactly what the doctor had ordered. Brooke was ready to come home at the end, but only because she missed her patients and her friends. But as long as she had Finn by her side, she could be literally anywhere and find happiness.

Of course he'd taken her to the perfect tropical paradise for their honeymoon, and she would swear her stomach had grown several inches while they were gone. She told herself it was the babies and not the huge quantities of food the two of them had consumed. Of course her stomach was growing, and he still had a six-pack—the good kind.

But now they were home and standing in Brooke's house. It was nearly empty, and for some reason that brought tears to her eyes. This place had been a refuge for her for years, and it had been all hers. She was sad to let it go but excited at the same time to move forward with her life.

Still she felt a tear fall down her face.

"Are you okay?" Finn asked as he stood behind her, his hands wrapped around her, resting on her belly.

She leaned back against him. "It's silly. This is just a home, but I have a lot of memories here. It's a bit more difficult to say goodbye to it than I realized it would be," she told him. She rested her hands on top of his and rubbed the smooth skin, feeling instantly comforted by simply touching him.

"You have memories here with your brother," he said. Maybe that really was the difficulty of letting it go. "And they are good, and you don't want to let them go."

"You might be right," she said with a sniffle.

"I have an idea I've been thinking about," he said.

"Really? What is it?" she asked him. She was already feeling better by nothing more than his touch and the sound of his voice.

"Why don't we keep the house as a place for families of the soldiers to stay in when they're visiting the new facility?" he suggested.

"Won't they have housing on the campus?" she asked.

"Yes, but I have a feeling the place will be packed, and it might be nice for someone to be a little ways away from the campus. This will be a special spot for special people. We can call it the Jack Garrison safe house," he said.

Brooke didn't try to hold back her tears this time. "Oh, Finn, no wonder I love you so much," she said as she turned and threw her arms around him. "What a beautiful idea. Yes! Yes! Yes! That's exactly what this house needs to be," she told him as she squeezed him tight.

He leaned down and gently kissed her, his hands running up and down her back in a soothing way that had her melting against him.

"I'm going to be sad when my belly is too big for me to nestle up in your arms," she told him.

"Your belly will never be too big. These arms can hold you and our babies at the same time," he assured her.

"I can't believe I fought so hard to not be with you," she told him in wonder.

"I love that you fought me. It makes the catch so much more," he said with a chuckle.

"So you think I'm a catch?" she asked as she leaned back and wiggled her eyebrows.

"I know you're a catch, Mrs. Anderson. I'm just the lucky bastard who caught you."

"Oh, Finn, I do love you . . . for time and all eternity," she said with a smile.

"That won't be long enough," he said.

Then they stopped talking as he kissed her before lifting her in his arms to make love to her one last time in the house they'd fallen in love inside.

And eternity truly wasn't long enough when it came to a love this pure.

EPILOGUE

The quiet of the veterans center property had been taken away as crowds of people milled about. A huge screen was set up behind an elaborate stage with chairs and a podium. The media was camped out, cameras on and scanning the crowds.

Noah looked out at it all, feeling slightly sick. This was the biggest project he'd ever worked on, and if he failed, he'd never have a career doing what he loved.

"Everything is ready. Take some air in, or you're going to hurl. And with this many cameras pointing at you, it will become a YouTube sensation within hours," Sarah said in a hushed whisper.

Noah took the suggested breath and felt his head begin to stop spinning. He was a confident man and hated the nerves rushing through him. He didn't need to focus on the entire project, just look at it piece by piece.

"How are you so calm?" he asked the woman he was becoming more and more obsessed with by the minute.

"I'm not calm at all. I'm just far better at hiding my nerves than you are . . . obviously," she said with a chuckle that didn't reach her eyes. She was just as scared as him, and she was right: she was a hell of a lot better at keeping that to herself.

"Good afternoon, everyone," Joseph said, not needing a microphone. The noise instantly died down as they waited to hear what the man of the decade—or century, more like it—had to say.

"I'm so very pleased by all the support and love we've received for this project. It started out about two years ago as my beautiful bride and I were talking about the poor care our treasured vets receive. So instead of just talking, we decided to do something about it," Joseph said before he paused to give a look so filled with love to his wife that Noah felt like an intruder.

"Joseph isn't known as a patient man, so he had this land purchased within a matter of days of our talk," Katherine said with a girlish giggle. She was speaking into the microphone, her delicate voice not possibly carrying to the back of the crowd without it.

"Time moves too quickly, and this project is important," Joseph said. "So we found the land, and then we had to build the perfect team."

Noah let out another breath as he and his brothers stepped forward. Cameras snapped, and he hoped he could get someone to give him a picture of him and his siblings side by side, united for the world to see. Brooke stood proudly at Finn's side, her rounded belly absolutely beautiful.

Sarah stood at his side as his partner on this project. He was hoping for it to become more than a working relationship, but so far she was proving to be quite elusive. He had no doubt he could win her over, though.

"I could talk all day about what we're doing here," Joseph said before chuckling. "But I think I'll let my brilliant architect nephew and his partner, the fantastic Sarah something, tell you in their own words."

The crowd laughed, always enjoying when Joseph spoke.

"You've got this, brother. Go wow them," Finn told him.

Noah gave his brother a nod, then took Sarah's hand and stepped up to the podium. He looked out at the crowd and felt his nerves instantly calm. No one was there looking at him as a failure. They all wanted to see this project succeed. And with him and Sarah leading it, that's exactly what would happen.

"Thank you for coming." Applause followed those simple words. "Let's begin, shall we?"

He didn't let go of Sarah's hand. He hoped he never had to.

ABOUT THE AUTHOR

Photo © John Evanston

Melody Anne is the *New York Times* best-selling author of several popular series: Billionaire Bachelors, Surrender, Baby for the Billionaire, Unexpected Heroes, Billionaire Aviators, and Becoming Elena. She's also written a young adult series and solo titles, including a thriller. Armed with a bachelor's degree in business, Anne loves to write about powerful businessmen and the corporate world. She's sold over seven million books to date and can be found on the world's most distinguished bestseller lists. Beyond that, she loves getting to do what makes her happy—living in a fantasy world. When not writing, Anne spends time with family, friends, and her many pets. A country girl at heart, she loves her small, strong community and is involved in many projects.

Keep up with the latest news and subscribe to her newsletter at www.melodyanne.com. You can also join her on her official Facebook page, melodyanneauthor, or on Twitter @authmelodyanne and Instagram at MelodyAnneRomance.